"WHERE IS THE BLOOD?"

The Master of Sinanju closed his eyes, as if too weary to display real impatience.

"If these animals are responsible for that," he said, indicating the lab where the body lay, "why is neither of them awash in blood?"

"I assume they licked themselves clean."

"There is not the scent of blood on these creatures," Chiun pointed out. "There is nothing here that tells me these creatures are to blame for anything other than being completely adorable. They are cute as buttons."

"Only if we're talking really ugly buttons."

"He did not mean it," the Master of Sinanju assured the BBQ. It moaned softly at him. Chiun squealed in delight.

"Give me strength," Remo muttered.

Other titles in this series:

Created by
WARREN MURPHY
and RICHARD SAPIR

THE Destroyer™

DEADLY GENES

A GOLD EAGLE BOOK FROM
WORLDWIDE®

TORONTO • NEW YORK • LONDON
AMSTERDAM • PARIS • SYDNEY • HAMBURG
STOCKHOLM • ATHENS • TOKYO • MILAN
MADRID • WARSAW • BUDAPEST • AUCKLAND

First edition November 1999

ISBN 0-373-63232-0

Special thanks and acknowledgment to James Mullaney for his contribution to this work.

DEADLY GENES

For "The Refreshments," whose album kept me going; and for Jimmy, Mary, Andy and Elizabeth—future fans, all.

As well as for the Glorious House of Sinanju, e-mail housinan@aol.com

1

They held a press conference to introduce it to the world.

It was smaller than the crowd expected, tipping the scales at just over 120 pounds. It was compact, but not in a menacing way. Its designers hadn't been worried about style; they were more concerned with practicality. And of its practicality, all were certain. Their success offered hope, so they said, of feeding all who were hungry in the world. There was only one real question that vexed the assembled press corps.

"Can we pet it?"

Dr. Judith White of BostonBio, Incorporated, smiled. "Of course you can. She's quite docile."

"She?" the Boston television reporter asked.

Dr. White nodded. "This one is female. We have four more like her and three males. Enough for a limited, controlled-breeding population."

The reporter worked for one of the three major Boston stations as the entertainment and human-interest correspondent, which meant that—unlike an anchorwoman—she could afford the extra forty pounds that cushioned her midriff and backside. The added weight had the effect of making her appear both nonthreatening to viewers when she was reviewing movies and hysterically funny any time she went white-water rafting or tried to saddle a horse.

The entertainment correspondent reached out and touched the creature on its broad nose. It blinked. She jumped back, startled.

"It's perfectly harmless," Dr. White assured her.

For the brilliant Judith White—the star of BostonBio's genetic-engineering department—affability was a supreme effort. She did not suffer fools gladly.

With the blessing of the higher-ups at BostonBio, Dr. White had called the local TV stations and newspapers in order to introduce what she called a "significant scientific achievement" to the world. She was surprised that of the few TV reporters who showed up to cover the great unveiling at BostonBio, all were human-interest correspondents. The greatest breakthrough in the history of science was being given the same treatment as a boat show or *Star Trek* convention. The only way it could have been worse was if the stations had sent the Boston weathermen, a collection of freaks so bizarre P. T. Barnum would have balked at exhibiting them.

"Oh, my. It has the saddest eyes I've ever seen," the female reporter said over her shoulder, smiling into her station's camera. She stroked the creature's nose.

"Yes," Dr. White agreed, without emotion. "Remember that its eyes are really irrelevant. *Bos camelus-whitus* is a laboratory specimen. It is no more a real living thing than any other human creation."

"*Bos* what?" asked the reporter.

"*Camelus-whitus.* That's its name."

The animal was in a low, straw-filled pen. Its head jutted out through a wide space in the metal bars.

"Someone around here called it a BBQ earlier." The reporter pointed over her shoulder to where a group of white-coated technicians stood.

The name made Dr. White stiffen. She wanted to glare at the men in the lab coats but kept her anger in check.

"An earlier incarnation of the animal was part horse," she admitted through clenched teeth. "That would make it a member of the *Equus* genus. *BostonBio Equus.* BBQ. I never much liked that appellation, however. Particularly since it has no relation to the animal standing before you."

The creature let out a low, mournful moan. The reporter moved her hand away in surprise. Hesitantly, she returned to stroking the animal's nose.

"It sounds like it's alive to me." The reporter smiled.

Dr. Judith White closed her eyes. Her patience was wearing thin.

"What you are touching is technically referred to as a transgenic nonhuman eukaryotic animal. Yes, it is alive. But it has been brought to life by artificial means.''

She went on to discuss the method by which BostonBio had isolated the DNA strands specific to certain traits in particular animals and piggybacked them on a simple bacteria. This bacteria—which, like all bacteria, furnished the raw material and chemical machinery for its own reproduction—was injected into the fertilized egg of an ordinary dairy cow. The result was a creature that was a combination of several animals.

The reporters paid no attention to the technical lecture being given them by Dr. White. They were all too busy lining up to take turns petting the animal, which regarded each of them with the same dreary pair of wide brown eyes. Occasionally, it would let out another doleful groan. Those television reporters who were petting the creature at these moments nearly squealed in delight, thinking how it would look on the evening's newscast.

One of the reporters turned to Dr. White. It was the same woman who had first touched the *Bos camelus-whitus.*

''It's adorable,'' she gushed. ''Are you going to market them as pets?''

''I can't believe this.'' Dr. White exhaled, finally showing her exasperation. ''I was careful to breed anything that could remotely be considered 'cute' out of them. The *last* thing I wanted was for people to think of these things as anything other than *food.*''

The reporter looked at the animal.

It stood about three feet high on short, stumpy legs. The body appeared too long for a creature so low. It looked almost like a huge basset hound. It had a mild hump, somewhat like that of a camel. The coloring was that of a cow—white with patches of black. But the black seemed washed out, as if the animal had stood too long in the sun. Unlikely, for according to Dr. White this creature had never seen the outside of the BostonBio laboratory. The wide head was a cross between cow, camel and something else vaguely sinister.

"It's so ugly it's cute." The reporter grinned.

"It is not cute, you fat imbecile!" Dr. White snapped, finally unable to contain herself. "It is *lunch.*"

The vapid smile faded like burned-off mist. The reporter's change in attitude sent ripples through the crowd. At her cue, the others began consulting their notes.

"BostonBio has had its problems with its genetic research in the past," the female reporter announced brusquely. "How do you respond to the allegations that your little experiment represents a danger to the human race?"

"Does it look dangerous to you?" Dr. White asked, exasperation showing in her flushed cheeks.

"*My* feelings are irrelevant. Please answer the question."

Dr. White sighed. Taking a deep breath, she began, "There have been precedents established on how to conduct this sort of research. I assure you that *everything* is perfectly safe. The literature I've passed out to you shows the applications of similar technology. For instance, more than a decade ago, the Supreme Court of the United States permitted the U.S. Patent and Trademark Office to grant a patent to a nonnatural, man-made microorganism that eats oil. This bacterium is not unlike the kind we used to create the *Bos camelus-whitus.* And I am sure you all know of the famous patented lab mouse that is being used in cancer research."

"That doesn't answer my question," said the reporter, who was never this zealous when her station was cramming her puffy white body into a bathing suit for its annual winter "getaway to the Bahamas" segments. Dr. White's outburst had turned her briefly into a real reporter. "Does this have any connection to BostonBio's troubles of two decades ago?"

Dr. White's mouth thinned. This was not the way she had wanted this press conference to go. "I know what you're talking about, and that was another corporate entity of BostonBio. No one even remembers what happened back then. We are talking about research that can save the human race, not harm it, and I am frankly more than a little annoyed that you would dredge up something from the past which could tarnish what we've achieved here. Now."

She pointed past the gathered press to the *Bos*

camelus-whitus. "That animal can go for long periods of time without water. We can thank the camel for that. Thanks to the cow, there is enough milk and meat to feed many. And we can be grateful to the snake for its slow digestive process."

Some of the reporters recoiled, thinking that they might have been touching a relative of the snake.

"Yes, the *snake*," Dr. White repeated, relishing perhaps a bit too much their discomfort. "It can go for as long without food as it can without water. And we can thank above all else the brilliant minds here at BostonBio for bringing everything together in that one, dumpy, pathetic, world-saving animal."

She gestured grandly to the BBQ. As if in response, the animal burped loudly. Eyes hooded morosely, it began languidly chewing its cud.

"One of those brilliant minds being *yours,* no doubt," the female reporter snipped sarcastically.

"Yes, actually," Dr. White admitted. "This is my project. From start to finish."

The reporter smiled tautly. "Would it cripple your genius ego to learn that this is a nonstory?"

Dr. White seemed stunned. "What?" she demanded.

"Well, this *is* Boston after all," the reporter replied with confident pride. "We're pretty used to scientific breakthroughs around here. Maybe if you could slap a saddle on that thing and take some kids for BBQ rides around Boston Common, maybe *then* it'd get on the news. You know, human interest and all. As it is it's all kind of ho-hum.''

"Ho-hum?'' Dr. White asked, stunned.

"Sorry," the reporter said with a superior smirk. Turning, she began looping the cord from her microphone around her long slender hand.

"You stupid, stupid bitch," Dr. White muttered, head bowed. She said it so softly few people heard the words.

"What?" asked the reporter blandly. She was handing her mike off to her segment producer.

"You stupid, fat, empty-headed, gluttonous cow!"

She moved so quickly no one could stop her. In an instant, Dr. White had sprung across the brief space separating her from the reporter. The gathered press blinked at the image. It was as if she had gone from one spot to the next instantaneously.

One strong hand grabbed the reporter by the throat. The other hand swung around and cuffed the reporter in the side of her softly bleached head.

"Stupid, fat cow!'' Dr. Judith White growled.

The reporter blinked in uncomprehending pain. A glimmer of fear registered in the back of her eyes as she watched Dr. White bring her hand back once more. The scientist's teeth were bared maniacally.

More hands suddenly reached around, grabbing Dr. White, holding her arms, preventing her from striking out again. Men in white lab coats tried to drag her away from the female reporter. Struggling in a blind rage, she seemed to hold them off for a moment. All at once, the fight seemed to drain from her, and she allowed herself to be pulled backward.

The reporter staggered back, as well. She fell into the concerned arms of her segment producer.

"You—you're *insane!*" she stammered, panting.

She felt the side of her head where the blow had registered. Her fingers came back smeared red. A trickle of blood seeped from her thin blond hairdo. It rolled down one overly made-up cheek.

"I'm *bleeding!*" the reporter shrieked. She wheeled on Dr. White. "You crazy animal, you *mauled* me!"

Dr. White was amid a protective gaggle of her subordinates at BostonBio. Some had released their grip on her; others still held her arms. She took several deep, steadying breaths.

"I'm fine," she assured her lab team. Hesitantly, the last few men let go of her arms.

"You are *not* fine!" the reporter screamed. "You're a *psycho!* This is unbelievable!" Her cameraman had found a clean handkerchief. She pressed it to the wound above her left ear.

Dr. White closed her eyes, patient once more. "This is all an unfortunate misunderstanding," she said slowly.

"What, you *didn't* just attack me?" the reporter screeched. She waved the bloody handkerchief at the rest of the gathered reporters. "You're all witnesses! I'm suing this whack-job's psycho ass! I'm suing BostonBio! I'm going to *own* you, lady!'' she yelled at Judith White.

Flinging the handkerchief at the feet of Dr. White, the reporter spun on her heel. She shoved her way past her producer and her cameraman, storming out into the hallway. She was followed by the rest of the Boston press corps.

Dr. White was left alone with her staff. No one said a word for a long time. The men remained around her, seeming to not want to disturb a single molecule in the room lest they stoke the ire of their famously volatile boss. At long last, it was Judith White herself who broke the silence.

''Well, that could have gone better,'' she commented softly. She pushed through the group of men, walking across the lab to her private office. She closed the door so gently it made the rest of the scientific team jump.

TEN HOURS LATER, Judith White quietly shut off the small television that rested on a shelf in her laboratory office. She tossed the remote control to her desktop, where it landed with a loud plastic clatter.

They'd ripped her to shreds. One of the stations had even gotten the assault on video.

She had not yet heard from her superiors at BostonBio, but it went without saying that they would not endorse her conduct. This was supposed to be the company's shining moment, and her temper had completely overshadowed the great press announcement. It was now unlikely that the networks would pick up the story. And even if they did, the story would feature a sensationalized look at Dr. Judith White herself and not her magnificent *Bos camelus-whitus.*

"Stupid, stupid, stupid," Judith muttered. The lab beyond was dark and empty. No one heard her words of self-recrimination.

Judith reached to her waist. She found a set of keys on a retractable cord. Pulling one free of the rest, she inserted it into the lock of a side desk drawer.

"Stupid, stupid, stupid," she repeated as she pulled the drawer open. She let the keys jangle back up to her waist. They sounded like clattering dog tags.

Reaching into the drawer, she pulled out a black plastic box with both hands, resting it reverently on her desk blotter.

She lifted the lid, revealing a soft foam interior. It was a drab gray and fashioned in the uneven egg-carton design. A series of vials rested in the box.

Judith removed one of the vials. It had a waxy corking substance in one end. The brown-tinged liquid in the vial appeared to be gelatinous.

With her free hand, she found a plastic bag containing an ordinary syringe inside the same drawer the box had been stored in. Tearing open the plastic with her teeth, she thrust the business end of the needle through the cork on the vial. She drew the viscous substance into the syringe.

Redepositing the half-empty vial inside the case, Judith rolled up the sleeve of her lab coat. She found a nice, fat blue vein at the crook of her arm and without a second's hesitation thrust the needle into it.

She depressed the stopper and watched carefully as every last drop of the gelatin substance disappeared from the clear syringe.

Quickly, Dr. White pulled the needle loose, dropping it inside the case. She flipped the lid closed and sat back in her chair, waiting for blissful nirvana.

The rush hit more quickly this time than last.

She shivered from the sudden cold. Her arms drew up tightly beside her body in spastic reaction. Everything—her eyes, her hair, her toenails—everything trembled wildly as the frigid sensation passed through her system like a melting glacier.

She could *feel* it. Could feel the raw sensation of fresh, surging power. The special treatments she had been giving herself made her feel invincible.

Judith White knew that she was almost there. She had more than touched the plain; she had *crossed* it. It was only a matter of stabilizing what she now felt. And she knew that moment was almost here.

She never wanted to come down.

A crash.

Sudden. Shocking.

Not from the euphoria she now felt. The noise was real. Out beyond the lab.

Someone complaining. Softly. The sound of rapid footsteps on shattered glass.

"Not now," Judith murmured to herself.

She wasn't ready.

More voices. Hushed, nervous.

She got to her feet. She had to steady herself against her desk as she made her way around to the other side. It was a challenge to stay upright as she staggered across the space between desk and door.

Her head was reeling. The voices seemed far away.

No. Close up.

She pulled open the door.

There was a narrow room off the rear of the main laboratory. It was supposed to be an extrawide corridor and storage area, and connected to another laboratory. Dr. White's team had redesigned the long chamber to house the BBQs. In her hallucinatory haze, Judith could see a faint amber strip of light coming from beneath the closed door to this room.

"*Quiet*," a hushed voice insisted.

"There's no one here," another rasped.

"Just be quiet, anyway," ordered the first. "Here, start with the ones nearest the door."

Dr. White heard the distinct, dejected lowing of the BBQs.

Not now, she thought. I'm not ready for this.

Holding on to metal lab stools and desks, she

made her way across the laboratory to the closed door. The single BBQ that had been brought into the lab for the press was still in its pen. The animal blinked at Dr. White as the scientist passed by, crawling hand over hand along the small fence that held the sad-eyed creature in place.

It seemed to take forever, but she finally made it to the door.

There were more than the original two voices by now. She could hear several more inside, grunting and swearing.

Judith fumbled for the doorknob. A distant, lucid part of her mind was surprised when she managed to catch it on the first try. She flung the door open wide.

The startled eyes that looked out at her from the long corridor did not belong to the BBQs.

There were a dozen of them. They wore skintight black mime leotards. Black gloves and black sneakers covered their hands and feet. Their heads were shielded by solid black ski masks. White eyes stared out through rough triangular holes in the masks.

The black-clad figures had been busy.

Most of the BBQs were gone. The last two creatures were even now being herded down the hall to the adjoining lab.

"What the hell do you think you're doing?" Judith demanded. Her voice was a guttural snarl.

Through her blurry, surreal vision, Dr. White could see that one of the floor-to-ceiling panes of glass in the next room had been shattered. More figures in black hefted a BBQ out the broken window. There was a fire escape beyond.

The figures nearby seemed paralyzed for a moment.

Judith staggered into the room.

If the injection would only clear... It didn't take long. Once it did, she'd be able to...

"*I'll* take care of her," snapped a gruff female voice.

One of the leotard-clad figures ran over to Dr. White. Judith held up one hand in an odd defensive posture. Her back arched visibly as she readied for the attack.

But the injection she had given herself was just too strong. Disoriented, she swung down at her attacker's head.

And missed.

She didn't get a second chance.

Something appeared in the hand of the dark figure. A flashlight. The beam played wildly across the wall as the intruder's arm swept up and then down viciously across the side of the scientist's head.

The pain was sharp and bright. It exploded from around the point of impact, racing through her already numb brain.

Judith dropped to all fours on the cold floor.

Weakly, she tried to push herself up. No good. She collapsed over onto her side.

A wave of blackness bled through her mind.

"There's another one in here!" she heard the woman who had struck her exclaim. The voice echoed.

Judith's distorted vision caught a final glimpse of black sneakers scuffing past her and into the main lab. They seemed fuzzy, far off.

There was a final, plaintive moan from the last BBQ.

Then a night shroud of warm oblivion swept in.

The wave of intense darkness engulfed Dr. Judith White.

2

His name was Remo, and he was explaining to the inmate that he had just masterminded a prison break. It was a tough sell, considering they were sharing a tiny solitary-confinement cell in the Supermax maximum-security federal prison in Florence, Colorado.

"What are you talking about?" Todd Grautski blinked, his voice thick with sleep. He was a gaunt man with a face that appeared to have been tied in a knot at one time and never completely unloosened. Wild eyes darted beneath a mop of uncombed, graying hair. His gray beard was like an unkempt ostrich nest.

It was dark in the small cell. A silvery pool of dull light spilled in through a barred panel in the door of the cell. The *closed* door.

The solemn red numbers on the cell's new digital clock told Todd Grautski it was after midnight. Grautski was suspicious of the clock, just as he was of all things mechanical. Unfortunately, the timepiece was not his.

"Keep your voice down," Remo whispered. He held a finger up to his lips. In the darkness, his deep-set dark eyes gave him the appearance of a shushing skull.

Remo was sitting on the edge of Grautski's bunk. The inmate tugged his blanket toward his chin as he sat up.

"What are you doing in here?" Grautski asked fearfully. His voice was stronger now that he was more awake.

Remo rolled his eyes. "I *told* you," he said, even more quietly than before. "I just engineered a prison break."

"So what are you doing here? Shouldn't you be outside?"

"Ohh," Remo said with a smile. "*Now* I understand the source of your confusion. You don't get it. I didn't break *out*. I broke *in*."

Grautski looked at the door. Still closed. There was no evidence that it had been opened since it had been locked with a chillingly mechanical click more than four hours before. However, there was still the vexing problem of the thin young man sitting on his bed. He wasn't a ghost; therefore he was real. He *must* have gotten in somehow.

Grautski wasn't sure if he should call a guard.

"Don't call a guard," Remo suggested, as if he had read Todd Grautski's mind. "They only get in the way. We want this to be neat, don't we?"

"Want what to be neat?" Grautski asked. He pulled the covers more tightly to his chin, as if the wool might protect him. There were a lot of people who wanted Todd Grautski dead. He had a sudden sinking feeling that his skull-headed visitor might be one of them.

The stranger's reply surprised him.

"Our *escape*, silly," Remo said.

"You're getting me out?" Grautski asked doubtfully. "Thanks but no thanks. I'll take my chances on appeal." Fearful of his guest, he pulled the blankets over his head.

"Don't you want to be free?" Remo asked Todd Grautski's trembling bedcovers.

"Go away," came the muffled reply.

"Don't you want to soar like an eagle over these prison walls?" Remo gestured grandly to the wall of the solitary-confinement cell. It was plastered with magazine pictures of naked women. He paused, studying the photographic images. "You know, when I was in prison they didn't allow dirty pictures," he commented.

"They're not mine," Grautski mumbled.

"They *mine*," interjected a voice behind Remo.

Remo had been aware of the second inmate since before he'd even entered the cell. But the man had been snoring softly until now. Remo turned to the speaker.

The face peering from the adjacent bunk was as black as the darkest cell shadows. Bloodshot white eyes stared at Remo.

"Do you mind?" Remo asked, irked. "This is a private prison break."

"You gettin' out?" the other inmate growled. He glanced at the closed door.

"No!" Todd Grautski mumbled through his blanket.

"Yes," said Remo.

"I comin', too," the other prisoner insisted.

"No," Remo said.

"*Yes,*" Grautski stressed. "You can go *instead* of me. And take your damn soul-stealing clock with you."

The second convict sat up, swinging his legs over the side of his bunk. "Don't mind him," he said, waving dismissively at the Todd Grautski–shaped mound of blankets. "He don't like any o' that technology stuff. You realize that is the one and only Collablaster you talkin' to?"

A flicker of something dark and violent passed across Remo's stern features. "I was aware of that," he said icily.

The second prisoner nodded energetically. "They call him the Collablaster 'cause he mail all kinds of dumb-ass bombs to all kinds of college types. Twenty years an' he only killed three guys."

"Allegedly," the Grautski blanket squeaked.

"*I* did more than that in one day," the inmate boasted.

At first, Remo had been irritated by the man's interruption. But as the other convict continued to speak, something familiar about him tweaked the back of Remo's consciousness.

"Do I know you?" he asked, eyes narrowed.

"Kershaw Ferngard," the prisoner announced proudly. "I in here for shootin' up a railroad car full of white folks. Allegedly," he added quickly. He winked knowingly.

Remo nodded. It seemed like an eternity ago, but he remembered the images of Ferngard on TV. His lawyers had attempted to use a "black rage" defense, his racial anger thus excusing him for the six people he'd killed and the other nineteen he had injured in his shooting rampage on the Long Island Railroad. Like Todd Grautski, Ferngard had dismissed his lawyers, opting to represent himself.

"What are you doing here?" Remo asked. "This is supposed to be solitary confinement."

"They paintin' my cell. I didn't like the color. Damn racist prison overcrowding." Ferngard hopped to the floor. "If we gettin' outta here, I needs my toofbrush."

"*I'm* not going anywhere," Todd Grautski's muffled voice insisted.

"Don't listen to Mr. Anti-Technoholic," Ferngard instructed Remo. He was fumbling in the medicine chest. "He be afraid ever since I plug my clock in this mornin'. When I turn on my razor, it took two guards wit mop handles to pull him out from under his bunk."

Ferngard turned. A bright pink toothbrush was clamped in his mitt. The handle was shaped like

Porky Pig. He clicked the business end between his molars. "Ready," he mumbled.

Remo looked from the eager face of Kershaw Ferngard to the quivering pile of wool that hid the infamous Collablaster. Remo was only here for Todd Grautski, but opportunities like this one rarely knocked.

Under the blanket, even though he was in his underwear, Grautski was beginning to sweat. It had gotten too quiet all of a sudden. He didn't like the sense of claustrophobia he got beneath the bedcovers. Solitary was one thing. He could handle that. He'd spent years alone in a cabin in rural Montana with nothing to keep him company save a battered secondhand bicycle and a vast stockpile of bomb-making paraphernalia. But this was too much.

Grautski was biding his time beneath the childhood safety of his covers when he felt a sudden coolness. As soon as the blanket was lifted, Kershaw Ferngard was dumped onto Grautski's prone form. Before they knew what was happening, both men were being knotted up like a bundle of rags inside the fuzzy prison-issue blanket.

"What you doing?" Ferngard demanded from inside the makeshift sack. "I drop my Porky Pig. Hey, get yo knee outta me eye," he snarled at Grautski.

"Shh," Remo whispered.

Beneath the 180-pound pile of wiggling Long Island Railroad Shooter, Todd Grautski tried to shove his hands out through the edge of the blanket. He encountered a tangle of thick knots. The intruder had used the four corners to tie them up inside the blanket.

Grautski suddenly heard a tiny ping of metal strike the concrete floor. "What was that?" he asked, panicked. "Was that an oven timer? I *hate* those."

"Shut up," Ferngard hissed from somewhere near Grautski's shins. He was straining to hear what was going on beyond the blanket. As he did so, the inmate had the abrupt sensation of rising into the air.

There was not a grunt from the man who was obviously carrying them. It was as if both men were no heavier than a duffel bag full of cotton laundry.

It took but a few steps for Kershaw Ferngard to know they'd gone too far to still be inside the solitary cell. By now they were gliding out through the open door to the small room.

"You really *did* break in," Ferngard said from the tangle of blanket, surprise and wonder in his muffled voice.

"Quiet," Remo replied in a whisper. "Try to act like a pair of smelly gym socks."

Ignoring the complaints that issued from the Collablaster, Kershaw Ferngard shifted inside the bundle. He jammed his fingers into one of the tangled knots. After a little jimmying, he managed to pry it open a few inches. He stuck one big eye up to the opening.

They were in the solitary-confinement corridor, slung over the stranger's shoulder like a hobo's bindle. Their combined weight was over three hundred pounds, yet the man moved with a confident glide through the deep shadows.

The place was eerily dark and silent. One wall was lined with closed metal doors. Beyond some of them, Ferngard could hear wet, muted snoring.

The concrete-walled corridor ended at a closed door. Beside it was a sheet of shatterproof Plexiglas. As they moved past the window, Ferngard saw a pair of guards beyond the thick pane. Both were sitting in chairs, heads back, mouths open. They weren't moving.

"You kill the guards?" the inmate asked, owl eyed. As he struggled to get a better look, Todd Grautski grunted.

"They're sleeping," Remo explained. "It's easier to break out that way." He held his finger to his lips for silence once more.

For the first time, Ferngard noticed how thick his wrists were. The man reached for the bolted door. "That'll set off the alarm," Kershaw warned.

"I *hate* alarms," Todd Grautski moaned. Quieter now, he seemed resigned to whatever fate this stranger had in store. "I should have said so in my Collablaster Declaration in the *New York Times.* They make a terrible electronic noise."

"Not if you treat them nicely," Remo said.

Remo tapped a single finger around the locking

mechanism for a tiny moment. Impossibly, the door popped obediently open. Just like that. The green light beside the panel didn't light up, nor did the loud buzzing noise that ordinarily accompanied the opening of the door echo through the hall. They were through the door and inside the narrow adjoining hallway in seconds.

"How'd you do that?" Ferngard asked, amazed.

"Like this," Remo said.

They were at the second security door to the solitary-confinement area. Repeating the motion, Remo sprang the second door as easily as the first.

"He didn't use any electronic gadget, did he?" the Collablaster asked worriedly.

"Yeah, he use a can opener," Ferngard replied, annoyed.

Ferngard felt the tension in Todd Grautski's legs. Mainly because they were wrapped around his neck.

"Ack," Kershaw choked amid the knotted tangle of Collablaster limbs.

"Hey, Frick and Frack, keep it down," Remo whispered. "This is where it gets tricky."

As Ferngard fought to disentangle himself from Todd Grautski's extremities, they slipped out into the general prison area. Skirting the main cells, Remo carried his bundle past the metal-railed lower tier of cells around to the hallway leading up to the cafeteria.

At several strategic points along the way, Ferngard saw more sleeping guards. Others were still awake, however. He could see them patrolling distant sections of the prison as they made their way inside the cafeteria.

"That was amazing," Ferngard whispered as Remo closed the door to the dining hall. "How come they didn't see us?"

"The eye sees only what it expects to see," Remo said.

"But the *cameras* do the rest," Todd Grautski cautioned. "They're *everywhere.*"

"Don't worry," Remo assured him. "They missed us."

"What about the *satellites?*" the Collablaster begged.

As he spoke, he felt the sudden impact of a hard surface beneath him. The knots in the blanket were unraveled. Grautski and Ferngard spilled out onto the cold cafeteria floor.

"Think galactically, act terrestrially," Remo told the Collablaster.

"What's that supposed to mean?" Grautski asked. He rubbed his bruised backside.

Free now, Ferngard blinked hard. A small piece of fuzz from the blanket had gotten stuck in his eye. "It mean you crazy for always worryin' 'bout satellites and microwaves an' shit like that."

All around was the airy mess hall. The big windows high above on one wall were covered with steel mesh. Occasionally, a searchlight would rake across the translucent glass.

"Bring your security blanket," Remo whispered as he walked to the window wall.

Grautski hesitated. Ferngard didn't. Scooping up the blanket, he ran after Remo. Grautski followed reluctantly.

"Who are you, man?" Ferngard asked hoarsely.

"Just a friend of humanity," Remo answered softly. The underlying tone of menace was lost on both prisoners.

"You really mean what you say to hair-dryer-puss?" Ferngard asked. "You was in prison?"

As he spoke, he glanced up at the windows. They were far away. Layers of imposing mesh coated them. The glass interior was crisscrossed with even more threads of steel.

"A long time ago." Remo nodded grimly.

"You don't look like the jail type," the inmate said. "You seem pretty damn straitlaced."

"I was framed," Remo said. "The guy who's my boss now set me up. I was sentenced to die in the electric chair. It didn't work. But as a dead man—at least officially—I was able to go places and do things that a living person would have a hard time doing."

They were at the wall.

"You really got the chair?" Ferngard asked, amazed.

"I don't like the electric chair," Todd Grautski said, wandering up behind them.

"You don't like de 'lectric *toaster,*" Ferngard snapped, peeved.

The Collablaster glanced from one man to the other. "The same technology produced them both," he argued weakly.

They ignored him.

"Sat, strapped, bagged and burned," Remo told Ferngard. He pressed his hands to the wall. It was cool to the touch.

"Wow. How many people you kill?" Ferngard asked.

Remo looked at him. His eyes were invisible beyond the deep shadows of his eye sockets.

"Today?" he asked.

"No, back then. When your boss set you up."

"One. But I didn't kill him."

"You got the chair for doing *one* guy?" Ferngard sputtered derisively. He tried to contain his laughter.

"It was a different era," Remo said. "People were punished for doing wrong. Not like now when any bored psycho with an automatic rifle can shoot up a whole railroad car full of commuters and end up in a cell crammed full of digital clocks and nudie magazines."

"Oh." Ferngard missed the sarcasm completely. "So what's the stuff you can do now that you couldn't do before?"

"This, for one," Remo said.

Remo reached out and grabbed Kershaw Ferngard by the collar of his white T-shirt. He flipped Todd

Grautski up onto the same shoulder. Remo pressed his free hand against the wall of the cafeteria.

Neither prisoner was quite sure what to expect. Even prepared thusly for the unexpected, both were still surprised when Remo's feet left the floor.

Ferngard's eyes grew wide. The one abraded by the tiny wool fragment was a watery red.

The cafeteria began to grow smaller. Row upon row of empty tables stretched out into the thick shadows at the far side of the large room.

He looked to the wall for some alternate explanation for this bizarre act of levitation. He saw only Remo.

Graceful in the precise way that spiders were not, Remo was using one hand and the toes of his leather loafers to carry them all up the smoothly painted cinder-block walls of the mess hall. There was not a hint of strain on his face.

"How you doing that?" Ferngard asked, astonished.

"You ask a lot of questions," Remo commented. The words came easily. It seemed that he should have at least grunted.

"If you could do this stuff, why'd you let your boss put you in the chair?" Ferngard pressed. He wiggled his toes. They moved through empty air.

"I couldn't do anything remotely like this back then," Remo explained. "Once I was officially dead, they turned me over to the Master of Sinanju."

"Sinanju?" Ferngard asked. "That like kung fu?"

"Think kung fu times about a billion," Remo said, "and you'll be scratching the surface. The Master of Sinanju trained me to be his heir. There's only one Sinanju Master and pupil per century, roughly. After bitching at me like a supermodel on a location shoot for about ten years, he made sure I was up to snuff for my mission in life."

"What's that?" Ferngard asked.

They were at one of the large windows. Ferngard was sure they'd have to go back down and find another way out once Remo realized that there was no breaking through. But to the inmate's surprise, Remo began working on the pane as he spoke.

"I'm an assassin," Remo said. "I work for an organization called CURE. It doesn't exist officially, and only me, my boss, my trainer and the President of the United States know it's around."

"A government conspiracy," the Collablaster breathed.

"The granddaddy of them all," Remo agreed.

Remo pressed Ferngard to the wall. Somehow the suction that brought them this far seemed to work straight through the Long Island Railroad Shooter's body. Remo used his free hand to pop the bolts around the securing cage at the corner of the window. He slipped each small bit of metal into the pocket of his chinos while he worked. Somehow he did this without dropping Ferngard or toppling Grautski off his shoulder.

"Yeah," Remo said, warming to his story. "CURE was set up years ago to work outside the Constitution in order to protect it. We take care of the cases that can't be handled in a strictly legal fashion."

He grabbed the mesh and peeled it back. There was a distant, soft creak of metal as the tiny links tore from concrete. The peeled-back section of mesh exposed a wide triangle at the corner of the window.

Remo went to work on the pane. He used the sharp edge of one index fingernail, which was slightly longer than the rest of his nails. The nail scored both glass and the interwoven fibers of metal sandwiched inside the thick pane.

With a soft pop, the large pane came free.

"Hang on for a minute," Remo said to Ferngard.

He hefted the prisoner higher, hooking the back of his shirt onto a twisted bit of metal. With both hands now free and only the weight of Grautski on his shoulder, Remo slid sideways across the windowsill, bringing the large section of glass with him. He settled the triangular pane inside the triangular section of wire mesh. It was a perfect fit. He coiled the bottom metal links to hold the glass in place. Once the glass was safe, he moved back over to Kershaw.

Slipping the inmate down from the makeshift

hook, Remo carried both men out through the window.

There was a narrow ledge rimming the upper portion of the cafeteria building. It wasn't nearly wide enough for someone to stand on. Yet Remo walked along the ledge as if it were the Coney Island Boardwalk.

"What really burns me is that if I *did* know how to do this stuff years ago, I could have escaped," Remo continued. "But the paradox is, if I'd escaped I never would have learned how to do this stuff." The brisk night wind blew through Remo's short dark hair. "You know what I mean?"

Neither man really heard Remo. They were too busy looking down at the empty prison courtyard three stories below. Todd Grautski muttered unintelligibly. Kershaw Ferngard clutched the prison blanket tightly to his chest.

"Less talk, more walk," Ferngard hissed.

They were at the corner of the building now. Remo began to descend the outer prison wall as easily as he climbed the interior cafeteria wall. He shifted the weight of the men.

"It's just funny how life is sometimes," Remo commented as they descended. "When I was in jail, the walls seemed so high, the bars seemed so thick and the guards seemed to be everywhere. I thought it was impossible to get out, so I just resigned myself to accepting the punishment I didn't deserve. Now it's a whole different ball game."

Ferngard felt the soles of his feet touch blessed terra firma.

Remo set Grautski beside him.

The Collablaster opened one eye. They were at the edge of the courtyard. In the daylight, a strip of brown grass and packed earth rimmed the space between the building and the exercise yard. At this time of night, all was awash in shades of black.

Remo beckoned the men to follow him across the paved yard. "*Everything* hasn't changed, though," he confided as they walked. "Chiun—he's the guy who trained me—he's become a real pain in the neck lately. He's locked himself in his room and won't come out. Says he's 'realigning himself with the forces of the cosmos,' or some kind of malarkey. But he doesn't fool me. Since when does cosmic realignment require you to yap on the phone all day and night? And our last bill had a ton of calls to Hollywood."

"Maybe you shouldn't talk so much," Todd Grautski said quietly as the main wall of the prison came closer. He never thought they'd make it this far. Now that they were so close, he allowed himself a flicker of hope. He wondered if the Feds had found *all* his bomb-making material when they'd searched his Montana property.

"I *know* this has something to do with that ding-dong movie of his," Remo pressed, ignoring the Collablaster. "Did I tell you he had a movie deal? At least I *think* he does. He told me about it a while back and then dummied up about the whole thing. He could be yanking my chain. He likes to do that. I can guarantee you, our boss isn't going to like it if he *does* have one.''

They made it across the yard with ease. Whenever a yellow searchlight threatened to drag across them, Remo pulled the men from the path of the beam. It was as if he had some unwavering instinct for avoiding light.

At the wall, the drill was the same as before. The prisoners were deadweight as Remo scaled the smooth surface.

''If he *does* try to have some stupid movie made, my boss is going to go ape-shit. He's a nut for secrecy. Chiun's name on the big screen would probably give him four simultaneous heart attacks. It'd certainly send him over the edge. Which, ironically, is where you two are going.''

They were atop the main wall. A narrow passage between two raised sections on either side of the wall connected the distant guard towers.

Beyond the wall, the convicts saw the first of the pair of concentric chain-link fences that encircled the prison. Once they were through the fences, they were home free. And this remarkable, heaven-sent stranger would have no problem with a couple of mere chain-link fences. Visions of guns and bombs and bloody corpses danced like sugarplums in the twisted brains of both men. There was only one thing wrong.

"What did you just say?" the Collablaster and the Long Island Railroad Shooter asked in unison. For some reason, they both felt as if they'd missed something very important.

Remo's deep disappointment was evident on his stern face. "You mean you weren't paying *attention?*" he asked.

"We heard most of it," Ferngard promised. "The secret organization and your boss and trainer and all. We just missed that last bit." He looked to Grautski, who nodded.

"The part about sending you over the edge?" Remo asked.

Ferngard smiled. "Yeah, that was it." The smile evaporated. "Huh?"

The inmate felt a strong hand press solidly against the center of his chest. Simultaneously, another hand shoved Grautski. Toppling over backward, neither killer had much time to consider his predicament. Their rekindled dreams of murder popped like pierced red bubbles.

As the inmates fell back to the prison courtyard, they fought for possession of the blanket as if it were a life preserver. The woolen corners flapped in the strong wind for the full three seconds it took them to strike concrete.

They hit with twin fat splats. The blanket settled like a heavy parachute onto their bloodied frames.

Remo looked down at the bodies of two of the most infamous murderers of the past decade. There was little satisfaction. It would have been nice to finesse these two.

He'd been told by Upstairs to make it look like a prison break, hence the blanket. Authorities would assume they'd somehow used it as a rope to scale the walls.

Someone had heard the bodies hit the courtyard. Searchlights raked the area, quickly settling on the prone corpses.

Up on the walkway, the bright yellow floodlights avoided Remo entirely.

A Klaxon on the main prison building blared to life, joined quickly by others. As lights switched on rapidly both inside and outside the prison, Remo slipped like a shadow over the wall. The next streak of light to pass where he'd been standing found empty air.

3

In the shadow-drenched administrator's office of a sedate, ivy-covered sanitarium on the shore of Long Island Sound, the man who had dispassionately framed a young Newark beat patrolman named Remo Williams for murder so many years ago was at the moment reading about another murder.

The man Remo had allegedly murdered had been an anonymous drug pusher, chosen precisely because he had been a blight on society who wouldn't be missed. The dead man this day was the owner of a small bookstore in Boston, Massachusetts. He had a wife, two children and a baby on the way.

Dr. Harold W. Smith read the AP report as it scrolled across one portion of his computer screen.

He used the screen-in-screen function on the monitor, which was buried under the surface of the gleaming onyx slab that was his high-tech desk. With this function, he was able to read several reports at once. All were the same. None were good.

There had been a break-in at BostonBio, a company at the vanguard of the genetic-engineering field. Reports were sketchy as yet, but the director of BostonBio's most promising new experiment had been assaulted in her lab. The prototypical animals that had been created by the company had been stolen. By whom and for what reason, no one seemed to have a clue.

In the dark isolation of his office, Smith read the scant details of the BBQ project. It was truly remarkable. The Boston press might have thought the news uninteresting, but Smith found it fascinating. And a bit frightening.

To think that Man had achieved a level of sophistication so great that he could now create a new and unique life-form...

There were moral implications, to be sure. But Smith had the soul of a bureaucrat, not a philosopher. While he understood why there would be trepidations for some when it came to the BBQ project, he saw it more as a practical matter. If the creatures were, as Dr. Judith White boasted, the solution to world hunger, then the project could not be jeopardized.

Smith paused at his work. The glowing keys of the capacitor keyboard, which was buried at the lip of his desk, grew dark as he removed his arthritis-gnarled fingers from the surface. He spun in his old leather chair, looking out through the one-way picture window behind him.

His gray face was reflected in the glass. All about Smith was gray, right down to his three-piece gray suit. The only hint of color in his entire gray-tinged spirit was a green-striped Dartmouth tie, which was tied to four-in-hand perfection beneath his protruding Adam's apple.

It was well after midnight. Long Island Sound was dark and foreboding. The few lights visible on the water at this time of night were startling in contrast with the depth of darkness. They almost seemed ethereal—angels beckoning the faithful home.

It was an oddly poetic thought for Harold W. Smith. One he would not have entertained when he'd first come to work in this plain administrator's office. The truth was, Smith held few such illusions in his youth. But the world had changed vastly since Smith had been appointed to this lonely post.

Smith was director of Folcroft Sanitarium in Rye, New York, the secret headquarters for the organization known only as CURE. In his position, he had seen much that was bad in America. It was CURE's charter to deal with each national crisis as it came along. But as Smith stared out into the inky blackness of eternity—a man in the twilight of his life— he thought that it might be nice for a change for CURE to be involved in something good.

The BBQ project seemed on the surface to be nothing *but* good. What could be more noble than a desire to feed the hungry? Smith wondered who might want to thwart such a plan.

According to a media report, Dr. White had attacked a reporter earlier in the day. Reading between the lines, Smith determined that it might have been frustration that drove her to do it. Perhaps whoever had stolen the animals was in collusion with the reporter. Perhaps it was partly vengeance, partly a desire on the part of the reporter to create a story. It had happened with the press before.

Whatever the reason, Harold W. Smith had made up his mind that CURE would do something good even before the blue contact phone rang atop his desk.

"Remo?" the CURE director said crisply into the receiver. His voice was squeezed lemons.

"Smitty, it's one o'clock in the morning. Who else would it be?" Remo's familiar voice replied.

Smith drew his eyes away from the black waters of the Sound. "I need not remind you that Chiun also has this number," he said.

"Chiun is still locked away meditating like some freaking Korean monk," Remo said, irked. Somewhere close behind him, a car horn honked.

"You are not home?" Smith asked.

"No way," Remo answered. "I'm hiding out at the airport. I've been getting this creepy Norman Bates feeling every time I look up at his window."

Smith didn't understand the cultural reference. He chose to ignore it. "What of your assignment?" he asked.

"You got a twofer, Smitty," Remo said. He actually seemed pleased. "You didn't tell me Kershaw Ferngard was in the same prison as Grautski."

"Yes," Smith said. "I heard he had been moved from New York. Minister Linus Feculent had been working to have him freed as a victim of racial injustice. The authorities thought it would quiet things down if he was not in close proximity to Feculent or network cameras."

"Well, if Dan Rather wants to interview either of them, he's going to have to bring a sponge and a pail."

Smith nodded in satisfaction. He swiveled in his chair, looking back out across Long Island Sound. There were no lights visible now. No angels guiding anyone home.

"I have another assignment for you," Smith said as he stared out into the lifeless black night.

"Fine with me," Remo said affably. "So long as it keeps me away from home."

Smith went on to quickly brief Remo about the genetic creations at BostonBio and the opportunity to use them as a cure to world hunger. He finished with the mysterious theft of the creatures.

"And you want *me* to go find them?" Remo asked once Smith was finished. He sounded surprised.

"It is not an ordinary CURE assignment, granted," Smith said. "However, the world stage is quiet at the moment. And it sounds as if the local authorities could use the help."

"Hey, you don't have to sell me on the idea, Smitty," Remo remarked. "It'll be nice to be involved in something that's sort of for the good of the world for a change.''

Smith was surprised that Remo shared his sentiment on the subject, but said nothing.

"There might be an added problem," he cautioned. "There was a murder in Boston a few hours ago. It was in the vicinity of the lab where the *Bos camelus-whitus* was created. The body of a local merchant was found mauled in an alley. His throat and abdomen had been shredded, and most of his organs had been removed.''

"Eaten?" Remo asked.

"Presumably."

"So these things are vicious.''

"I am not certain," Smith admitted slowly. "I saw raw video footage of the creatures posted on the home page of one of the local network affiliates. They seem docile. But as we both know, looks—as far as the ability to kill is involved—can be deceiving.''

"So much for helping out mankind," Remo said, dryly. "Sounds like these dips have turned Bean Town into *Jurassic Park III*.''

"It is possible that this attack has nothing to do with the lab specimens," Smith said. "There have been cases of wild animals in urban areas before. Wolves and coyotes in Central Park and moose running loose in Boston, for instance. This *could* be a big cat that has somehow made its way into the city. It might have nothing at all to do with the BBQs.''

"Within walking distance of the lab?" Remo said doubtfully. "Don't bet the sanitarium on it, Smitty."

"Be that as it may, I want you to learn what you can and report your findings back to me."

He gave CURE's enforcement arm the address of BostonBio and the full name of the director of the BBQ project.

"Dr. Judith White," Remo said. "Got it."

Smith was about to hang up.

"And Smitty?" Remo offered hesitantly.

Smith paused. "Yes?"

"If you hear from Chiun, don't tell him I was itching to stay away from home. If it puts him on the snot, he'll say I misaligned him again. I can't take another two months of him locked away straightening out his pretzeled psyche."

"Very well," Smith agreed. He severed the connection.

After he had replaced the blue receiver, Smith's gaze strayed back to the window behind him and the water beyond.

It was very late. He should begin to think about going home for the night.

As he stared off blankly into space, a light suddenly appeared like a sparkling diamond on the surface of the water far away.

One of Smith's angels?

Smith sat up more alertly in his chair. He stared at the distant light. As quickly as it had appeared, it vanished from sight.

　　Sitting behind his comfortable desk in his familiar Spartan office, Harold W. Smith got a sudden, unexplainable twinge of concern. Though he tried to dismiss it, he could not. Frowning, he turned back slowly to his computer.

4

By the following morning, Boston's local media outlets were all eagerly linking the gruesome death of bookstore owner Hal Ketchum to the theft of the BBQs from the genetics laboratory of BostonBio.

Mutant Monsters Panic Hub! screamed the headline of the *Boston Messenger,* a paper not famous for its temperate reporting of the news. In an editorial, the more sedate *Boston Blade* managed to link the entire series of events to supply-side economics. Not surprising. The paper regularly blamed everything from teen pregnancy to the JonBenet Ramsey murder on the devil decade of the 1980s. For their part, the local television stations were no less gleeful to throw gasoline on the raging fire of hysteria.

A BostonBio security guard was scanning a bored eye along the lines of typically vitriolic *Blade* text when Remo Williams stepped through the gleaming glass doors of the corporation's main office complex. Sunlight streamed in across the floor as Remo approached the desk.

The guard didn't look up from the paper. ''I am not a spokesman for BostonBio. I am under contract

not to discuss anything that occurs within the buildings or complex of BostonBio. No one at BostonBio
is granting interviews at this time. Please leave me
the hell alone.''

His nasal voice was bored as he ran through the
speech he had repeated at least three dozen times
since his shift started at seven that morning. When
he was finished, he crinkled the paper, folding it to
the sports section. He didn't get a chance to check
on any of Boston's chronically losing teams.

"I'm not a reporter," Remo explained to him.

The guard looked up, surprised the visitor hadn't
left. His nose bumped a laminated ID card.

"Remo Post. Department of Agriculture," Remo
said, holding out the ID. "I'm here about last night's
theft.''

The guard snorted, putting his paper aside. "You
and everybody else." He took Remo's identification,
inspecting it carefully. "You don't look like an agriculture agent," he said eventually, looking up over
the card.

"The corn-husk hat gave me dandruff, and my
sorghum pants chafed," Remo said.

Peering across his foyer desk at Remo's tan chinos and white T-shirt, the guard seemed doubtful.
He finally shrugged, sliding the card back to Remo.

"What the hell. After yesterday, we'll all be out
on our ears anyway. Third floor." He picked his
paper back up, jamming his nose back inside the
sports pages.

"I'm gonna take a leap and chalk this all up to crummy security," Remo muttered to himself.

Leaving the vigilant security guard to read his paper, Remo crossed over to the elevator.

THREE STORIES ABOVE the BostonBio lobby, Dr. Judith White was throwing a fit. According to the tally kept by her lab staff, it was her seventh that morning.

"I can't *believe* this shit!" she screeched. She waved a copy of the morning paper that one of her staff had had the temerity to bring in that morning. "You're all a pack of sniveling Judases! You're buying into this character assassination! *I'm* the one responsible for this project, not any of you! I could have fired every last one of you, and the *Bos camelus-whitus* project would have gone on!"

With angry fists, she balled up the newspaper, flinging it at the man who had pulled it from his desk drawer when he thought Dr. White was busy in her office. It struck him loudly in the forehead. She'd thrown it with such ferocity, he hadn't even had time to duck out of the way.

"You people *all* make me sick!" she screamed. Spinning away from the guilty-faced staff, she marched back inside her office. The high lab windows shook with the violence of her slamming door.

The lab staff didn't seem to know how to react.

It had been this way all morning. Dr. White had refused treatment for her injury from the night before. It was probably a mistake, since the blow to the head she had received seemed to have made her even more vile-tempered than usual. Of course, her mood might not be the result of a concussion. Dr. Judith White had been perched on the edge of sanity for a long time. The stress of the BBQ theft might just have been the thing that finally toppled her over.

In any event, without their lab specimens, there was nothing much for the lab technicians to do. No BBQs meant no work. The lab staff had merely stood around for the past two hours, anxiously awaiting the next outburst from their project director.

It was into this tense atmosphere that Remo strolled.

Inside the lab, Remo flashed his bogus Department of Agriculture ID at the first unoccupied white coat he met. The man was a microbiologist with a pronounced overbite, a receding hairline and a name tag that identified him as Orrin Merkel.

"Post," Remo said, tone bored as he repeated his alias. "Investigating the theft of the cookouts last night."

"Of the what?" Orrin asked, perplexed.

"Those animal jobbies in the paper," Remo said, himself confused. For a moment, he thought he was in the wrong lab. "Didn't you build them here?"

"Oh," Orrin said. "The *BBQs.*" There was an angry snort from behind a distant closed office door. "That's not their real name," he said, pitching his voice low. "And Dr. White doesn't approve of the nickname."

"She's the one who was here when they were stolen?" Remo queried, jabbing a thumb at the door. Orrin nodded. "Thanks."

Remo headed for Dr. White's office.

"Uh...I don't think you want to see her," Orrin said, hurrying up beside Remo. "Guys? Help?"

He glanced around for support, but when Remo's purpose became clear, the rest scattered from the room like frightened cockroaches. Orrin was left alone with the agriculture man.

Remo was steering a beeline for the door.

Orrin had to leap across a desk to get in front of him.

"You *really* don't want to see her," he insisted.

Remo stopped. "Why not?"

Orrin shot a worried look at the door. He lowered his voice to a conspiratorial whisper. "For one thing, she's a drug user," he confided. "Heroin, I think."

"The director of this lab uses heroin," Remo said skeptically.

"She shoots up after hours. Some of us have seen her. So far it hasn't affected her work." Orrin considered. "Although I guess it could account for her mood swings. Sometimes she's a real *B-I-T-C-H,* if you know what I mean."

"Nope, I don't," Remo said. "But then, spelling's not my strong suit. After ten years with the department, I *still* spell *agriculture* with *two* *K*s.''

"There's a whole psychiatric textbook back there," Orrin whispered, nodding to the door. "Aside from the drug use, she exhibits strong antisocial tendencies and, as far as anyone here can tell, she is one hundred percent, completely and totally amoral. Possibly sociopathic, as well."

"Doesn't sound like the woman who's going to cure world hunger," Remo said.

Orrin bit his lip. "There's *some* good in everybody, I guess. Dr. White might be a lot of things, but she's also a genius. Maybe she's just misunderstood."

"I'll be sure to put that in my report to the undersecretary for husking and threshing," Remo said.

He sidestepped Orrin. Despite frantic gestures from the microbiologist, Remo knocked on the closed office door. Orrin was across the lab and out the front door before Dr. White even had a chance to respond.

"Hurry up and come in already!" a gruff female voice barked in response to Remo's knock.

After the impression he had gotten from the young scientist, Remo wasn't sure precisely what to expect beyond the door. When he pushed the door open, any preconceived notions he might have had melted in a stunned instant.

Dr. Judith White was beautiful. Her black hair was long and full around her face, shaped vaguely in the tousled, confident manner of a lion's mane. Her nose was aquiline, her dark red lips full and inviting. The teardrop shape of her green eyes was vaguely Asian.

As far as her body was concerned, the parts Remo could see as she sat behind her desk would have turned a *Playboy* model green with envy. When she stood in greeting, he realized that the same model would have gone from green to blue before dropping dead from terminal jealousy. In Dr. Judith White, the female form had achieved a level of physical perfection unheard-of on Earth.

When she smiled, a row of dazzlingly white teeth gleamed brilliantly, framed between perfect lips. The smile was not one of politeness. It was more a perturbed rictus.

"What do you want, Mr. Post?" Judith asked.

Remo was confused at her use of his cover name.

"Have we met before, Dr. Boobs?" he asked absently. He was staring at her ample chest.

"What?" she said, voice icy. Her eyes could have cut diamonds.

"Hmm?" Remo asked. He pulled his gaze up to her face. It was an effort. They liked it where they were.

For some reason, Judith seemed annoyed. She scowled as she retook her seat. "I heard you mention your name to Orrin, the Dweeb." She waved a hand toward the lab. "These morons haven't figured out yet that I can hear everything from this office."

Remo looked through the open door to the spot where he had spoken to Orrin Merkel. It seemed too far for her to have heard his conversation with the microbiologist. He was frowning when he turned back to her.

"Washington sent me to investigate the theft of your BBQs," Remo said. He took a seat before her desk.

Cluttered bookshelves lined the walls behind Dr. White and to her left. To the right, half-raised mini-blinds opened on the well-tended grounds of BostonBio.

She shuddered, closing her eyes with overempha-sized patience. "*Please* don't call them that," she said.

"Isn't that what everyone's calling them?"

"Everyone's wrong. They are *Bos camelus-whitus*. BCW would be more accurate than that other ridiculous appellation."

"But nowhere near as lunchbox ready," Remo pointed out.

His smile was not returned.

"Yuck it up, Post," Dr. White said, flat of voice. "In the moment it takes you to chuckle, hundreds of human beings starve all around the world."

"If the alternative's getting mauled by one of your *Boss cactus-whiteouts,* maybe they're better off," Remo suggested.

Dr. White snorted. "That bookstore owner, right?" she said skeptically. "I'm sick of hearing *that* one, too. I don't know who killed that guy, but I can guarantee you it wasn't one of my BCWs. They literally would not harm a fly.''

She was passionate about the animals, Remo could see. And that passion was possibly blinding her to the fact that the animals she had created might actually be killers. He chose to drop the subject.

"Any idea who might have taken them?"

"I already *told* the Boston police who did it," Judith said crisply. "But in case you didn't know, the mayor in this town is about as dumb as a WB sitcom. He's barred the cops from looking where they should. All because of stupid political correctness. The world is going to *starve* because of PC politics."

"I'll bite," Remo said. "Where do you think they are?"

This time Judith White's smile was sincere. "HETA," she announced.

Remo frowned. "Where have I heard that before?"

"It's a wacko animal-rights group," she explained, sinking back in her chair. "Humans for the Egalitarian Treatment of Animals. They have an ad campaign on TV I'm sure you've seen. They sponsor all sorts of animal-adoption stuff, fight animal testing in labs, that kind of thing. Celebrity endorsers line up around the block for them."

"Oh, yeah." Remo nodded. "What makes you think they're the ones who stole your animals?"

"*Someone* in this lab has loose lips," Judith said. "Whoever it is must have bragged about my breakthrough. Since the birth of the first *Bos camelus-whitus* eight months ago, HETA has been stepping up activity against BostonBio."

"Maybe it's a coincidence," Remo suggested.

"No way, sugar," Dr. White insisted. "BostonBio has a good record with animal testing. There are much bigger, more well-known targets in the area for them to go after. The timing was just too perfect. No, if you want my advice, brown eyes, you'll go after HETA."

"They have a local office?"

Dr. White nodded. "In Cambridge," she said.

"Can I borrow your phone book?" Remo asked.

Dr. White's eyes narrowed. "What for?"

"My ability to channel addresses is on the fritz."

Judith closed her eyes and leaned her head back, exposing her long, white neck. She lowered her head back down, slowly opening her eyes as she did so.

"I'll take you," she said with a heavy sigh. Pushing off her desk for support, she rose to her feet.

"That isn't necessary," Remo told her.

"Look, I've got nothing better to do. I'm facing suspension and possible criminal action for assaulting a ditzy reporter yesterday. The only thing that'll keep me here are those animals. I was planning to take a spin over to HETA myself. You can be my muscle."

Skirting her desk, she stepped from the office,

stripping off her white lab coat as she walked. Her chest bounced purposefully.

"Do I have a choice?" Remo asked the empty room.

He was surprised to get an answer.

"No," replied the distant voice of Dr. Judith White.

5

Sadie Mayer joined HETA because that nice lady from *The Olden Girls* told her to.

Not personally, of course. Sadie had never met a celebrity in her life. And if she did, good gosh, whatever would she say to them? No, Sadie had been encouraged to join the organization by a thirty-second commercial spot featuring *The Olden Girls* actress run by the animal-rights group during *Wheel of Fortune*.

Sadie wasn't an activist. She made this clear to anyone who said so. She always associated real activism with those dirty people from the sixties. Also, activism seemed to mean burning something. Either underwear for feminists or draft cards with hippies. Sadie didn't like to burn things.

No, her brand of activism was simple and flame free. It involved a big yearly check, occasionally stuffing and sorting envelopes and twice a month volunteering to man the phones at the local Cambridge headquarters of Humans for the Egalitarian Treatment of Animals.

Today was Sadie's Thursday to sit behind the

HETA reception desk licking envelopes. Her hands and tongue were deeply involved in her work when she spied a vaguely familiar figure step through the front door of the building. The woman was in the company of a young man.

The woman seemed very businesslike in her smart blazer and tweed skirt. Very much like Hillary Clinton. He, on the other hand, looked like a typical bum. Sadie considered anyone who didn't dress like Lawrence Welk on Saturday night to be a bum. By her definition, all three of the sons she had raised were bums.

Sadie held her disdain in check as the pair strode across the small lobby to her plain schoolmarm's desk.

"Can I help you?" Sadie asked, drawing the flap of a business-size envelope across her dry-as-dust tongue. The sealing gum tasted vile. She put the envelope in a box with the other five dozen she had sealed. Thanks to her inability to produce saliva, they were all already coming unglued.

"We want to see—" Remo began, Department of Agriculture ID in hand.

"Where's that weed Tulle?" Judith interrupted.

Remo shot Judith a withering look.

Sadie paused in midlick. "*Mr.* Tulle?" she asked scornfully. "Is *that* who you mean?" She drew the envelope the rest of the way across her tongue. It popped open as she placed it in the Out box.

"If he's the guy in charge," Remo supplied.

"Oh, he's in charge, brown eyes," Judith snarled to him. "He's the biggest cashew in this can of assorted nuts."

"Crazy woman make nice-nice now," Remo suggested through tightly clenched teeth.

Judith wheeled on him. "Well, I don't hear you saying anything," she snapped.

"That's because you haven't given me a chance," Remo replied sharply.

"Look, is he here?" Judith demanded, spinning back to Sadie.

She moved so quickly that it startled the old woman behind the desk. Sadie jumped in the middle of licking an envelope. The paper edge sliced at an angle across her parched and bumpy tongue, opening up a thin bloody crease.

"Look what you made me do!" Sadie complained.

Angry, the old woman stuck out her tongue, pressing her dentures at the center. She could feel the pain of the paper cut across the whole width of her tongue. Turning her eyes downward, she tried to see the small wound.

"Dith ith goin to hur fo daith," Sadie griped.

As she sat examining her wound, Sadie was startled by a hand reaching for her. She looked up to see that the woman who had caused her to injure herself was actually reaching out a hand as if to touch Sadie's tongue.

Sadie jumped back.

"What the hell are you doing?" Remo asked Judith. He placed a firm hand on her forearm, arresting it in space.

Judith paused, as if startled. She looked at her own hand, suddenly thinking better of whatever she had intended to do. Quickly, she withdrew her arm.

"I'm sorry," she said curtly to Sadie. She glanced over her shoulder at Remo. "It's all right, you know. I *am* a doctor, after all."

That's when it hit Sadie.

"You're *her!*" the older woman cried sharply, forgetting her injured tongue. "The one from the TV. The lunatic from BostonBio who assaulted poor Sally Edmunds."

Judith rolled her eyes. "I give up. His name is Curt Tulle," she said to Remo. "*You* do better." Stepping back, she crossed her arms over her ample chest.

"Thank you." Remo nodded.

Without another word to Sadie, he sidestepped the old woman's desk and walked up the hallway that stretched away behind her seat. Surprised but obviously pleased at his decisiveness, Judith fell in behind him.

"I'm starting to like you, brown eyes," she said.

"My name is Remo," he said, peeved.

"Blame your parents for that," Judith suggested.

As they strolled down the hallway, Sadie shouted loud protests, threatening to call the police. Remo and Judith ignored her.

There were a few doors lining either side of the short corridor. Most were closed.

"That one." Judith pointed to the second office from the end.

Remo had sensed the steady heartbeat coming from beyond the closed door. He assumed Judith had been here some time in the past to know Tulle's office.

Remo didn't bother to knock. He pushed against the chipped, green-painted surface of the old wooden door. It creaked painfully open on the cramped office of the Boston director of Humans for the Egalitarian Treatment of Animals.

Curt Tulle looked up from his desk. At least Remo assumed that's who it was. He couldn't quite tell if the thing he was looking at was human under all that fur.

Curt wore a raccoon hat, the kind made popular during the 1950s. A long, draping woman's mink coat was buttoned tightly up to his neck. The neck of the HETA director was wrapped, in turn, by a dark ermine stole. The clasp holding the wrap in place made the head of the hapless creature appear to be biting the animal's tail.

To Remo, there was no more accurate a phrase to describe the look on Curt Tulle's face as that of an animal caught in headlights. It was sheer, blind, frozen terror.

"Keep the windows rolled up and your hands in

the car,'' Remo suggested over his shoulder to Judith.

As Remo spoke, Curt Tulle finally found his voice. "Who are you?" he demanded angrily. "Who let you in here?"

The ermine stole was already stuffed inside the drawer. He seemed to remember the raccoon hat abruptly, snatching it from atop his head. The drawer opened again, and the hat was flung inside. Curt slammed the drawer loudly shut a second time. A few shimmies of his shoulders loosed the mink coat. He kicked it into the well under his desk.

"I guess the only thing about fur that's murder is the price," Remo commented.

"Filthy hypocrite," Judith snarled, her voice a low growl.

When she moved toward Curt, Remo had to intercept her.

Her passion gave her extra strength. Remo had to exert surprising force to pull her away. He scooted her back behind him.

"Let's put the good-cop–psycho-cop act on hold, shall we?" he suggested to White. To Curt, he said, "We're investigating the disappearance of the PDQs from BostonBio."

"BCWs," Judith hissed angrily.

"BMWs," Remo corrected.

"Hey, I know you." The HETA director squinted. He was looking at Judith White. His deer's eyes grew even wider. "You're the crazy scientist who's trying to play Mother Nature."

This time Remo didn't move quickly enough to stop Judith. She darted around him, leaping and sliding across Curt Tulle's desk in a single fluid move. Along the way, she scooped up a letter opener that had been lying next to a banker's lamp. The green-shaded lamp went flying as Judith kicked around, dropping in beside the startled HETA director. With one hand, she grabbed a clump of thin hair, pulling back his head. The other hand aimed the business end of the letter opener into Curt's Adam's apple.

"Where are my animals?" she screamed.

Curt choked fearfully. "I don't *know!*" he cried.

"You're *lying!*" she snarled.

"No! No, I'm telling the truth!" His desperate eyes sought out Remo. "Say something!" he pleaded.

"I'm not cleaning up the body," Remo cautioned Dr. White. Stepping back, he settled comfortably into a chair, pleased for a change to farm out the heavy lifting.

Curt was sweating. Judith's voice was close to his ear, hot and menacing.

"I know there are HETA-funded terrorists who *live* for this crap. You paid them to break into my lab, didn't you?" She jerked his head back harder. *"Didn't you!"*

"Possibly!" Curt admitted. Perspiration had broken out across his upper lip.

"Possibly?" Remo asked from across the room.

Curt tried to shrug. "We *do* disperse funds from this office," he admitted. "I can't always say for sure where the money goes to ultimately. Legal reasons."

"I'll legal you a blowhole," she barked, pressing the blunt knife into his flesh.

"Please!" Curt begged.

Remo interjected. "Who do you think took the animals?"

"No one knows for sure," Curt replied nervously. "But I was talking to a HETA sympathizer in Salem a few hours ago. A guy named Billy Pierce. He hinted around that he might know something. I told him I didn't want to know. *Please.* You've *got* to believe me. I don't know *anything.*"

"Truer words have never been spoken," Judith growled.

She wrenched Curt's hair one last time before flinging the terrified HETA director face first onto his desk.

The letter opener had inadvertently punctured a small spot on Curt's neck. A drop of deep red blood clung to the end of the blunt knife. Judith seemed surprised at the sight of the blood. She held it before her eyes, as if shocked that she could have performed an act of such violence. She snorted once deeply—angry at herself—and then flung the knife away.

"Coward's blood. I can smell it a mile away,"

she announced contemptuously. She twirled away from the desk. "Are you ready to go, Hank Kimble?" she asked Remo.

Remo got slowly to his feet. "I'm guessing you don't get many Christmas cards," he ventured.

Without another word to the shaking HETA director, the two of them left the office.

In the hall, they nearly tripped over Sadie Mayer. Rather than call the police, the old woman had opted for eavesdropping outside Curt Tulle's door. She dogged them to the lobby.

"Scumbag son of a bitch!" Sadie yelled. "Filthy bastard scum-sucking bum."

"You're sweet," Remo commented at the front door. "Do you French your father with that mouth?"

"Son of a bitch bum!" Sadie screeched. She stabbed an angry finger at Judith. "He who sleeps with dogs winds up with fleas!" This was apparently a caution to Remo.

"That reminds me. Honey, we're low on flea powder," Remo said to Judith.

"Shut up, idiot," the scientist snarled impatiently, shoving her way through the front doors.

"Goddamn son of a bitch bum!" Sadie shrieked at him.

"When did Boston start dumping testosterone in the drinking water?" Remo asked.

In response, Sadie tried to kick him. Avoiding her

bone-and-bunion-filled Reeboks, he slowly trailed Judith White outside.

REMO AND JUDITH WEREN'T GONE more than one minute when a set of keys jangled outside the steel alley door near Curt Tulle's office. The fire door opened silently. A pair of dark-clad figures clicked the door shut behind them.

Stepping carefully, the two shapes moved swiftly up to the HETA director's office.

Curt had knotted his ermine stole around his neck once more and was stroking the soft fur in a gentle, soothing manner. Sitting behind his desk, he looked up with a start when the new pair of visitors slipped into his office.

The man and woman were both somewhere near forty. They wore jackets over their black leotards. Their ski masks were stuffed into their coat pockets. Dressed too warmly for the early-autumn day, both of them were sweating profusely.

The HETA man nearly jumped out of his skin when he first saw the couple. When he realized that he recognized them, his face relaxed somewhat.

"My God, you scared the hide off of me." He tugged off the ermine stole, stashing it away once more.

"What's the matter with you?" the man asked.

"Didn't you *see* them?" Curt said, agitated.

"We came in the back." This from the woman.

Curt took a deep breath. "Judith White was here."

"The Beast of BostonBio?" the woman asked, aghast.

Curt Tulle nodded. "She had some buck with her. They're looking for those whatever-they-ares. The BBQs."

The woman smiled smugly. "They'll never find them."

Curt looked up sharply. "You know where they *are?*"

"Of course we do," she retorted. "Who do you think liberated them?"

"You're going to *love* what we have planned for them," her companion declared excitedly.

The HETA director could think only of the crazed look in Judith White's eyes. When the man opened his mouth to speak once more, Curt Tulle fixed it so he didn't hear a word of what he said.

As the couple detailed their diabolical plan, Curt clapped his hands firmly over his ears. Rubbing his nervous bare ankles against the comforting fur of the mink coat beneath his desk, Curt drowned them out by screaming the words to "Puff the Magic Dragon" at the top of his voice.

6

When he was fifteen years old, young Billy Pierce's mother assured her son that he'd grow out of his terrible case of acne.

"Don't worry, Billy," Mrs. Pierce had said, with the quiet confidence only a parent could muster. "It shows up for maybe a few years and then it's gone forever. And I don't know what you're worried about anyway. You're still the handsomest boy at Salem High School."

As far as looks were concerned, Billy deluded himself into thinking that maybe his mother was right. Perhaps underneath the layers of oozing pustules and bloody scabs was another Rock Hudson waiting to break out. Billy never did find out.

Handsome was in the eye of the beholder, and any girl who beheld Billy from freshman all the way to senior year saw only "Zit-Face" Pierce. The acne, as well as the nickname, followed him to Salem State College.

Even when Billy graduated from college with a degree in English, the name dogged him. Perhaps it was his acne, perhaps it was his attitude, but whatever the reason, he couldn't find a good job in town. He settled for employment in a small local fast-food establishment. Leftover pizza and as many French fries as he could filch didn't help his cratered complexion.

When he finally couldn't stand it any longer, Billy went to see a doctor. He subjected himself to ten full minutes of poking and prodding by the middle-aged physician. Finally, the doctor sat down in a chair before the twenty-three-year-old acne sufferer. He stayed a safe distance from his patient, seemingly afraid some of the worst of Billy's sad affliction might erupt with Vesuvian violence.

"Billy," the old doctor asked seriously, "when was the last time you took a bath?" He tried not to inhale too deeply.

"Baths are for the Man," Billy retorted.

The doctor shook his head somberly. "No, Billy. Baths are for people who want to be clean. You are without a doubt the filthiest thing on two legs I have ever seen."

How could Billy explain it to the old, un-hip fossil? It was the early 1970s, and fashionable dirt was in. This lack of personal hygiene among the avant-garde was so chic it predated grunge by twenty years. In 1972 everyone who was anyone had long, scraggly hair and looked like they'd just crawled out a sooty tailpipe.

Billy decided at that moment that the doctor was

a quack. He also resigned himself to a life of lingering acne.

Almost thirty years later, nothing much had changed for Billy Pierce.

He still had the same job. He still lived at home with his mother. And his face still looked as if it had seen the business end of an acid-filled squirt gun. But now his long hair was greasier and thinner, his forehead stopped somewhere near the back of his head and his belly hung hugely over his belt, completely obscuring his large peace-symbol buckle.

And the single major change for Billy Pierce over the years was his allegiance. Since, sadly, there was no longer a war in Vietnam to protest, he had to find something else to occupy the self-righteous part of his moral and political soul. Necessity had forced Billy to throw his support behind the liberation of animals from their human overlords.

But it wasn't like the old days.

When he was protesting the war in Southeast Asia, he felt like part of a larger community. There were songs and sit-ins and marches on Washington. As an animal-rights activist, he toiled mostly in isolation and anonymity.

That was what he was doing today.

He had gotten the special blueprints from the Salem city hall. They were a little old, but very detailed.

A cracked coffee mug his mother used for gardening held down one curling corner of the large roll of paper. Dirt had dried in the bottom of the mug. Water-damaged paperbacks that had been stored in the basement four years ago when the cellar flooded held down two other corners. Billy was using his hand and elbow, alternately, to keep the last corner from rolling up.

As he looked over the plans, the bare fluorescent bulbs above him cast weird shadows across the table. Billy was trying to figure out what he would need.

Wire clippers. Probably. Maybe bolt cutters.

Would he be able to pick the locks? He doubted it. But if he couldn't pick them, he knew the bolt cutters probably would do him no good on the locks. Billy had never had much upper-body strength.

Maybe they weren't locked at all. After all, the interspecies prisoners couldn't very well escape by reaching out through the bars. Maybe they were just hooked closed.

Of course! The keys would be on the premises!

It would help to know where they were. Billy vowed to do a little more reconnaissance before D day.

As his fat, grimy finger traced a path through the rooms on the blueprints, Billy heard a noise upstairs. It was the sound of someone stepping lightly across the kitchen floor.

Billy was startled by the noise. His mother was supposed to be at bingo until ten.

"Ma?" he yelled in the direction of the creaky wooden stairs. "Ma, is that you?"

No reply. At least not a vocal one. The gentle, padding footfalls became more focused. They moved in a direct path for the upstairs hallway where the cellar door was located.

Billy instantly panicked. Someone had obviously learned of his plan.

His hand sprang away from the blueprints, which immediately curled up, rolling with such force that they pushed away his mother's soiled mug. It fell to the floor, breaking into a dozen large pieces.

Billy didn't care. He had already turned away from the table and was waddling frantically toward the musty-smelling bulkhead at the rear of the basement.

The upstairs cellar door opened. Precise footfalls struck the staircase behind him.

Across the basement, Billy stumbled on the first concrete step. Toppling forward, he skinned his hands on the third. He pushed his ample girth back upright.

It was cold inside the bulkhead, with a thick earthen odor.

Billy grabbed desperately at the latch, twisting it wildly. With a single, violent push, he attempted to shove the flat door up into the yard. He found that he wasn't strong enough to budge the door more than an inch. Late-afternoon sunlight streamed in through the narrow crack for a tantalizing moment before the door clanged back loudly over his head, like the lid of a coffin.

He tried again. Too late.

A strong hand grabbed him by the shoulder. He felt his massive frame lift off the steps. Billy's feet rose from the short concrete stairwell, and he soared backward into the cellar, landing atop the very table where he had been sketching out his great mission. The old table shattered to kindling beneath his great bulk.

Billy rolled over onto the pile of debris, eyes blinking back shock and pain. For the first time, he beheld the face of his attacker. *Attackers.*

"Are you trying to *kill* him?" Judith White demanded. She stood, her face a mask of accusation, near Remo Williams at the dark opening to the bulkhead.

"I wouldn't have had to grab him if he hadn't heard you stomping around like a drunken bison upstairs," Remo countered.

"Stomping?" Judith retorted. "I'm as silent as a cat."

"How silent do you think a 115-pound cat would be?" he asked, irritated.

"A lot quieter than you," she replied angrily.

"Listen before you answer, lady. Have you heard me scuff my foot once since you met me?" Remo demanded. "Have you even heard one single footfall?"

Judith paused. Her temper seemed to dissipate somewhat.

"No," she conceded. The admission appeared to puzzle more than anger her.

"And while we're at it, you're not exactly a poster child for subtlety after that performance back in Boston," Remo pointed out. "So back off."

Leaving the cowed geneticist, Remo marched over to Billy Pierce.

The aging hippie was picking himself out of the rubble of his mother's shattered sewing table. As he dragged himself to his feet, he shook loose the remnants of one of the wooden legs, which had somehow gotten stuffed up the right leg of his bellbottoms.

The same hand that had thrown him halfway across the room now lifted him the rest of the way to his feet. Remo deposited Billy on the concrete floor.

"Okay, Wavy Gravy," Remo said, "what do you know about the stolen animals?"

"I didn't do anything yet!" Billy begged. The words tumbled out. "All I did was get the plans from the city hall. That's legal. You can't do anything to me if I haven't done anything yet. Besides, I wasn't going to steal them. I was going to *free* them. And I wasn't even going to do *that* 'cause you can't prove I was."

As he spoke, he indicated the curled-up blueprints

on the floor. Remo raised an eyebrow. Silently, he gathered up the plans, drawing them open.

He glanced at Billy. "These are to the Salem dog pound," Remo said, reading the border caption.

Judith bounded forward, snatching the blueprints from Remo. "You put my BCWs in a *dog* pound?" she barked.

"B-whats?" Billy asked, confused. "I don't know what you mean. I was planning to liberate the Salem dog pound. That's what all this is about." His eyes narrowed. "You're not with the city?"

"No," Remo snapped, shaking his head.

Judith had had enough. She shoved Billy roughly in his flabby chest. "Where are the laboratory specimens you stole from BostonBio last night?" she ordered.

At the mentioning of the genetic firm's name, Billy Pierce's eyes grew wide amid his acne-flecked face. He tried to bolt again, but Remo held him fast. His legs kicked for a moment in air like a frozen cartoon character's. When he realized that he was making no progress, he reluctantly surrendered.

"Where are they?" Remo asked, his face hard.

Billy was panting from his exertions. Remo had to lean back to avoid the foul vapor that oozed from his mouth.

"You won't turn me in if I tell you?" Billy asked hopefully.

"I'll turn you into hamburger if you don't," Remo warned.

Billy spoke quickly. "I don't really know about the BBQ liberation per se," he said.

"*Liberation?*" Dr. White scoffed.

He seemed surprised. "Don't you agree that all animals have a right to freedom?" Billy asked.

"The BCWs don't have a clue what freedom is," the geneticist snapped. "They were conceived in a test tube and born in a lab. They are *things. Not* animals."

"*Where?*" Remo stressed, steering Billy back to the matter at hand.

"I'm not really sure," he said. "I'm supposed to meet some people from the Animal Underground Railroad near the Concord rotary tonight. There's some farmland on Route 117 near there. They're going to smuggle the BBQs to freedom."

"Freedom!" Judith screamed, exasperated. "They're glorified lab rats! They have no natural instincts except for what I've bred into them. They've got no sense of how to survive in the wild. If you morons let them go off and fend for themselves, they'll starve to death in a week!"

Billy Pierce puffed out his wounded chest. "Says *you*," he said bravely. He instantly regretted his daring.

Judith's eyes squeezed to angry slits. Without any warning, she sprang into action.

One hand was held up and away from her body. The other was tensed in a fist near her abdomen.

The loose hand swooped down toward the dirt-smeared throat of Billy Pierce.

There was enough power behind the blow to sever the aging hippie's carotid artery. Her long nails could have shredded his neck to the point that he would have bled to death before the paramedics arrived.

Of course, to do this, she would have had to make actual contact.

The hand flew down. Billy's eyes widened in shock.

The vicious, fatal contact was inevitable.

Her hand mere inches away from the creased and crusty flab, Dr. White was stunned when her narrow wrist met something powerful and unyielding. A strong hand wrapped around her forearm, locking it in place. The hand had moved much faster than her own blow. She blinked back her surprise.

"What the hell do you think you're doing?" Remo asked. His hand was wrapped around her wrist. Her claws were frozen three inches away from Billy's filthy neck.

Though she said nothing, her eyes shot daggers at him. She looked back to Billy and snarled. Billy fell back in fear, stumbling into an unused workbench. He dropped loudly onto a wobbly metal stool, panting madly.

"Listen, lady," Remo growled. "I don't know what kind of junk you're pumping into your veins, but it's making you a real pain in the ass."

Her head snapped around to Remo. She regarded him coldly for a moment. With surprising strength, she wrenched her hand free. Remo let her.

"I was a pain in the ass before I started shooting up," she snapped.

"There's something to be proud of," he said aridly.

Without another word, Judith skulked off to a dark corner of the basement. She stood there in the shadows, her eyes trained suspiciously on the two men. Remo felt her gaze was directed more at him now than at Billy Pierce.

He had gotten a strange sense of calm from her back at HETA headquarters when she'd assaulted Curt Tulle. It was the same here. Her heart thrummed low and constant in her chest. It wasn't the erratic heartbeat of someone who had just attacked another human being.

The drugs. Had to be. Whatever she was injecting must have been a weird combination of both stimulant and calmative. Probably something she had synthesized herself.

It figured. The woman who was hell-bent on feeding the world was a certifiable lunatic.

Remo turned his attention away from the lurking shape of Judith.

"Can you get in touch with your friends before tonight?" Remo asked Billy.

"No," he admitted, gulping. His eyes strayed beyond Remo to the half-shadowed face of Dr. White.

Remo could sense that he was telling the truth. "Looks like we're going to have to wait until tonight to get your overgrown lab rats back," Remo called to the scientist.

"Tonight?" she said, suddenly shocked. "What time is it?"

"Five after four," Remo said.

"Damn!" She flew out of the shadows. "I have a *Hot Copy* interview at five. I have to get back to the lab. Let's go, brown eyes."

"Get a cab," Remo replied flatly. "I'm staying with Stink Boy. Besides, you scare me." He sank to a lotus position on the concrete floor.

Billy's eyes were sick when he realized his guest was staying.

"But I'll miss my interview," Judith complained.

"Reschedule. If you're nice, maybe he'll let you assault him tomorrow."

Judith scowled. "But this may be the last chance I get to ingratiate myself to these media jackals."

Angrily, she raced up the cellar stairs. Remo heard her on the phone a moment later. Seconds later, the screen door to the kitchen slammed, and Judith left the house. Presumably to wait at the curb for the taxi.

Remo relaxed. Finally, some peace and quiet. He smiled placidly at Billy Pierce. Billy smiled weakly back, his broad face a sheen of sweat.

Remo took a deep, calming breath. And gagged.

"Try to stay downwind, would you, pal?" Remo said to Billy.

7

They had planned to rent the truck in New Hampshire so as not to draw attention to themselves, but someone pointed out that a rental truck driving around in Massachusetts with New Hampshire plates might draw more attention than one with Massachusetts plates. The conspirators had fretted over this for a time, finally deciding to pick up a truck in Massachusetts after all, but from far away. They chose one from an agency in Worcester.

"What's your destination?" asked the bored clerk at the Plotz truck-rental station. His pen was poised over the white rental forms.

"Omaha," blurted out Clyde Simmons.

"Seattle," said Ron DePew just as quickly.

They looked at one another in horror.

"We're piano movers!" Clyde Simmons shouted, as if sheer volume could mask the obvious discrepancy in their cover story.

Since it happened to be his last day, the clerk didn't care. The story worked. With enough cash to cover the fee, they were on their way. They were expected to deliver the truck to the Plotz agency in

Omaha—they had settled on Clyde's cover destination—by noon three days hence. Of course, the truck would never arrive.

"Smooth as silk," Ron boasted proudly as they drove the truck from the lot. He began peeling off the obvious false mustache he had picked up at a novelty store.

"Smoother," Clyde replied in a drop-dead-cool tone. Like an even cooler Barry White.

"Oww!" Ron screamed in response. When Clyde looked over, he saw that his partner was sitting in the passenger's seat holding what appeared to be a limp caterpillar. Bits of bloody flesh clung to it.

That day, Clyde and Ron learned two things. First, they were both cool as cucumbers. Second, it was not wise to stick on a phony mustache with Krazy Glue.

The blood on Ron's face had coagulated by the time they reached the Medford collective. Clyde had opted to leave his mustache on.

The farm was set back on a busy road. A thick stand of trees blocked the eight-acre spread from prying eyes.

Clyde and Ron turned at the familiar tin mailbox and steered onto the bumpy dirt road. They were bounced and jostled crazily in their seats as they drove beneath a canopy of trees toward the distant barn.

Twilight had fallen on New England. The faint smell of an illegal outdoor fire wafted in through the open cab window, carrying with it the hint of autumns long past.

Clyde broke through the copse of trees and got his first complete view of the barn. An excited tingle fluttered at the pit of his stomach. So focused was he on his ultimate destination that he didn't see the two black-clad figures standing in the middle of the path until the last second.

"Shit!" Clyde shouted, slamming on the brakes.

The big truck skidded several yards to an abrupt halt. Ron was flung forward into the dashboard, smashing his forehead painfully. He fell back into his seat, teeth bared, clutching at his newest injury. A cloud of dust poured up from the rear of the truck, blanketing the cab, swirling in through the open windows.

Through the dirty haze beside Clyde, a black ski mask appeared. A gun muzzle poked in through the window.

"Hey! Whoa! Calm down," Clyde suggested, raising his hands. The truck continued to chug softly.

"Watch it," Ron warned from the other side of the cab. Another ski-masked figure had climbed up to the passenger's door. A rifle jammed Ron's ribs.

"State your purpose," the driver's-side ski mask insisted evenly.

"Jeez, Sam, you know our purpose."

Clyde promptly reached over and pulled off the

man's ski mask. The cherubic face beneath was pale and startled.

"Hey, gimme that," the man whined. The gun withdrew.

Clyde held the mask away from Sam's grabbing hands.

"Are they ready for us?" he asked while waving the mask. He nodded to the barn.

"Yes," Sam said. He snatched at the ski mask once more, this time pulling it from Clyde's grip. His expression was angry as he dragged it back down over his face.

Sam's big nose stuck through the right eye hole. He tried twisting the mask back in place—a difficult feat with an automatic rifle in one hand. An ear popped through the left eye hole. He poked himself in the eye with his gun barrel and yelped.

"Keep practicing," Clyde droned. "Maybe someday you'll be able to dress yourself without Mommy's help."

In the passenger's seat, Ron snorted. The facial movement split his false-mustache scabs.

"We can't be too careful in this operation," Sam cautioned through a mouthful of wool. "Command has learned that forces are already aligning against us."

"Really?" Clyde asked. "Well, if they do show up, don't stand in the road like a couple of doofuses. I almost ran you over."

Clyde stomped on the gas, and the rental truck

lurched forward. Sam and his leotard-wearing friend had to hop into a fresh cloud of dust to keep from being carried along to the barn.

Yet another man in ski mask and black leotard rolled open the main barn door at Clyde and Ron's approach. After they had guided the truck inside the big interior, the door was quickly rolled shut.

Clyde shut off the engine.

The men climbed down from the cab. Stale dry hay crunched beneath their work boots as they walked around to the front of the truck. Two familiar faces greeted them.

Clyde and Ron had met Mona and Huey Janner at a HETA rally several years before. They were a couple of renegade animal-rights activists who were in charge of the East Coast division of the Animal Underground Railroad.

The couple who had slipped into the Boston HETA office after Remo and Dr. White's departure still wore their black leotards, this time without concealing jackets. They carried their ski masks in their hands.

Mona was a mousy figure with intent, unblinking eyes.

"Were you followed?" she said. She spoke in an infuriatingly precise, overpronounced, snippy fashion. Eight parts Susan Hoerchner mixed with two parts Jeremy Irons.

"No," Clyde replied. "At least I don't think so."

Mona's thin mouth grew even thinner. Her lips all but disappeared in her grimace of disapproval.

"There is an agent from the Department of Agriculture looking into the liberation," Mona instructed. "He was at HETA headquarters in Boston today."

"Did he find out anything?" Ron asked, concerned.

Mona laughed derisively. "You know Tulle. What do you think?"

"I don't like this," said Clyde worriedly. "Washington wasn't supposed to be in on this so soon."

"Actually, we're not sure what Curt might have told them," Huey Janner interjected.

"Them?"

Huey glanced at his wife for permission to speak. Her eyes didn't object. "Dr. Judith White was with him," he announced somberly.

All of their faces took on the expression of people who had just learned that Grandma had been dug up and fed to the dogs down the street.

"So what do we do?" Clyde blurted.

"Continue as planned," Mona said, voice steely. She turned abruptly, marching away from the truck.

The rest hurried to keep up with her purposeful stride.

"Is that smart?" Clyde asked.

"The crisis is too urgent to worry about being smart," Mona said crisply.

Ron glanced nervously at Clyde. "What if we get caught?" he asked.

"Deny everything," Mona instructed.

They had reached another wooden door leading into a separate wing of the barn. At one time, the property had been a dairy farm. Mona dragged the door open, revealing a long, dimly lit interior. Dozens of hay-filled stalls lined either side of the old-fashioned walls. Most were empty. The nearest eight were not.

Mona took a gas lantern down from the wall. She led the small group to the closest stall.

For the first time, Clyde and Ron got a look at the new species of animal known as *Bos camelus-whitus*. Sixteen sad eyes peered out from the stalls all around them. Ron squatted down next to the nearest BBQ.

"Wow," Ron exhaled. He tipped his head thoughtfully. "It looks so harmless. Did one of these really kill that guy in Boston?"

"That's ridiculous," Mona snapped. "We had them with us the entire time. It's a media fabrication." She looped her lantern onto a hook next to the stall. "Take this one," she said, pushing the half-open gate wide.

Huey went inside and took a leash down from the wall. He snapped it onto the collar, which he had put on the animal earlier that afternoon. Not a choke collar. Mona had been clear about that.

"Only one?" Clyde asked, surprised. "What about the others?"

"They're too hot right now," Mona explained. "We get them out one at a time. All at once risks getting them *all* caught. And we don't want that to happen."

"No," Clyde reluctantly agreed, knowing that if the animals were caught, so was he.

Huey led the beast out onto the floor. It wasn't clear whether the difficult time it had walking was due to its stumpy, genetically engineered legs or to complete apathy. Judging by the look on the animal's supremely uninterested face, Clyde guessed it was the latter.

Mona's husband coached the lethargic animal out into the main barn.

"I've already set up a meeting with the Midwest Underground. By the way, Billy Pierce is going to be there to help with the exchange."

"C'mon," Ron complained, "not Zit-Face Pierce."

"He is a sympathetic biped and should be treated with respect," Mona chastised. "I contacted him when I thought we would have to move all eight of the creatures."

"Call him and tell him we don't need him."

"I tried, but there was no answer. He must already be on his way."

They were at the rental truck. Ron unlocked and opened the rear door. He and the other two men hefted the creature up into the hot interior. Although it only weighed about 110 pounds, the BBQ was awkward deadweight. It took a lot of grunting and straining from the three of them to put the oddly shaped animal inside. Once they were through, the BBQ stared out at them with its large, sad eyes.

Clyde pulled the door shut on the mournful animal.

Mona marched the men around to the cab. "The exchange will take place at the Concord checkpoint at nine o'clock sharp. Remember, obey all traffic rules. You don't want to be stopped for something stupid."

"Right, right, right." Clyde nodded. He thought he had been nervous about this operation before, but he was even more anxious now that he knew someone from Washington was already on the case. He was sweating profusely. Cold droplets spilled from his armpits down the interior of his flannel shirt.

"And wear your disguises," she commanded as they climbed inside the cab. In the lamplight, Mona Janner peered up at Ron DePew, as if seeing him for the first time. Her eyes narrowed. "What happened to your lip?" she asked.

In the rear of the truck, the BBQ moaned sadly. Up front, Ron also moaned.

8

Remo knew what commuter traffic was like in this part of the state, so he had struck out early for Concord. It was a good thing, too. The methodical deconstruction of every crucial roadway in Massachusetts had reached its fourth straight decade. As a result, the traffic was bumper-to-bumper for much of the ride. The hour-or-so trip from Salem took nearly four hours.

Orange plastic safety barrels were spaced along every torn-up road. The breakdown lane had been turned into a regular traffic lane, and the regular traffic lanes had been turned into endless gravel riverbeds.

Massachusetts State workers were sluglike artists, and the highway was their canvas. Every road in the state highway system seemed to always be a work in progress.

Remo was grateful to find a stretch of relatively unscarred pavement starting about a mile away from Concord's medium-security prison.

He thought of Todd Grautski and Kershaw Ferngard as he drove past the high-walled facility. Remo regretted not picking up a newspaper. He would have enjoyed seeing the unfailingly inaccurate accounts of how the two men had met their end.

Steering onto the rotary near the prison, Remo circled halfway before heading off on Route 117. A few hundred yards beyond the rotary, Remo pulled his rental car over onto the soft shoulder of the road.

Leaving the engine idling, he got out.

The pounding had stopped somewhere near Burlington. That was good. It was bad enough trying to steer through a million edgy Massachusetts drivers without the added distraction of the incessant drumming that had been coming from the rear of the vehicle.

At the back of the car, Remo pretended to be supremely interested in his taillights while waiting for a break in traffic. When there was enough space between yellow headlights coming off the rotary, Remo leaned over and popped the trunk. He was instantly enveloped in a malodorous cloud of body odors mixed with stale pizza.

A filthy, flabby hand grabbed at the lip of the trunk. A wide, balding head popped into view after it.

"I couldn't *breathe* in there, man!" Billy Pierce gasped. He gulped deeply at the cool night air.

"If you couldn't breathe, you'd be dead," Remo said, himself breathing shallowly at the edge of the cloud. "Which I'm going to be if I stand here one more minute."

Leaving the trunk open, Remo went back to the front of the car. He slid in behind the steering wheel.

The massive shift of weight at the rear of the car a moment later told him that Billy Pierce had climbed out. The trunk slammed shut. Another moment and the door across from Remo opened. Billy slid in beside him. The car instantly listed to the right.

Remo had powered down all four windows before stopping the car. Billy's broad index finger immediately made a move to the window control switch on his door.

"Leave it," Remo commanded. He was looking over his shoulder, waiting for a break in traffic.

"But I'm cold," Billy complained.

"Fat people are never cold," Remo argued.

"*I'm* cold," Billy repeated. "And it's glandular." The sweat from his long trip in the trunk dripped down his massive frame. It had chilled him the moment he had come in contact with the crisp night air.

"The window stays down," Remo said firmly.

As Remo pulled back out onto the road, Billy Pierce crossed his arms tightly. The shivering, aging hippie settled into sullen silence.

THEY DIDN'T DRIVE FAR.

The farm came up quickly on the left. There were two large fields bisected by a dark public road that ran up between them. Remo pulled off the main route and onto the narrower side road. The black-shrouded road stretched off into darkness far ahead.

Remo and Billy got out of the car.

"Where are they?" Remo asked.

"They wouldn't be out in the *open*," Billy said, rolling his eyes, as if Remo knew nothing of covert operations. "They want to do this in secret. There's an access road at the edge of the woods beyond the field. The trucks will be there."

Remo looked at the nearest field. It was thick with early-autumn corn. The stalks grew high above his head.

"Okay, east or west woods?" Remo asked.

Billy scratched his grimy head. "Um..."

Remo closed his eyes. "Great," he muttered with a deep sigh. "Okay, here's what we do. I'll take east—you take west. If you even think you've found your little buddies, come back to the car. I'll meet you back here in twenty minutes. And in case you have any ideas about bolting..."

Remo reached out and tweaked Billy's ear. The pain was so horrific and engulfing, the animal-rights terrorist didn't have time to scream. When Remo pulled his hand away, Billy sucked in a deep breath. He nodded his understanding.

Standing in the middle of the road, Billy began scratching his head again. "Er...just one question," he began sheepishly.

Once Remo had aimed him west, Billy started out across the road. He vanished amid the corn a few seconds later. Remo heard him crunching and stomping and swearing his way through the stalks.

"Give me strength," Remo groaned. Turning, he headed into the nearer stalks of tall corn on the opposite side of the road from the animal-rights activist.

A moment later, the field swallowed him up.

CLYDE SIMMONS HAD PARKED the rental truck at the end of the access road twenty minutes before. He and Ron DePew were standing outside the truck now. Waiting.

A small brook trickled off into the distance. The constant, nearby noise of running water coming from the intense darkness tensed Clyde's already jangled nerves. He checked the luminescent face of his watch. It glowed eerily green.

"They're late," he said.

"Just so long as they get here before Zit-Face," Ron replied. He was gingerly touching the sticky, coagulated mess beneath his nose where he had reglued his false mustache. He'd accidentally put it on upside down. The bristles had stuck up his nostrils and made him sneeze for much of the trip from Medford until he'd snipped most of them off with a pair of key-chain fingernail clippers.

"He's late, too," Clyde noted.

"Mmm," said Ron. He scratched at one end of the mustache. His face contorted in pain. "Ouch!" he yelped.

Clyde glanced at him. "Leave it alone," he said, annoyed.

"I *can't*," Ron complained. "It itches."

"Take it off, then."

"Mona told us to leave them on."

"Mona isn't here," Clyde said, a cold edge in his voice. "And even if she was, she doesn't know everything."

"You wouldn't say that if she *was* here."

"Yeah, well...maybe," Clyde admitted, perturbed. He stared off into the night.

There was no sign of the second truck anywhere. Just the endless babbling brook. Occasionally, the sound of a car would echo across the gently bowing cornfield. Clyde sighed loudly, looking back to the rear of the truck.

He and Ron were standing near the grille. Together they had managed to get the BBQ out of the back. It was tethered at the rear of the vehicle, out of sight. Every few minutes, the creature would low plaintively. It was almost like a cross between a cow's moo and a sheep's bleat, without being fully either.

Ron stroked the mustache as if trying to massage the itch away. "You don't like Mona much, do you?" he asked.

"Yeah, right," Clyde mocked. "We get the grunt work and she gets the glory."

"There hasn't been much glory yet," Ron pointed out.

Clyde smirked derisively. "Are you kidding me?

With what we've got tied back there?'' He jerked his head to the rear of the truck. ''She's about to go national. *Without* either of us.''

Ron continued to toy with his mustache. ''Still, it's worse for Huey. He's married to her.''

Clyde looked at his partner as Ron played with his mustache. He had been doing it since they'd left Medford. Something in Clyde finally snapped.

''Enough is enough,'' he growled.

Clyde grabbed one soggy end of sagging horsehair. With a mighty wrench, he ripped the mustache from Ron's face.

Ron DePew's shriek of pain was muffled beneath a pair of horrified, snatching hands. Ron's palms clamped firmly over the injured area as his body reacted to the blinding shock of sudden, intense pain.

''Shh,'' Clyde admonished. He dangled the false mustache between two disgusted fingers. Ron's discomfort had the instant effect of lightening Clyde's mood.

''That *hurt,*'' Ron's muted voice whimpered.

''It's better to get it over with fast. Like a Band-Aid. Here.'' Clyde shoved the mustache back at Ron.

''Get that away from me,'' Ron complained. Removing his palms from his face, he felt at the raw flesh on his lip. His fingertips came away wet. Blood. ''You ripped half my frigging face off!'' he cried.

"Quiet," Clyde ordered. He cocked an ear to the cornfield. "Did you hear something?"

"No," Ron whined. He wasn't paying attention to anything beyond his injured upper lip. He continued prodding at his face.

After a moment, Clyde relaxed. "Nerves," he said, shaking his head.

"Who cares about your nerves?" Ron said, his lips twisted. He mumbled from the corner of his mouth. "Can you see teeth through this?" He pointed at the biggest lip hole.

THE FAINT AROMA of Ron DePew's blood carried back on the chill autumn breeze. Somewhere at the rear of the truck, unseen by the HETA activists, a pair of nostrils pulled in the heady scent of fresh blood. A primitive hunger stirred.

And as the two men stood, unwitting in the dead of night, confident, stalking feet began to slip silently through the darkness toward the cab.

REMO FOLLOWED the narrow path between the rows of corn. Crickets chirped loudly all around him.

The aroma from the field was intoxicating. Remo had to concentrate to keep his mouth from watering.

As a Master of Sinanju, Remo's diet was severely limited. But he'd been delighted to learn after more than twenty years of little more than rice, fish and duck that corn was an acceptable alternative to his customary staples. Acceptable to everyone, that is, save the Reigning Master of Sinanju. To appease Chiun, Remo had promised to strike corn from his diet forever. He only wished he could banish the desire.

Burying the urge to gorge himself, Remo plowed forward.

At the edge of the woods far away, a lone cicada screeched at the night. It was followed by a second, then a third. The symphony reached a crescendo before cutting off entirely. The short lull was broken as the first cicada took up its whine once again.

There were no signs of human life yet. The wind was blowing north to south, so no softer sounds or subtle smells were brought to Remo from either field. If the HETA trucks were at the edge of the dark woods that loomed ominously ahead of him, he wouldn't know it until he was nearly upon them.

Because of the direction of the wind and the limitations of his own senses, Billy Pierce had dropped off Remo's personal radar once they were an acre or so apart. The animal-rights activist's cursing, stumbling trip through the cornfield had faded into other background noise.

Nearby, Remo sensed a single, small heartbeat. Probably a raccoon or skunk. The creature waddled awkwardly through the rows of swaying corn a few yards away.

The wind shifted briefly once, doubling up on itself before switching southward once more.

Skunk, Remo noted. Definitely a skunk.

But up ahead was still a blank slate. Even so, if the trucks were there, he'd know soon enough.

As silent as the very air itself, Remo pressed forward.

THE GROUND RACED UP to meet Billy Pierce.

Muttering unhappily, he pushed himself to his feet.

His palms stung where he fell. Putting them up to his face, he examined them carefully in the moonlight.

They were bleeding. The scraping wounds he'd gotten while trying to escape from his bulkhead earlier that day had reopened. The right palm was worse than the left. He must have landed on a jagged rock.

He wiped the thin smear of blood and grime on his ragged bell-bottoms. It wasn't clear whether this helped to clean the dirt from his hands, but it seemed to satisfy Billy. He stumbled forward.

He wasn't aware how far he had actually traveled across the field until he was all the way through it.

Billy tumbled over a raised lip of earth and fell with a heavy thud through the last row of corn. The stalks crunched loudly beneath his great girth.

"Damn," he griped, as his massive belly oozed in both directions, settling out on either side of his prone body.

He floundered for a moment, grabbing at the

ground before him with his still stinging, bleeding hands.

Somewhere nearby, he heard the sound of a small river gurgling off into the night.

His hands sank into the earth. It was muddy to the touch.

"Great," he groused. "I fell in water."

Although he was ordinarily averse to the thought of washing any part of his anatomy, the pain in his hands was so great as he pushed himself laboriously to his knees that, for a moment, he considered actually dipping his hands in the stream and swishing them around a little to cool the stinging sensation. But as he leaned his hands against his large thighs, Billy realized that the water sound was too far away for him to have landed in the river.

That was odd.

Kneeling at the edge of the cornfield and puzzling over the strange, unexplained wetness on his hands, Billy was surprised anew. As luck would have it, he had plopped out of the woods at the precise spot he had been looking for. No more than three yards away was the HETA rental truck.

It sat quiet and unmoving on the narrow access road. The rear door was open wide. The weak cab dome light was turned on.

Billy wasn't sure what to do.

There was no sign of his HETA confederates nor of the animal they were supposed to be moving.

He was supposed to go meet Remo at the car, but

there didn't appear to be anything to show him. And the last thing Billy wanted to do was to inspire Remo's anger yet again. Frowning, he decided to investigate a little before going off for his rendezvous.

Billy struggled to his feet.

He wiped the strange slick fluid from his hands as he stepped carefully over to the truck. Whatever it was, it felt sticky on his pant legs. Not like mud.

At the rear of the truck, he found the leash that had been used to tie the BBQ to the vehicle. It was snapped in half. Standing on tiptoes and leaning inside the rear of the truck, Billy saw none of the animals.

Frowning in confusion, he walked around to the cab.

He noted the ghastly stench as he approached the front of the truck. Far worse than the odor people claimed he made. This was like rotting roadkill.

Below the open cab window, Billy suddenly remembered the strange fluid on his hands. The dome light was weak, but good enough to see by.

He examined his hands. They were slick and red. Red?

Experimentally, he sniffed the substance. As he did so, he glanced over to the edge of the cornfield.

And froze.

It was there. Near the edge of the field. He had fallen right next to it and hadn't seen it.

The body had been ripped to shreds. The face was ghastly white, the dead mouth open wide in shock.

Billy recognized the man. Ron DePew.

It was blood on his hands. *Ron's* blood.

Billy staggered back, falling against the cab.

Away from the body. *Get away!*

Billy stumbled around the front of the cab.

Another body. Flat on its back. Stomach open wide.

Blood. Blood everywhere.

On the ground, on the body. On the face.

Eyes looking up at him. Feral, angry. The creature had been feasting on the second corpse. It lifted its head out of the stomach cavity, entrails dripping from its slathering, crimson-smeared mouth.

Hideous, blood soaked. And *familiar.*

Panic gripped his thudding chest.

Billy twisted, tried to run. Too late.

The creature bounded toward him. A single leap and it was upon him. One curled paw lashed down toward his neck, talons curled in violent rage.

Blood exploded from his throat, spattering across the grille and windshield of the silent truck.

And in his last moments of life, Billy Pierce reacted to fear and brutal death with the same blind instinct used by the first ancestors of humanity to scamper down from the trees.

Billy screamed.

REMO HEARD the terrified shriek from the distant edge of the opposite field.

He had just given up his futile search at the edge of the woods and was turning back in Billy's direction.

The sound shocked him to action.

Rather than follow the paths through the high corn, Remo threw himself into the nearest stalks. While he ran, he slashed his hands left and right.

Corn stalks toppled and crumpled, falling back in his wake. He moved through the first field like a determined thresher, reaching the road's edge in less than fifteen seconds.

He broke into the open near his rental car. There was another vehicle parked up the road. Remo had no time to see who it might be. He bounded across the desolate street and plowed into the opposite field of corn.

His hands were slicing blurs as he hacked a beeline passageway through the tall corn to the point where Billy's scream had originated.

He exploded through the second field and onto the narrow access road.

The stench of blood was powerful, mixed in with the odor of digestive fluids and exposed bowels.

Remo saw the gutted body of Ron DePew first.

Eyes keenly trained in Sinanju followed the bloody path Billy Pierce had unwittingly left from the edge of the cornfield to the front of the rented truck.

Remo found Billy. What was left of him.

The body had been mutilated. The face and neck

were ripped to shreds. The large chest was open. White ribs shone like orderly piano keys through the split casing of frail human flesh.

In spite of the gruesomeness of the attack, Billy had fared better than Clyde Simmons.

The other HETA member had been the main course in a grisly buffet. His stomach cavity had been split open wide. The spine was visible on the opposite side of the large hollow. There were no organs left.

Blood washed the area, turning the earth to sticky mud.

Remo tuned his senses to their limit. Obviously, an animal was responsible. And the HETA people were supposed to be exchanging the BBQs tonight.

The cicadas and crickets continued their nightly serenade. In the distance, a car engine coughed to life. But in all the night sounds, Remo could not locate those of even a single large predator.

Settling for the next-best thing, Remo went to the edge of the area soaked with blood. As expected, he found a set of tracks leading away from the bodies.

They were odd. A ball-shaped indentation preceded by a strange clawing hook. The imprint was nothing he was familiar with. A BBQ.

The path led back into the cornfield.

Loping, Remo followed the trail through the acres of soughing corn. The path ran parallel to the one he had made, though it was much clumsier than his own. He followed it out to the road.

By the time he reached the blacktop street, the dirt of the field had cleared the blood from the animal's foot pads. Once Remo reached the road, he was unable to determine where the creature had gone.

He looked up to where the road disappeared in the darkness. Nothing. Back in the other direction, he saw a lone car turning onto the main route toward the prison.

He'd lost it. The BBQ was gone.

RETURNING TO THE BODIES of the HETA men, Remo crouched down to examine the carnage.

It was a grim sight.

Now that he knew what kind of footprints the BBQs made, he could see the animal's imprints all around the body of Clyde Simmons. They were everywhere—one atop the other.

Remo traced them back to the original set. The last ones made before the initial attack. These ones ran up along side the truck.

At the rear, he found the snapped leash. The animal must have been left there. It had broken free before going on its violent rampage.

Remo's eyes narrowed as he examined the ground.

"What the dingdong?" he said, brow furrowed.

Hands on his knees, he examined the ground carefully.

The imprints back here weren't the same ones as

at the front of the truck. These were heavy, clumsy hoofprints. Not the cautious, delicate ones that had been made around the HETA bodies.

Remo bit the inside of his cheek in concentration. Try as he might, he couldn't come up with a suitable explanation.

He went around to the truck's cab. Leaning in, he pulled on the headlights.

The wooded area in front of the truck was immediately bathed in a wide yellow glow.

He went back to the bodies.

The tracks were still the same as before. And still different from the ones in the back.

Staring at the problem wouldn't bring a solution. There was nothing more he could do here. Let Smith try to sort out the mystery.

As he was turning to go, he noticed something odd about the body of Billy Pierce.

"What the hell?" Remo said, puzzled.

He squatted down next to the body. With careful fingers, he reached to the edge of the raking wound in Billy's chest.

An object clung to the flesh. It was hard and thin and shaped like a waxing moon.

Remo plucked the object free. He examined it in the glow of the headlights.

Going back to the cab, Remo found a few white envelopes with the HETA address embossed in the upper left-hand corners lying on the dashboard.

He took one and stuffed the unfamiliar object inside.

A souvenir for Smith. Something else to confound the CURE director.

Shutting off the cab lights, he jumped down to the ground. Envelope in hand, Remo stole off into the night.

9

As the first bleary streaks of dawn began to rake the gray-tinged sky over Long Island Sound, the light of the new day found Harold W. Smith already at work.

Smith had taken care of the day's sanitarium business in the predawn darkness. It was the work of CURE to which he now devoted himself.

After a scant ten minutes perusing the digests culled by CURE's basement mainframes during their sleepless night patrolling the electronic netherworld of the World Wide Web, Smith had determined that there was nothing that would require calling Remo off his BostonBio assignment.

Things were quiet in the world. What Smith saw now were the usual mundane, day-to-day affairs that the Folcroft Four—his name for the quartet of mainframes—collected from a wide variety of sources.

A crooked judge in Fresno.

A seeming new drug pipeline from South America.

Rival Mafia factions involved in a turf dispute at a New England fishing port.

Nothing worthy of Remo's particular talents.

Smith accessed the latest information on the BBQ situation. As he expected, there was nothing new. It was early yet. If Remo had already found the creatures, it might not be reported to the press for several hours.

He hoped that Remo was successful. In his rock-ribbed Yankee soul, Smith could not fathom why someone would want to derail a project devoted solely to the benefit of mankind. But then, Smith's analytical mind had always had difficulty comprehending irrationality.

As he pondered the BostonBio situation, his computer emitted a small electronic beep. Smith adjusted his rimless glasses as he turned his attention to whatever it was the Folcroft Four had found. Nimble fingers accessed the new file. He was surprised to find that it was related to Remo and Chiun.

The program was part of a complex system Smith had established to keep track of CURE's operatives. It trolled the Net in search of their names, credit-card uses, bank withdrawals or anything else that might be of import.

Smith's bloodless lips pursed as he read the report.

Ordinarily, the computer system would disregard the telephone bills Remo received at the home he shared with the Master of Sinanju. It was only programmed to respond in the event of a large anomaly

in any of the monetary transactions of either Remo
or Chiun.

As Smith scanned down the lines of the phone
company invoice, he was dismayed to see dozens of
long-distance phone calls. All were to the same four
numbers in California. Smith recognized the 818
prefix of Burbank and the 213 of Los Angeles.
These showed up more than any other.

The total bill came to $587.42.

Smith knew Remo all too well. There was no way
CURE's enforcement arm would have stayed on the
phone with *anyone* that long. It had to be Chiun.

But whom would the Master of Sinanju be calling
in California? Especially when Remo said the old
Korean had been meditating in isolation the past
several weeks.

Remo and Chiun's last assignment *had* taken
them both to California. It was possible that Chiun
had met someone there with whom he was now con-
versing. The thought troubled Smith. The wizened
Asian had a habit of blurting out the nature of his
work to anyone who would listen. Fortunately, the
people who heard his claims of being a master assassin in the employ of America were either eventual victims of CURE or merely disregarded Chiun
as a delusional old man.

The Master of Sinanju was up to something. What
it was, Smith had no idea. But over the years, he
had developed a keen sixth sense when it came to
the wily old Korean. And whenever Chiun got in-

volved in something new, it usually wound up costing Smith money. Reminding himself to ask Remo about the bill, Smith switched back to his regular work.

When his desk phone rang forty-five minutes later, however, Smith was so engrossed in his work that he forgot completely about the outlandish telephone bill.

"Smith," he said crisply, receiver tucked between shoulder and ear.

"Morning, Smitty."

In the kitchen of his condominium more than 150 miles up the East Coast, Remo kept his voice low. Since his return home the previous evening, there had been stirring sounds coming from the Master of Sinanju's bedchambers. Chiun's meditation phase seemed about to end, and Remo didn't want to be blamed for causing cosmic disturbances in its waning hours.

"What have you to report on the BostonBio situation?" the CURE director asked.

"You mean you haven't heard?" Remo said, surprised.

Smith got an instant sinking feeling in the churning pit of his ulcer-lined stomach. "What is wrong?"

"I guess that means you haven't." Remo took a deep breath. "Remember that little murder thing near the lab?"

"The bookstore owner? What of it?"

"Looks like BostonBio had better dust off its liability policy."

Smith's prim mouth thinned. "How can you be certain the creatures were responsible?" he asked.

"Because I saw what these things are capable of last night," Remo said, voice grim. "Let's just say they're not candidates for the petting zoo at Santa's Happy Village."

Before Smith could press for details, a screen-in-screen file automatically opened at one corner of his buried monitor. AP text appeared in even lines.

"One moment, please," Smith said to Remo.

Using his keyboard, Smith clicked the window to full size. He quickly digested the wire-story report.

"Remo, there was an incident last night west of Boston. Two trucks were found in the woods near Concord prison. Six mutilated bodies were discovered near the vehicles. They were flagged due to their similarity to the original death near BostonBio."

In his Massachusetts kitchen, Remo frowned. "I didn't know about the second truck or the other three bodies."

"They were found a half mile away from one another," Smith explained. "Obscured by woods."

"Hmm," Remo mused. "Anyway, looks like the BBQs are going postal. Oh, and HETA's in on the party, too."

"The animal-rights group?" Smith queried.

"It was their commandos who swiped the one-eyed, one-horned, flying purple people-eaters from BostonBio. The local HETA chapter had set up a switch last night with a group farther west. They were doing the whole *Born Free* thing until their cargo got the munchies."

In his Spartan Folcroft office, Smith removed his glasses. He massaged the bridge of his patrician nose.

"How many of the creatures escaped?"

Remo hesitated. "This is where it gets a little tricky. My best count puts it at one."

Smith paused for a moment before speaking. He lowered his spotless glasses to his onyx desk, hand rock steady.

"Remo, that is impossible, given the number of deaths. Surely while one of their fellows was being mauled at each truck, either one or both of the remaining two HETA people could have sought shelter in the cab or trailer. There *must* have been more than one."

"Should have been. *Wasn't,*" Remo insisted. "Only one as far as I could tell." He hesitated to relay the next bit of information. "Although there *were* two sets of tracks."

"Explain."

Remo went on to tell him about the footprints at the rear of the truck and the distinctly different tracks that led into the cornfield.

"You could not be mistaken?" Smith said once he was through.

"No way, Smitty," Remo insisted. "Two sets of tracks. One animal. I'm sure of it."

Smith considered. "That is a mystery," he admitted. "However, we are dealing with what is essentially a new life-form. It is possible that this ability to alter its step is some form of self-preservation endemic to this species. Perhaps it only surfaces during a killing phase."

"Oh, and there was something else," Remo said. "I found something in a gash the BBQ made in one of the bodies."

"Oftentimes a tooth or claw is left behind after a particularly savage attack," Smith said. "Which is it?"

"Next mystery," Remo replied. "It's neither. Whatever it is, I overnighted it to you last night. You should be getting it some time this morning."

"I look forward to receiving it," Smith said, intrigued.

"Jeez, Smitty, you're awfully calm about all this," Remo complained. "These things have racked up a pretty hefty body count. I figured you'd want me to squash them."

"If it comes to it, that may be our only option," Smith said somberly, replacing his glasses. "For now we should concentrate on locating the creatures and returning them to BostonBio. Dr. White is the one person in the world suited to learning the true nature of what has transpired there."

Remo snorted derisively. "Humanity's destined

for the short end of the food chain if we dump our fertilized eggs into *that* bottomless basket.''

"I am aware of Dr. White's shortcomings," Smith admitted. "I have been studying her background information. She is quite brilliant but obviously unstable. Her assault against a local Boston television personality two days ago is just the latest incident in a long line of aberrant behavior. She has a police record going back to her college days. However, that does not make her any less important when it comes to understanding these animals."

"Is she on drugs?" Remo asked abruptly.

Smith frowned. "*Most* of the charges brought against her were drug or alcohol related. The last was two years ago. I believe police found PCP in her car."

"Bingo," Remo said.

"Is that significant?" Smith asked.

"No," Remo replied. "Just explains a lot."

Smith forged ahead. "In spite of her personal failings, Dr. White is your best ally in understanding these animals."

"If it's a choice between the lady or the tiger, I'll take my chances with door number two," Remo muttered.

Before Smith could respond, the text shifted on his monitor once more.

"Hold, please," he said, distracted.

Smith found that his computer had dragged yet another news story from the Internet. According to the identification code the CURE mainframes had given the latest data, it was cross-referenced with the two earlier suspected BBQ attacks. Smith scanned the report quickly.

"Oh, no," he said after he was through. His voice was hollow.

"What's wrong?" Remo asked.

"It appears we no longer have Dr. White's expertise to fall back on," Smith replied.

"Why not?" Remo asked.

Smith scanned the story again, on the chance that he had read it wrong the first time. He had not.

"Another mutilated body has turned up," the CURE director said tightly. "This one on the grounds of BostonBio. The *Boston Blade* is reporting that the body is that of Dr. Judith White."

10

Initial reports in the local press of the death of Dr. Judith White appeared to be greatly exaggerated.

When Remo returned to the lab at BostonBio, he found the scientist upright, alert and in the middle of throwing a characteristic fit of temper.

"Get that thing out of here!" Dr. White screamed. Her beautiful face curled into wrinkles of intense displeasure as the forensic team attempted to heft the mangled body into a black-zippered morgue bag.

Remo was careful to avoid the wide area of drying blood that had spread out around the body.

As he walked by, he leaned in to get a glimpse of the ghostly white face of the latest BBQ victim. The glassy, frozen-in-death eyes of Orrin Merkel stared up at him.

Judith sat on a desk beyond the cluster of police and medical examiners. A cigarette dangled from between her perfect red lips.

"You're alive," Remo commented as he stepped over to her. There was a hint of undisguised disappointment in his tone.

Judith raised a single eyebrow as she peered over at him. Taking her cigarette between her slender fingers, she blew a huge cloud of smoke at the ceiling. "Isn't the Agriculture Department usually busy pimping out bees and stomping on boll weevils?" she replied sarcastically.

"I haven't graduated to bugs yet, so they assigned me to you. The papers had you dead," Remo pointed out. He glanced back, surveying the scene.

"The papers *want* me dead. Trust the *Blade* to screw up a free lunch. I'm the one who reported the body. They somehow twisted that into me *being* the body."

The police forensic team had succeeded in dropping the largest section of remains into the thick black bag. Remo saw that the stomach cavity had been ripped open. Like the corpse of Clyde Simmons the night before, the scientist's organs had been removed utterly. His abdomen was like an open, ghastly red bowl.

Remo nodded to the corpse. "Orrin," he said.

Dr. White blew another cloud of smoke, this one from the corner of her mouth. "What's left of him." She didn't seem disturbed in the least.

"Shouldn't you ratchet down the Bette Davis act a few notches? After all, this does let your BBQs off the hook."

Although the freshly mutilated corpse of her lab assistant hadn't succeeded in agitating her, Remo's words seemed to. Judith stubbed her cigarette out on the desk's surface. Sliding to her feet, she beckoned Remo to follow.

They walked to a rear door of the lab, Judith allowing the last thin veil of smoke in her lungs to escape along the way.

She pushed the door open. The corridor beyond was lined with the pens from which the animals had been stolen two nights before. Remo was surprised to see one cage was occupied.

An odd-looking creature with huge, sad eyes looked mournfully to him as he stepped into the hall, which connected the two laboratories. The animal's foot-long legs were far too short for its large body. It moaned softly.

"A BBQ?" Remo asked, surprised.

Judith's face was serious. "I found it here this morning when I came in."

"These things have a *homing* instinct?"

Judith seemed hesitant to speculate. "I guess they must. Unplanned on my part. How else could it have gotten back here?"

"I went to the HETA meeting place last night. They were only planning on exchanging one animal. It got away."

"And this is it." She gestured to the BBQ. It backed away from her hand.

Remo shook his head doubtfully. "I don't know." He frowned. "If this is the one from last night, it would have had to travel twenty miles through pretty tough terrain."

"It might be something I didn't foresee," Dr. White admitted. "We've all heard stories about dogs and cats that travel clear across country in order to find their masters."

"Lady, that's not Lassie and you ain't exactly Timmy."

"It's *possible*," she stated firmly.

He pointed at the creature's stumpy legs. "This thing would have a hard time walking to the wall and back without collapsing. There's no way."

"Maybe it isn't the one from last night, then," she admitted. "Maybe it's one of the other ones."

"Yeah. And my vote it's the one that killed that guy near here the other night."

Dr. White no longer seemed as certain as before.

"Possibly," she said. "But I'm not convinced," she added quickly. "These deaths could be the work of another animal. Or a human being." Inspiration struck. "A *serial* killer."

"Back at the Agriculture Department, we call that grasping at straws," Remo said. "The only link between the murders are those things." He nodded to the BBQ.

"Deaths," she interjected.

"What?"

"If they *are* the work of the BCWs—and I'm not conceding they are—then the proper word would be *deaths.* An animal does not murder. It kills. Perhaps to eat, perhaps to survive. But an animal does not murder."

"That's a tortured exercise in semantics," Remo noted.

"No," Judith said firmly. "That's the law of the jungle. Survival of the fittest." There was passion in her eyes.

"I don't think *natural* selection has anything to do with anything that's gone on around here," Remo said, deadpan. "And I think the six dead HETA people would back me up on that."

"There were more deaths?" Judith asked.

Remo nodded grimly. "Last night. With the other two, it's human race, zero—BBQs, eight and counting."

"My *God*," Judith croaked, aghast. She turned away from Remo. Staring out one of the barred windows along the side of the room, she shook her head in slow horror.

"I'm sure mankind'll be touched you're finally coming around," Remo commented dryly.

"Screw mankind," she groaned. "Where does this leave the *BCW* project?" She bristled at his look of disgust. "I *mean* it," she complained. "The brass here is already riding me about the incident with that ditz reporter. The BCW project has been hit with *major* bad press *and* HETA sabotage. And to top it all off, I heard from my lawyer this morning. That Tulle twerp is suing me for assault. Can you believe it?"

"You shish kebabbed his carotid with a letter opener," Remo pointed out.

"There are some species that would see that as a *mating* ritual."

"Only the Klingons," Remo suggested.

She wasn't listening. "I was complimenting that hypocritical toad. Not that any of you males deserve it. There aren't any *real* men left in this world." She raised her hands before her as she spoke, palms open and fingers unfurled—penitent claws.

Remo was hardly listening. While Dr. Judith White's parts were all in the right place, her personality was more effective than a cold shower. A feminist lament at this juncture merely worked to clinch an already closed deal.

"Tell me when you're finished," he offered blandly. He wasn't even looking at her. He was peering down at the BBQ, trying to decide if it could be a killer. Big, guileless eyes looked back at him.

Still staring out the window, Judith snorted loudly. "You know what's *really* pathetic? You're the closest thing to a real man I've met in a long time."

"Look harder," he instructed.

Annoyed, she glanced at Remo again. All at once, her hard expression melted. It happened with bizarre rapidity. Something sparked in the back of her green eyes.

"You *are* a real man, aren't you," she growled. It was not a question. It was a statement of fact.

"I pee standing up." Remo nodded absently.

Judith bit her lower lip in deep concentration. Abruptly, she reached a clumsy hand out for him.

Remo was still studying the BBQ when he sensed the hand swinging toward him. He ducked beneath it.

"I'm sorry," he said, forehead furrowed. "When did this turn into our first date?"

She didn't answer. Her hand snapped out again. As before, Remo ducked away. He was astonished to find that he had inadvertently moved directly into the path of her other swinging hand. He ducked out of the way an instant before she could cuff him in the side of the head.

Remo felt the tiniest brush of her fingertips at the ends of his dark hair.

"Let's get physical," she purred playfully.

It was amazing to him that her blow had nearly registered. Remo was long used to the attention he received from the opposite sex. His Sinanju training had made him alluring to women. They sensed he was somehow superior to other men. Like all animals, they wished to breed with the best their race had to offer.

But this time was different than normal. There were none of the "stirring of passion" signals from Judith. Her porcelain skin wasn't flushed. No increased perspiration. Her heartbeat even remained constant.

Remo took a step back, amazement giving way to annoyance.

"Lady, whatever you're on, cut the dose," he groused.

"Don't knock it till you've tried it," she replied.

Briefly, Remo wondered if he shouldn't yell to the cops in the next room that there was an attempted rape in progress. It looked as if all the guns, Mace and billy clubs in town wouldn't quell Judith's animal lust.

But just as he thought he'd have to take drastic steps, an anxious face suddenly poked through the doorway at the end of the hall.

"Dr. White, come in here!" the man called urgently. The scientist ducked back inside the second lab.

Judith stopped her advances.

Just like that. Like flipping off a switch.

Smoothing the wrinkles in her short skirt, Dr. White spun from Remo. Without a word, she stepped briskly down the hall to the adjoining lab. It was as if the previous three minutes had never happened.

"So *that's* what it's like to be a White House intern," Remo commented to the lone BBQ.

Not knowing what to make out of what had just occurred, he trailed Judith to the second lab.

As he walked away, Remo failed to notice that the BBQ had backed to the rear of its stall. There was fear in the backs of its sad eyes.

THE WINDOW THROUGH WHICH the HETA commandos had spirited the BBQs two nights before had been boarded up. It was scheduled to be replaced later that afternoon.

Remo noted that the janitorial staff had neglected to pick up all of the traces of broken glass on the floor of the lab. Tiny shards sparkled in dusty corners beneath lab tables and heat registers.

He found Judith and the rest of her white-coated team standing around a twenty-four-inch television that sat on the same shelf as a large coffeemaker. Half-filled mugs littered the shelf.

Remo instantly recognized the man on TV. A bandage covered the letter-opener wound in his neck.

Curt Tulle stood before a podium on which were arranged a dozen microphones, all bearing logos from various local and national news outlets.

"...was not involved. I want to make that absolutely clear," Curt intoned, his expression grave. "Nor was the national HETA organization. This creature was entrusted to us by an anonymous individual after news of the BBQ deaths was made known."

The camera shifted jerkily to one side. Remo spotted the familiar shape of a BBQ standing on a raised platform next to Curt. It chewed unconcernedly as a few camera flashes popped around it.

"They've only got one?" Judith demanded of her staff.

"That's all he's admitting to," said a woman in a white lab coat.

The camera swept dizzyingly back to Curt Tulle.

"Reports say these things are killers," a reporter shouted.

"*We* are the killers," Curt said sadly. "Every helpless bunny, mouse or puppy that is killed in the name of so-called scientific research is the victim of government-sanctioned murder. If this creature before you kills, it is a fitting irony that it does. I wonder how many animals the butchers at Boston-Bio slaughtered in order to manufacture the very thing that might bring about their own end?"

"What about those who say these things are monsters and should be destroyed?" another reporter called.

"If they *are* monsters, they are *our* monsters," Curt said righteously. "If they need to feast on human flesh in order to survive, we should provide it to them."

"Are you actually recommending we feed human beings to these things?" the reporter asked, amazed.

"If it is necessary, yes." Curt nodded. "As I understand it, our nursing homes are overcrowded. Perhaps the BBQs would be satisfied with a diet of our elderly or infirm. At least until their ultimate release."

"Release?"

Curt nodded happily. "I have been in touch with Bryce Babcock, the secretary of the interior. He is quite keen on the idea of releasing them into Yellowstone or another national park. You recall he championed the wolf-release program of a few years ago.''

''Wouldn't that endanger park visitors?''

''Again, a small price to pay. And if I am able to recommend an appetizer to Secretary Babcock, I will be certain to mention that Dr. Judith White of BostonBio would make a delicious meal. These are *her* babies, after all. She should share responsibility for feeding them.'' Absently, he touched the wound on his neck as he spoke.

In the BostonBio lab, Dr. White lowered her head. ''Shut it off,'' she ordered levelly.

Her staff didn't move quickly enough.

''Shut it off!'' Judith roared.

Someone nearby fumbled with the remote. Curt Tulle collapsed into a single pixel. The tiny spot of white faded to darkness.

She stayed very still for a long time. Finally, she raised her head. Her eyes searched for Remo. She found that he was nowhere to be seen. He had slipped away while she was watching the conference.

''HETA says they're going to fight for ownership with us in court,'' one of her staffers—braver than the rest—offered. ''Until then, he promises they'll keep the BCW safe,'' he added weakly.

Ever so slowly, Judith stared at the man, dead eyes locking on the nervous assistant, who suddenly looked like a hunter confronted by a grizzly.

''Like hell,'' she muttered.

The office had been shrouded in oppressive, lengthening shadows, seemingly for hours. At long last, day finally collapsed completely into night. When the gathering darkness became too consuming, Curt Tulle was forced to turn on his desk light.

Pieces of the green glass shade were in the trash. The result of Judith White's attack. White light from the naked bulb spilled out across walls and ceiling.

Curt's weak eyes avoided the bare bulb. The light was just another thing to fear. He'd been an absolute nervous wreck since before the press conference.

If Mona Janner hadn't forced the lone BBQ on him, he would never have gotten involved in this. But she knew his Achilles' heel. The one thing that the HETA membership would have found completely unacceptable if it were to become public knowledge—his private passion.

Lost in thought, he stroked the nutria fur choker that was clipped around his neck. It always soothed him.

Until today.

With the bandage beneath it, the choker didn't fit

as snugly as usual. It bunched up awkwardly at the side of his neck, chafing slightly.

Reminded once more of Dr. White, Curt shivered.

It was all Mona's fault. Curt was content to quietly head up the Boston HETA office. He'd always protested the right things. Occasionally, he'd appeared on local television. All very quiet, very subdued.

Not like Mona. She was a doer. One of the passionate loudmouths who had invaded the movement in recent years. She'd do and say anything to further their cause.

Personally, Curt didn't like the new brand of activism that had flooded the movement. As far as yesterday's confrontation was concerned, Curt would have preferred to settle his differences with Dr. White and BostonBio in a court of law. Where there would be bailiffs with side arms to keep the half-crazed scientist in line. Now Mona had even screwed that up. All for those stupid lab animals.

The whole BBQ business made Curt intensely uncomfortable.

The agitation he was feeling toward this whole sorry enterprise had clearly and distinctly cried out for the big guns. He had been forced to break into his personal store. Sitting alone in his Boston HETA office, Curt Tulle was decked out in full, glorious regalia.

In addition to the nutria choker, he wore a pair of alligator boots. Although they made his ankles sweat, the feel was exquisite. Well worth the exorbitant cost.

Specially made sealskin trousers gently caressed his thighs. He had insisted that his seamstress use the skins of *baby* seals. Everyone knew they made the best material.

A suede belt held the pants up. Again, *young* lambs were the best choice for suede—at least as far as Curt was concerned. And he was paying the bills, after all.

He wasn't wearing his favorite mink coat, opting instead for the long black sable—which he broke out only on special occasions. A pillbox hat made of the gorgeous fur of the Arctic blue fox perched at a rakish angle atop his head.

His ermine stole lay limp across his desk blotter. Curt stroked the fur carefully and evenly as he sat at his desk.

The animal didn't respond, which was how he liked it. For although he was head of the Boston branch of the most famous animal-rights group in the nation, Curt Tulle absolutely detested animals. From a personal perspective, the only good animal was a dead, skinned and processed animal. Ideally, one that excited a powerful tactile response.

The hypocrisy he displayed in his public and private attitudes was reconciled in his mind by the fact that he cared more deeply for the world than other people. Sure, he hated having living animals around *him*. But he fought tooth and nail to keep them everywhere else. And if a few random housewives were mauled by mountain lions while out jogging or a couple of kids were bitten by rattlesnakes while playing in the sandbox, Curt could live with it. Just as long as every last animal in his own backyard was caught, caged and crushed.

Curt was stroking his ermine and thinking about how nice it would be to live in a giant animal-free bubble when he heard a loud thud from the hallway beyond his closed office door. Sadie.

Curt exhaled. This was Sadie Mayer's second night this month to help out behind the front desk. The old woman was supposed to leave at nine.

Curt didn't like Sadie. He much preferred the energetic young college girls with leftist political leanings who migrated to town every fall. They were certainly easier on the eyes. But Sadie and her ilk were necessary to keep around if only to cover the phones during the long summer months.

Right now it was late September, the fall semester was well under way all around Boston and Curt Tulle absolutely did not need Sadie Mayer stomping around giving him a heart attack in the middle of the night.

Frowning, Curt pulled off his fox-fur hat. He left it on his desk, stepping out into the hallway.

It was cold in the hall. The alley door was open. Sadie.

"Stupid old bat." Curt shivered. He went to close the door.

He knew where she'd be. Ever since Mona and Huey Janner had dumped off the BBQ that morning, Sadie had been sneaking back to see the animal. He'd caught her a dozen times in the storeroom near his office, petting the dull-looking creature on its long snout.

The thought of actually touching a living animal gave him a further chill. He shuddered beneath his sable as he walked past the rear storage room on his way to the alley exit.

The storage room door was ajar. Of course he'd been right. Sadie had no sense of how valuable the BBQ was. To her, it was just another animal. She'd be knitting it a sweater next.

Agitated, Curt pushed the door.

Something blocked the way.

The painted wood surface was rough to the touch as he pushed again. Harder.

Whatever it was shifted clumsily. The door pushed the inert object farther into the room as Curt shoved his way inside. Grumbling, Curt stepped inside.

He found Sadie instantly. She was the thing that had been blocking the door.

Curt gasped.

The old woman sprawled on her back in the shadowy room. Her eyes were open and milky. The bundles of slick, squishy organs that had—for the last seventy-six years—resided within the delicate shell of Sadie Mayer's abdomen were now spread haphazardly around the room. The wooden floor was awash in blood.

Horrified, Curt staggered back into the wall. His heel caught part of Sadie's liver. He skittered sideways. Feet slipping out from beneath him, he crashed to his side on the sopped floor. The train of his sable coat rolled through pools of viscera as he clawed at the wall, trying desperately to get back to his feet.

His alligator boots lost their footing again, and he fell once more, this time face first into the thick puddle of blood.

Curt screamed. The noise caught in his throat, and he choked on the sound. Whimpering, crying, he pulled himself to his knees. Fumbling at the door, he dragged it through the half-congealed ooze. Like a baby, Curt crawled on his hands and knees out into the hall.

Panting, heart pounding madly, he fell to the floor outside, hands coated with Sadie's blood.

He was sobbing now, unable to hold back the panic and horror.

The blood. So much blood.

Sadie. Petting the BBQ. He remembered chasing her out of that room earlier in the day.

Now she was dead. Alone in that room. And dead.

In spite of the intensity of his hysterical attack, something significant dawned in the back of Curt Tulle's reeling, confused mind.

Sadie. In that room. Alone.

Alone.

The BBQ was gone!

The thing *was* a killer. Mona Janner had dumped a vicious monster in his lap and taken off.

He cried, whimpered. Blood everywhere.

It wasn't in the supply room.

It was free.

Somewhere else in the building.

He needed to get away. To *safety.*

The urge to flee swelled like a surging tidal wave in the mind of Curt Tulle, suppressing all other thoughts.

He pushed himself back to his knees.

Too late.

He heard the footfalls—confident, focused. *Felt* the pressure on his back.

It came from the direction of the alley door. The *open* door. Too late to run.

A blow to the neck.

No. Stronger than that.

Blood erupted onto the floor beneath him. No longer that of poor Sadie. It poured as if from a running faucet from the open gash in his neck.

Another blow. This one on his back. Clothes tearing. Claws ripping into flesh.

The world slowed to a distant, lazy pace. Like a film run in slow motion.

He felt himself being lifted from the floor. The ceiling came very close. Twisting, bleeding, he was flung like a rag doll down the corridor. He arced up to the ceiling, shattering a bare hanging bulb. He felt the pain from the broken glass in his cheek. More blood.

The floor raced up quickly to meet him. He plummeted down, crashing in a bloodied ball into the corner near the bathroom.

Footsteps padded closer again.

Sniffing.

Another noise. This one at the front door.

Everything vague, hazy.

A snort very close. Retreating footsteps.

Weakly, Curt lifted his head. He saw the familiar black-spotted flanks of the BBQ vanishing into the shadows at the end of the corridor.

Blood ran from his forehead into his eyes. He lost focus.

"I *hate* animals," he wheezed.

As the pain of death dragged slowly up his battered body, Curt allowed his head to thud back to the floor.

Remo had to wait until the last of the straggling reporters had left before approaching HETA headquarters. Since he lived in the area, he didn't want to run the risk of being seen. It had been eight years since his last date with the plastic surgeon's scalpel, and he had no interest in going back.

On the sidewalk, Remo tested the doorknob. Locked.

With a tight twist and gentle shove, he popped the lock. Tiny shards of metal skittered across the floor as Remo stepped inside.

The moment he entered the foyer, he was assaulted by the familiar, distinct smell of human death.

Remo slipped around Sadie Mayer's desk. He found Curt Tulle's body in the hallway beyond.

The HETA director lay twisted against one wall. A streak of blood lined the floor where he'd skidded to a final, fatal stop.

At first glance, Curt didn't appear to be the victim of a BBQ attack. His stomach cavity was still intact.

As he approached the body, Remo sensed a

thready heartbeat. Curt coughed once, lightly. Foamy blood bubbled out between his lips.

Crouching down beside the HETA director, Remo checked his pulse. Almost nonexistent. And his wounds were extensive. Curt hadn't much time left.

The HETA man seemed to respond to the delicate touch of Remo's hand. His unseeing eyes rolled around. His head shifting slightly even as he stared blankly at the ceiling.

White lips parted.

The word Curt repeated would have been inaudible to every human set of ears on Earth, save two.

"...ona...Mona...Mona," Curt gasped.

"Is that who did this to you?" Remo prodded gently.

Curt coughed. A string of sticky dark blood dribbled down his chin.

He seemed to want to shake his head but could not. *"BBQ,"* he whispered. "Mona's...gonna kill me," he exhaled.

Curt's head lolled to an awkward angle. A final trickle of blood gurgled up between his lips.

Face severe, Remo left the body.

There was more blood in front of the supply room. Inside he found the remains of Sadie Mayer.

The old woman's wounds were consistent with the other BBQ attacks. She had been killed first and then methodically eaten. Curt looked more like the victim of a savage assault.

Remo concluded that the BBQ had had its fill

with Sadie. By the time it reached Curt, it was sated. The creature had been playing with its food.

Farther down the hallway, Remo found the same tracks he had seen in the Concord cornfield. They led into the alley.

He hurried outside.

As before, the blood faded after only a few yards. This time the trail seemed to end more abruptly than before.

The BBQ was gone.

As he crouched to examine the final, bloody print, Remo wondered once more what kind of animal could change its footprint when it killed. It was baffling.

The mark he looked at now was clearly a paw print. The BBQ left *hoof*prints.

The creatures from BostonBio were deliberate genetic mutations, so anything was possible under the circumstances.

Still…

Privately, Remo hoped that Chiun would be done with his meditations soon. He'd hit a stone wall on his own. Maybe the Master of Sinanju could shed some light on this mystery.

Remo turned away from the last print.

As he headed from the alley out onto the street, Remo failed to notice that the alley door to the HETA headquarters had been wrenched open. From the outside.

13

When word of the latest deaths attributed to the escaped BBQs broke on the eleven-o'clock local news, a palpable panic settled over Boston and its surrounding suburbs.

Phone lines became tangled from eleven o'clock until the wee hours of the night as viewers called friends and relatives to warn them in case they hadn't heard the latest terrifying news. Police stations all across eastern Massachusetts were flooded with unconfirmed BBQ sightings.

Assurances from BostonBio that the animals were perfectly harmless were ignored. And rightly so. The death toll was now up to ten, including one of the crazed geneticists who had actually worked on the insane project. At the moment, there were more human casualties than there were BBQs. Under the circumstances, no one in their right *mind* would believe BostonBio.

HETA had grown silent on the location of the remaining animals in its possession. BostonBio had retrieved only one. For all anyone knew, the other seven could be God-knew-where eating God-only-knew-whom. And there was nothing anyone could do about it.

With Curt Tulle dead, the authorities didn't even know whom in the HETA movement to arrest. But even if they'd thrown a net over the entire animal-rights group, it would still take years of court fighting, plea bargaining and actual prison sentences to get them to reveal the location of the creatures. In the meantime, Boston's citizenry hunkered down behind locked doors, fearful to even step outside lest they be attacked and consumed by one of the marauding beasts.

Nationally, the BBQ story had been back-burnered the previous evening. But the latest developments would bring more notoriety. The deaths at HETA and the one confirmed at-large BBQ would doubtless be the lead story on all four networks the next day.

Already, the national press was circling. *Nightline* was devoting its entire program to coverage of the panic in Boston. A representative of the show had contacted BostonBio in order to get Dr. Judith White on the program. The genetics firm had bluntly informed the show that Dr. White was on indefinite suspension.

The premier geneticist of her generation had gone from brilliant genius to embarrassing outcast in just over forty-eight hours.

Flouting her suspension, Judith was sitting in her darkened lab hours after the murders at HETA HQ.

The bluish light from the flickering television screen bathed the room in uncertain shadows. Her eyes were at half-mast as she watched her name being dragged through the mud by troglodytes who couldn't even begin to grasp her genius.

On a rational level, Judith understood why BostonBio had suspended her. They had considerations separate from hers to deal with. Most of them legal. But on a visceral level, she hated every last one of the gutless imbeciles who was allowing this televised crucifixion to continue. It was not only bad for BostonBio and Judith White, but it was also bad for the *world*.

They'd hung her out to dry.

Management had decided that the best defense under the circumstances was to say nothing. The opposition had roared into the vacuum left by the company's absence. Without even token resistance from BostonBio, the media were having a field day.

In the wake of Curt Tulle's death, HETA sent in emissaries from its national offices to man the Boston franchise. Judith was watching some of them on the lab TV.

Three actresses from the *The Olden Girls* were among those who had been flown in. The feeble-witted women from the popular 1980s sitcom sat behind the temporary head of Boston HETA as he addressed reporters.

"Curt Tulle is a martyr to animals and all living things *everywhere!*" the man screamed. For some reason, he felt compelled to shout every statement. "I only hope that I can live up to his great standards!"

"Are you the permanent head of Boston HETA?" asked one of the reporters. Unlike the press at the previous news conference, this woman was a network correspondent.

"I am part of an interim ruling council! Since arriving earlier this evening, I have been ably assisted by Ms. and Mr. Janner, who have been more than helpful at this moment of great crisis!" He indicated a pair of figures standing at the rear of the crowd behind the podium.

Huey fidgeted uncomfortably. Mona glared defiantly at the home viewing audience.

"Will your group surrender the remaining BBQs?"

At the question, Mona's and Huey's eyes grew as wide as pie plates. They were visibly relieved an instant later to find that it hadn't been directed at them.

"This is a *plot!*" the national HETA man yelled, ignoring the question entirely. His arms flapped crazily. "The government—in league with the fiends at BostonBio—have made it their mission to wipe out HETA! For without HETA, there will be no opposition to them, and without opposition, dear friends, they will be able to come into your homes and take *your* pets for their horrible experiments!

That is their ultimate goal! The animal Holocaust has begun!''

Judith White stared at the laboratory television, eyes level, face unreadable.

A reporter asked one of the women from *The Olden Girls* what she thought of the BBQ situation. The woman had also played the lustful host of a cooking show on the old 1970s *The Sherry Taylor Hoore Show.*

''I like kitties,'' said the elderly woman, her dull eyes wetly earnest.

Judith slammed her palm so savagely against the television the plastic chassis cracked. The TV winked off.

Her lip curled, revealing perfect white teeth.

The black box from her desk lay open on the table next to her. She had already filled one of the syringes with the brown gelatinous fluid from one of the vials that rested on the foam interior of the box.

She gathered up the syringe. With a lunge more appropriate to a game of darts than an injection, she jammed the needle into a pulsing blue vein in her arm.

With her thumb, she pressed the plunger down, forcing the brown liquid from the syringe. It oozed soothingly into her bloodstream.

Even as she felt the liquid enter her and mix with her warmly flowing blood, she knew it would be the last.

Judith shuddered wildly. The sensation was like

that of hands of solid ice gripping her spine. Her back arched at the frigid sensation.

The liquid coursed through her.

The last.

Her head spun. As before, but not like before. Far away, but not too far.

Light...spinning.

The last.

The BBQs were the most important thing now. Important to her. And to the *world*.

Her final injection. She was there.

A jolt. Snapped back to reality. The icy hands flew from her spine. Her head cleared. The effect was not as it had been all the other times.

And there was something else....

"Dr. White?"

The voice came from behind her. She turned slowly, a smile curling the edges of her red lips. One of her geneticists stood at the mouth of the corridor that linked the two separate laboratories. Alone.

"I'm surprised you're here, Dr. White." His return smile was uncertain.

"Just finishing something up," she purred. She slipped down from the table on which she'd been perched. One hand snapped closed the lid of her special black box.

"I—that is to say, *we* heard. All of us. We think it's terribly unfair what they're doing to you." The scientist frowned somberly.

Judith's hand slipped across the smooth surface

of the black case. One finger caressed the interlocking double-*B* BostonBio logo. Her eyes rose to meet those of the young man. They locked.

"Bullshit." Judith grinned.

The geneticist shifted uncomfortably. He hadn't expected to see his boss here so late. In fact, like most of his co-workers, he had prayed she would never return to her post at BostonBio.

"I...um..." the man mumbled.

"Shut up," Judith cooed. Her smile never wavered.

She slid around the table, revealing long, flawlessly tanned legs. Slowly, Dr. White sashayed over to the man. As she walked, her short skirt wrinkled up around her thighs.

The young scientist gulped, trying not to stare.

"Um...there are two of them," he stammered. As he spoke, he looked at her ample chest. His own words seemed to startle him. Quickly, he jerked a thumb over his shoulder. "Two *BCWs,* I mean. Two. In there."

Judith kept walking. "Mm-hmm." She nodded.

"It's just, I thought there was only the one. At least, there was only one earlier today."

"Now there are two," Judith agreed. "One *plus* one."

She was beside him. He jumped when her hand reached out to him. But this had nothing to do with Dr. Judith White's notorious vicious streak. Her warm palm gently traced the contours of his cheek. He shivered at her touch.

"Dr. White, this…uh…probably isn't a good idea."

"Of *course* it is," she replied in a hoarse whisper.

Her face came in close to his, sliding cheek-to-cheek. Beside his face, warm lips brushed softly against his ear. He felt a gentle tug of perfectly polished enamel as her teeth pulled lightly at his earlobe.

"Have you eaten yet?" Judith asked breathily.

In spite of himself, the geneticist closed his eyes, surrendering to the seduction. Dr. White was an insufferable bitch, but she was also the most gorgeous female of the species he had ever encountered. But her non sequitur food question puzzled him back to reality.

"What?" he asked. "Yes. Yes, I have." She was still nibbling on his ear. He closed his eyes, trying to recapture the mood of a moment before.

"It's been a few hours for me," she exhaled hotly. Her breath tickled the soft hairs around his ear. "I'm hungry again."

The geneticist had closed his eyes, his head tipped invitingly to one side.

"Mmm. We can get something after," he moaned.

Judith's teeth chewed farther up his ear. She was beyond the lobe now, encompassing almost the entire ear.

"Maybe a little something to tide me over," she hissed.

Teeth became fangs. With a savage bite, she clamped firmly onto the young man's ear. A jerk of her face wrenched the ear from the side of his head.

Shock suppressed the urge to flee. Stunned, the scientist pulled away, falling to his knees. A frantic hand clamped the side of his head.

He found to his horror that his auditory canal was open wide to air. Blood poured across the gaping hole. The sticky liquid coursed around his shaking fingers.

Fear. Shock. He wheeled to Judith White.

He saw his ear for the last time. It was balanced on the tip of her tongue like a single red-tinged potato chip. She smiled as she flipped the clump of skin and cartilage back into her bloodred mouth. A few quick chews followed by a solitary gulp, and the ear was gone forever.

"I bet you can really hear my stomach rumbling now," she said with a broad grin. Blood filled the spaces between her flawless teeth. *His* blood.

He was too frightened to speak. Too scared to scream.

And as the young geneticist's eyes pleaded for mercy, Judith White padded forward. To feed.

14

Remo stood alone, a silent sentry at the front window of his Quincy condominium.

The street beyond was eerily calm. Night shadows skulked near curb and corner.

Few cars traveled the roadways so late on a normal night. This night there were far fewer than usual. The BBQs. Fear of the beasts had rippled out from Boston into the outlying communities.

Of course, the odds were astronomical against anyone encountering one of the creatures, even if all of the remaining animals were at large. But that didn't matter to the population of Boston and its suburbs.

Even Remo wasn't immune to believing that he might actually spy one of them. In his case, however, it wasn't fear, but hope. He wanted more than anything to corral the BBQs and return them to BostonBio.

The BBQ project was on the verge of collapse, yet its original goal—to feed the starving world—was noble. If the project was at all salvageable, Remo would do whatever he could to help.

And so he waited. Staring out at the dark and empty street. Half-expecting to see a herd of wild BBQs thunder past his home, yet knowing full well that he would not.

There seemed to be one silver lining in the events of late.

The noises had started filtering down from upstairs an hour ago. No more were they hushed, one-sided conversations. These were packing sounds. Whatever business Chiun had been up to, it appeared to be coming to an end. He was putting away his candles and incense.

After standing alone for what seemed like an eternity, Remo finally heard the door to Chiun's room sigh gently open. He didn't hear a footfall on the stairs, nor did he expect to. Only when he detected the familiar rhythmic heartbeat did Remo turn.

The Master of Sinanju sat angelically on the floor in the center of the living room, as if he'd been there since the floorboards were nailed in place. He wore a brilliant sapphire kimono, adorned with swirling purple peacocks. The flowing robes were arranged around his bony knees.

The wizened Korean seemed as old and wise as Time itself. His ancient skull was covered with a sheet of skin like thin, seared parchment. Twin tufts of yellowing-to-white hair sprouted out above each shell-like ear. A thread of beard adorned his chin. Youthful hazel eyes regarded Remo from amid knots of wrinkled lids.

Remo's smile was thin but genuine. "Welcome back to the land of the living, Little Father," he said.

"Thank you, my son," Chiun replied. "You managed to keep your screaking and clumping within acceptable limits during the weeks of my spiritual journey. You are to be commended." He tipped his head in an informal bow.

That Chiun should emerge from hiding in such a good mood was cause for concern to Remo. He pushed thoughts of their recent trip to Hollywood from his troubled mind.

"I have a problem," Remo said, returning the bow. When he lifted his head, he saw that Chiun was no longer looking his way.

The old man was craning his neck in birdlike curiosity as his gaze moved from one corner of the room to the next. When he looked back to his pupil, a confused shadow had settled over his bright eyes.

"Where is my gift?" he asked with simple innocence.

Uh-oh, Remo thought. He immediately racked his brain.

It wasn't Chiun's birthday, not that they celebrated it anyway, thanks to Remo. Christmas was three months away, though rarely were gifts exchanged between them on what Chiun considered a pagan celebration of the birth of "that nuisance carpenter." That left the Feast of the Pig and the anniversary of the day they'd met. But the Feast of the Pig was still some time off, and Chiun had never seen the day of their first meeting as something worth rejoicing over. Indeed, for the first ten years of their association, the only way Remo ever knew the date had rolled around yet again was from the appearance of a black armband over the Master of Sinanju's kimono sleeve.

He came up empty. Remo bit his cheek. "Gift?" he asked guiltily.

"It is customary after a journey, is it not?" Chiun replied, a creeping tightness to his singsong tone.

Remo let the captured air escape from his lungs. "It's customary to *give* gifts, Little Father. Not *get* them. Besides, you didn't go anywhere."

The cloud of Chiun's brow darkened. "You are telling me you got me nothing?" he accused.

Remo's eyes darted left and right. He was trapped.

"Nothing," he blurted, "except that I felt kind of sad without you here to talk to. And now that you're back, I'm sort of happy." His hesitant voice grew stronger. "So I guess that's what I got you. A son's love." He smiled hopefully.

In spite of himself, a spark of warmth ignited the old man's eyes. An upturned flicker brushed the vellum corners of his thin lips. He forced it away.

"In lieu of a brass band, I suppose it will have to suffice," Chiun sniffed. "Next time I return from a pilgrimage of self, however, I expect a present with a price tag." He fussed with the hems of his kimono.

"One Mylar balloon coming up," Remo promised, relieved to have dodged the bullet. "Anyway, a lot of junk's been happening since you pulled your 'Louisa May Alcott does Hollywood' routine."

Chiun's eyes instantly narrowed. "You have not been listening in on my telephone conversations?" he accused.

Remo sighed. "No," he said.

"Good," Chiun responded. "For there were none."

Remo didn't bother to mention the fact that the last phone bill he'd seen would have choked a horse.

"Chiun, I have a problem."

"That is nothing new. Speak, O Giver of Cheap Gifts."

"Smith has given me an assignment. A genetics company has created an artificial animal that can feed the world. But it looks as if the animal is vicious. People have died."

"All people die," Chiun said, dismissing the last of what his pupil had said. "We know this better than any. As for the rest, I do not understand this nonsense of an artificial animal, yet I know well of many animals deemed vicious."

"The fact that it might be a killer isn't the only problem," Remo explained. "A couple million and a good PR firm could help BostonBio wiggle out of that. The weird thing for me is the tracks these things leave."

He explained to Chiun the stark difference between the hoofprints of the BBQ at rest and the paw prints it made following its murderous attacks.

Chiun frowned thoughtfully. "A bird walks, yet it flies," he pointed out. "A duck does both, yet also swims."

"The BBQs don't have wings," Remo said. "And they'd need pontoons to float. They just have big clumsy feet that somehow morph into something delicate when they kill."

Chiun's frown lifted. "Do you remember, Remo, the riddle of the Sphinx?"

"Sure," Remo said. "You told me it back when you were dragging me all around the world during the Sinanju Rite of Attainment. The riddle is, whose face does the Sphinx wear? And the answer is the face of the Great Wang."

Lines of frustrated annoyance creased the old man's parchment skin.

"Why is it, Remo, that you appear never to listen to a word I say, yet apparently absorb just enough to aggravate me at a later date?"

Remo offered a confused half smile. "Luck?" he suggested.

Chiun's gaze was flat. "I refer to the Egyptian riddle. What is it that walks on four legs in the morning, two legs at noon and three legs at night?"

"Everyone knows that one," Remo replied. "The answer is a man. He walks on four legs in the morning of his life because he's crawling. As an adult, he walks on two feet. And when he's old, he uses a cane. Three legs. But you told me that was a child's riddle.''

"And I was correct. For I am aged by anyone's estimation, would you not agree?" Chiun asked.

"Only to those who don't know you like I do, Little Father," Remo said warmly.

"Do not be maudlin, Remo," Chiun chided. "There are those who *think* me old. Yet I do not require a cane. And so you see the true nature of all riddles." He nodded sagely.

Remo's face clouded. "I do?" he said.

"Yes," Chiun responded. "The answer is that riddles are a foolish waste of time." He rose from the carpet like a puff of escaping steam. "We will learn the true secret of this animal when we see it."

With that, the old Asian padded from the room.

As he watched the frail figure pass out into the hallway, Remo felt his heart warm. Even though his mentor technically hadn't gone anywhere, it still felt good to have Chiun back.

"I know where we can find one," Remo called after his teacher. He hurried out into the hall. A moment later, the front door clicked shut.

They were not gone more than two minutes before the phone began ringing urgently.

The desperate jangling echoed into empty, darkened rooms.

15

Smith let the telephone ring precisely one hundred times before finally replacing the receiver. Obviously, Remo was either out or was not answering his phone. As for Chiun, the old Korean rarely deigned to answer the telephone.

The CURE director was sitting in his cracked leather chair. Around him, his austere Folcroft administrator's office had been swallowed by shadows. A single drab bulb glowed atop his desk.

It had been many hours since last he slept. Gray eyes burned behind rimless glasses as he stared at the silent blue phone.

All but a skeleton crew remained at Folcroft so late after midnight. Without a major crisis for CURE, it was late even for Smith to be working. But he had been waiting for something specific.

The envelope sent by Remo had arrived late in the morning of what was now the previous day. Under the guise of an FBI investigation, Smith had immediately forwarded the mysterious object contained within it to the Smithsonian Institution for analysis.

He had then sat back and waited.

Day stretched into night and had moved on into the postmidnight hour of the following day before the results finally came back. When the answer was at last sent back along the circuitous electronic computer route Smith had established to ensure secrecy, the CURE director found it as puzzling as Remo's mystery of the BBQ tracks.

He had seen the object with his own eyes before sending it along to the Smithsonian. It was small and half-moon shaped. The tough material was cupped and came to a curving point at the far end.

The object Smith had seen jibed perfectly with the determination of the Smithsonian. He rebuked himself for not coming to the same, obvious conclusion.

Forensic scientists at the Washington institution had concluded that the item was nothing more than a woman's artificial fingernail. The kind glued on to increase normal cuticle length and strength.

In his report, the Smithsonian scientist who had forwarded his conclusions to Smith asked if the nail was part of an FBI serial-killer investigation. In his final e-mail, Smith issued nothing more than a blunt thank-you.

Smith reread the report displayed on his monitor as he considered whether or not he should try to call Remo again.

Pam Push-On Nail. The Smithsonian had even determined the specific brand of artificial nail.

Remo claimed to have found the fingernail in a wound of one of the BBQ victims. Smith considered briefly that Remo might be playing some kind of sick joke. He decided almost as soon as the thought occurred to him that this wouldn't be the case. Remo's sense of humor had never been so inappropriately ghoulish.

Which left Smith with a new baffling mystery.

The six HETA people in Concord had been men. Only Remo and a single BBQ had been in the area. How and why was the fingernail left in one of the bodies?

Smith stared, unblinking, at the report, hoping somehow that some new insight would leap out at him. But it remained little more than words on a screen. Even so, for some reason, this new information gave him a feeling of inexplicable dread.

Tearing his eyes from his computer screen, Harold Smith snaked an arthritic hand to the phone.

Maybe Remo was home by now.

16

The parking lot of BostonBio was virtually empty. Remo assumed the few parked vehicles belonged to security guards or janitorial staff.

He expected he might find some resistance at the front desk due to the lateness of the hour, but the Department of Agriculture identification he had been using for the past few days got both him and Chiun onto the elevator. The lift carried them silently up to the third floor.

The impersonal silver doors opened into a long hallway, bathed in darkness. Remo led Chiun to the door of the lab where he had first met Judith White.

"No key," Remo said. "Guess we do it the old-fashioned way." He reached for the knob, planning to pop it open.

Reading his intentions, the Master of Sinanju held a staying finger to Remo's bare forearm.

"You are hopeless," Chiun muttered.

The old Korean inserted a long index fingernail into the space between lock and door frame. He wiggled it as a burglar would a credit card. The lock clicked obediently. Sliding his nail back out, Chiun pushed. The door swung dutifully into the room.

"Show-off," Remo said.

"If you would surrender to the inevitable and grow your nails to their proper length, you would not have to crash and smash your way through life," Chiun sniffed.

"Don't start," Remo warned.

They slipped inside the lab, silent wraiths.

The lights were on. Diffused fluorescent bulbs shone from fixtures all along the interior ceiling. More light spilled from the corridor that connected this lab to the next.

Judith White's office door was ajar. Although her lights were on, as well, they sensed no life signs.

"Death stalks this place," the Master of Sinanju intoned.

Remo nodded. "A scientist was killed here yesterday."

Chiun shook his head. "No," he announced, button nose upturned. "This death is recent."

Remo pulled at the air. Immediately, the tang of human blood flooded his nostrils. It came from the corridor where the BBQs had been stored.

Exchanging a single tight glance, both men began to move across the silent lab. They were as stealthy as jungle predators when they reached the door.

The wide corridor where Judith had made her sloppy pass at Remo was well lit. The BBQ pens were to their left. As they moved into the long room,

Remo was surprised to find more than one of the cages occupied.

Two BBQs looked up as they entered the room.

"This is the creature of which you spoke?" Chiun said, his voice pitched low. His eyes were razor slits.

"Yeah." Remo frowned. "But there should only be one of them here." He glanced down the hall.

The lights were on in the adjoining lab. Gliding weightlessly forward, their feet sliding in perfect concert, the two Sinanju Masters made their cautious way up to the other lab.

They saw the body instantly. Freshly dead, it lay in the center of the room. Their senses told them he was alone. Sliding into the lab, they hurried over to the body.

It was like the others. The stomach cavity had been torn open, organs consumed. One of the ears was missing.

But unlike the other victims, this man appeared to have been slaughtered and eaten at a more languid pace. There wasn't as much blood on the floor as before. Most of it had pooled in the stomach husk.

Standing over the body, Chiun peered down at the hollowed stomach cavity. His face betrayed no emotion.

"This is the work of an animal," the Korean pronounced.

"That's what everyone's saying." Remo nodded.

Chiun tipped his head, considering. It was clear something weighed on his mind.

"Care to let the rest of the Scooby Gang in on whatever's got your spider senses tingling?" Remo asked.

Chiun gave him a withering look. "Will there ever come a time when you shut your mouth and open your eyes?"

Remo frowned deeply. "That like one of those 'Do you plan to stop beating your wife?' questions?"

"Pah!" Chiun exclaimed. He spun on an impatient heel, heading back to the corridor.

Remo had to jog to catch up to the swirl of dancing silk. He found the Master of Sinanju standing before the two caged animals. Remo noted that the latches on the cage doors were secure.

"Do you still not see?" Chiun pressed.

"You mean how do they let themselves out, kill and then get back in?" he ventured.

"Are you so blind?" Chiun asked brusquely. "Where is the *blood?*"

Remo looked around. He looked down the corridor to where they'd found the body. Finally, he looked back to Chiun. His expression was sheepish.

"What blood?" he asked.

The Master of Sinanju closed his eyes, as if too weary to display real anger.

"If these animals are responsible for this death, then why are they not flecked with blood?"

Remo looked more closely at the nearest BBQ. Its pale skin was as clean as a whistle. So was the other animal's skin. There were no darker patches on their black spots.

"Maybe they licked it off," Remo suggested.

"They could not clean away the scent of so fresh a kill from their breath," Chiun pointed out.

The Master of Sinanju squatted down before one of the BBQs, hazel eyes intent. The odd-looking animal stared blankly back at him.

"These things are genetically engineered," Remo offered. "Maybe they absorb smells like a box of baking soda in the fridge."

"I know of this 'genetical,'" Chiun said. "It is the name applied to inferior breakfast cereals that masquerade as a famous product. Beyond that, these creatures are guilty of nothing more than being completely adorable."

Remo blinked blandly. "Come again?" he asked.

When Chiun looked up at him, his face was beaming. "Surely you must agree they are as cute as buttons."

"Only if we're talking really ugly buttons."

"Hush, Remo," Chiun admonished. "It will hear you." Sticking his bony arms between the bars of the cage, he pressed his hands against the animal's triangular ears. "Pay him no heed," the Master of Sinanju cooed.

The BBQ moaned softly. Chiun squealed in delight.

"I hate to break up this Kodak moment, Marlin

Perkins, but we've still got a hollowed-out scientist in the pantry.''

Chiun's expression dismissed this as irrelevant.

"Do you think Smith would allow me to take one of these marvelous creatures back to Sinanju?'' he asked.

"Does the phrase 'no way in hell' mean anything to you?''

"I will assure him that I will feed it and walk it every day,'' the old man said, not listening. Chiun patted the BBQ on its long snout, his expression wistful. "Did you know, Remo, that Master Na-Kup is still heralded in the scrolls of Sinanju for bringing a camel back to my village? It was a gift from a lesser pharaoh. He called it a Mountain Beast for the shape of its hump. All the village gathered around to see it. The people were quite impressed.''

"They were probably cranking its tail to see which way the money came out,'' Remo said. He didn't like where this was heading.

"Na-Kup did nothing more to distinguish himself as Master but lug one mangy camel back from Egypt. Yet here it is three thousand years later, and he is still known to all as Na-Kup the Discoverer. Surely I would be remembered even more fondly in years to come were I to return bearing something more exotic on my proud shoulders.''

"I'll buy you a cockatoo,'' Remo said dryly.

"Master Cho-Lin already discovered those lice-ridden buzzards centuries ago.'' Chiun scowled.

"Or do you not remember the fifteen hundred lines in the scrolls devoted to Cho-Lin and his Speaking Bird?"

"Sounds like a bad Vegas act," Remo commented.

When Chiun raised baleful eyes to Remo, they widened in surprise. He was looking beyond his pupil.

In the infinitely short space of time that Chiun noticed Dr. Judith White, Remo became aware of her, as well. Her step was so soft, her heartbeat so low, she was at the mouth of the corridor before either of them was aware of her.

Near the BBQ pen, the Master of Sinanju stood rapidly. The lines of his face bunched into knots of ominous tight wrinkles.

"Judith?" Remo queried, alarmed.

She was framed in the doorway to the main lab.

Judith White was awash in blood. Her lab coat and the front of her form-hugging dress were streaked with crimson.

"Remo?" she asked, her throaty voice oddly hesitant and distant. She reached out a hand to him.

All at once, Judith's eyes rolled back in her head. Legs buckled. Without another word, she collapsed to the cold lab floor. Fainted dead away.

17

"Are you certain Judith White was not responsible?" the lemony voice of Harold W. Smith pressed.

Remo was on one of the lab phones. The ambulance carrying the near comatose BostonBio geneticist had left for Boston's St. Eligius Hospital five minutes before.

"What kind of dippy question is that?" Remo asked.

"You just told me she was still on drugs," Smith stressed.

While waiting for the ambulance to arrive, Remo and Chiun had done some snooping around. They'd found the black box with its vials and syringes in Judith's office.

"Drugs don't turn you cannibal, Smitty," Remo said.

"No, but perhaps she was acting in a drug-induced rage."

"Doesn't wash. This guy wasn't just killed. His *insides* were gone. My money's still on the BBQs."

A harrumph sounded across the room.

The Master of Sinanju sat, cross-legged on the

floor. Beside him one of the BBQs stood tethered to a desk leg. Chiun was nose to nose with the creature.

"You *did* say she was covered with blood, yet did not appear physically injured in any way."

"Probably fell over the body and then stumbled around in shock afterward," Remo suggested.

"If Judith White were to blame, it would explain the artificial nail you found in the body in Concord."

Smith had mentioned the Smithsonian's conclusion.

"I'll check out her hands next time I see her," Remo promised. "*If* we ever see her alive again."

"Why? Is there a danger to Dr. White?"

"I don't know," Remo admitted. "Depends on what kind of junk she was pumping into herself. It seemed like she'd doubled the dose after finding the body. Her heart rate was down to next to nothing. Even Sinanju can't hear someone's heart when it's between beats. According to the guards around here, she wasn't skulking around the building anywhere, so she was probably in her office the whole time."

"And no one else was in the lab?" Smith questioned.

"Just her and the BBQs."

"*BBQs?* Remo, you told me yesterday BostonBio had only one of the creatures back in its possession."

"As of tonight, it's two. I'm guessing it's the one

from HETA headquarters. These are *homing* monsters, Smitty.''

''This is puzzling,'' Smith mused. ''If you feel Dr. White is not responsible for the most recent death, then we are left with only the animals themselves as suspects.''

''Don't forget HETA,'' Remo suggested. ''But they couldn't have gotten in here without the guards seeing them.''

The thought occurred to both men simultaneously.

''The window,'' Remo said, remembering the avenue HETA had used to first gain entry to the lab.

''See if it has been repaired,'' Smith instructed.

''I'm on it. Hold the phone, Smitty.'' Remo placed the receiver on the desk and hurried into the connecting hallway.

Chiun was off the floor the instant Remo slipped into the hall. Abandoning his BBQ, he hurried to the phone.

''Hail, Smith the Generous,'' Chiun intoned, pressing the receiver to a shell-like ear. He pitched his voice low.

''Master Chiun,'' Smith said, surprised. ''Remo had not told me you had concluded your meditations.''

''Remo has lived a lifetime of forgets, Emperor,'' Chiun replied. ''Unlike your noble self. He was without my guidance for the duration of my philosophical pilgrimage, yet was there a single gift waiting for me upon my return? No. But his thoughtlessness no longer surprises me. And, anyway, I knew that *you* would not make the same error. And so I must rely on you, Smith the Dependable."

Warning lights had already flashed on in the CURE director's mind the minute a gift was mentioned. He'd dealt long enough with the wily Korean to know the beginning of a setup. Not daring to even breathe lest he unwittingly agree to some new demand, Smith prayed for Remo's rapid return.

"The boy is inconsiderate," Chiun continued. "Not at all like you. Many are the times I have told him, 'Learn from your emperor, Remo. Make a lesson of his renowned philanthropy.' Of course, if you ask him, he will doubtless say that I have never said this to him," Chiun added quickly. "The depth of his forgetfulness is unending. But know that a day does not go by wherein I do not shout the glories of your munificence down into the empty well that is Remo's skull."

Chiun paused. He frowned. A muffled gulp was all that issued from the earpiece.

"Is there something wrong with your breathing?" the Master of Sinanju queried.

Smith exhaled loudly, inhaling rapidly. "No," he panted, trying to catch his breath. "No, I am fine."

Chiun nodded. "Excellent. So tell me, Emperor. Where may I retrieve my gift? Or have you dispatched it by herald? I cannot wait to see what it is. Do not tell me," he said hastily. "It will ruin the surprise."

"Er...actually, Master Chiun..." Smith began hesitantly.

"Yes?" Chiun's eyes were already narrowing with cunning.

Smith forced the words out all at once. "I did not know it was traditional to give a gift at such a time."

Chiun allowed the ensuing silence to bear the heavy burden of his great disappointment.

"You got me nothing?" he asked eventually, voice small.

"I am sorry," Smith apologized.

"Oh, no, that is fine," Chiun replied quietly, bleeding from every word.

The old Asian sounded genuinely despondent. The amount of gold Smith shipped yearly to the North Korean village of Sinanju as retainer for Chiun and Remo's services was so generous, the Master of Sinanju could have indulged any whim. Yet Smith could not help but feel a twinge of guilt.

"I could yet get you something," Smith suggested, rapidly adding, "something *small*."

Chiun sniffled. "That would be most kind, but not necessary," he moaned sadly.

"I insist," Smith said. Already he was wondering what there was around the sanitarium that could be packaged as a gift. Mentally, he had already dropped a few notebooks and pens from the supply room into a box when Chiun broke in.

"Since you insist, there *is* something that I would

like,'' the Master of Sinanju volunteered, his voice strong once more. ''A minor boon.''

Smith felt the trap snap shut. ''What is it?''

''A piffling thing,'' Chiun responded. ''I would not abrade your tender ears with its name. Say but the word and I will take this trifle as my own, in your generous name.''

''Master Chiun, if it is within my power to grant it to you, I will. But I need to know what it is you want.''

Chiun frowned deeply. The fool wasn't making this easy.

''I am not sure what it is called,'' the old Korean said. ''White nomenclature is still difficult at times. Remo called it an ABC, or letters equally inappropriate. It is an ugly name for a beautiful animal.''

''Animal?'' Smith asked. ''Chiun, do you mean a BBQ?''

''Remo told me it was an ABC.'' Chiun's voice was puzzled.

''Those animals are not mine to give,'' Smith said.

The chill raced with blinding speed over the fiber-optic line. ''You are going back on your word?'' Chiun said coldly.

''I gave you no word,'' Smith replied firmly. ''And given all that has happened, it is likely those animals are vicious. Furthermore, they are the property of BostonBio.''

''One would not be missed.'' Chiun insisted.

"There are only eight altogether."

"A clerical error." Chiun waved angrily.

"Please understand," Smith said reasonably, "they might still be bred and distributed around the world someday. If they are indeed harmless, I will get you one then."

"But *everyone* will have one then," Chiun whined. "I will not be lauded as Na-Kup if I drag home any common American thing. Why not lug a telephone or television?"

Chiun's lament sparked a memory for Smith.

"Now that you mention the telephone, Master Chiun, I could not help but notice the large number of calls you placed to California while sequestered."

Chiun's sulking tone instantly transformed to low menace. "You monitor my conversations?" he accused.

"Not the calls themselves," Smith explained hastily. "But the times and dates of all long-distance calls are recorded on the bills I pay. Are you involved in something I should know about?"

Chiun heard the gliding approach of Remo's loafers.

"My involvements are my own, Smith," Chiun said flatly.

Unfurling his hand, he let the phone clunk to the desk.

When Remo entered the room an instant later, Chiun was settling back down before the tied BBQ. The animal lowed. The old man scowled at it.

Remo scooped up the receiver. It was warm. He shot a glance at Chiun as he spoke. "Windows are all set, Smitty. Broken one's been replaced. Nobody came or went that way."

Smith seemed relieved to be speaking to Remo. "Still," he said. "Our prime suspects in all of this remain the animals and HETA. I will have tests performed on the creatures there. With so recent a kill, it should be a simple matter to determine whether or not they were responsible for the body you discovered tonight."

All at once, a thought occurred to him. Smith's chair squeaked as the CURE director sat up straighter.

"I don't know why I did not think of it before," Smith said excitedly.

"What?"

"One moment."

Remo heard Smith's fingers drumming rapidly at his special keyboard. After a few short minutes, Smith returned to the phone, voice flushed with success.

"I believe I might have something," he said. "I checked the HETA membership rolls in Boston and cross-referenced them with credit-card payments at area grain and feed stores. One store in Leominster keeps popping up."

"Where the hell is that?"

"It is not important," Smith said. "The credit

card used there belongs to one Huey Janner. He and his wife own a farm in Medford.''

''So?''

''They have ordered large quantities of diverse food items over the past three days. Hay, meatless dog food, bulk oats and so forth.''

''They never ordered anything like that before?'' Remo asked, picking up the thread.

''No,'' Smith replied. ''Theirs is a vegetable farm. They do not allow animals on the premises for either food or as beasts of burden. Understandable, given their membership in the HETA organization.''

''How do you know that?''

''I accessed their Web page.''

''So much for the pristine country life,'' Remo said dryly. ''We'll check it out.''

''If you do find the animals there,'' Smith instructed, ''and they give you any indication that they might be dangerous, it would be in the best interest of all for you to destroy them.'' His instructions were clinically blunt.

Remo looked back to Chiun. The BBQ was in the process of licking the old man on the nose. Hearing Smith's words, the Master of Sinanju's face grew appalled.

''Find someone else,'' Remo said firmly.

''But if they are as vicious as they now seem to be, they cannot be allowed to survive,'' Smith argued.

Chiun wrapped his bony arms protectively around the BBQ's thick neck.

"No way, Smitty," Remo said emphatically. "The Old Yeller guilt-o-meter is already cranked up to high. I'll find them, but I'm not going to kill them."

"It may become necessary," Smith warned.

"Let somebody else do the honors. I'm not a butcher."

The emphatic manner with which he delivered the words sounded odd, even to Remo. Given his profession, it seemed hypocritical for him of all people to be so passionate in his refusal to euthanize the BBQs. The seeming contradiction merely acted to further firm his resolve.

Smith seemed displeased with his objection. "Very well," he relented. "But at least return them to BostonBio. Any difficulties with the creatures can be resolved then."

Stemming any further complaints from CURE's enforcement arm, Smith severed the connection.

Across the room, Chiun continued to hug the BBQ close to him. The animal was oblivious to the protective arms.

Remo closed his eyes. So much death in what was supposed to be a simple, altruistic assignment.

And in his heart of hearts, Remo hoped fervently that the BBQs were not responsible for all the evil he had seen of late. There were already too many species of killer animals in the world.

18

She was no longer Judith White. Yet, in so many vitally important ways, she still was.

It amazed her every time she thought about it.

Thought. Rational, *intelligent* thought.

The thing that lay beneath the cool sheets in the hospital bed at St. Eligius Hospital understood that this was what made all the difference in the world. Thought. The ability to think, to reason. It distinguished her from all other animals on Earth, save one.

Thin gossamer streaks of white moonlight, mixed with the waxy yellow glow of parking-lot lights, spilled across her quietly resting form. The smells of the ward the humans had brought her to flooded her senses.

All the ointments and medications, the stale meals and bad perfumes, nervous sweat and soiled linens—she took them all in.

She smelled the humans. Each odor individual and distinct. To the creature that had been born Judith White, they were not fellow men. They were meals.

The humans had Meals on Wheels. Judith White had her own version of that. Meals in Shoes.

She snorted at the amusing thought.

"Meals in Shoes," she muttered softly, smiling. "Delivered warm right to your door."

"Excuse me?" whispered a voice from the hall.

Judith had heard her coming, of course. But she was surprised the nurse heard her voice. Human hearing was just about the worst of any animal in the world. But occasionally one surpassed the rest. Not difficult to do, given the commonness of human limitations.

Judith remained still. Her eyes were open barely a slit. Only enough to see. In the 3:00 a.m. darkness of the room, her whites wouldn't be seen.

Predictably, the nurse attributed the soft voice to a dreaming patient. The woman tiptoed quietly into the room, her white sneakers virtually soundless on the linoleum. To Judith, she might just as well have stomped in wearing tap shoes and a suit of armor.

The nurse checked the patient in the next bed, an obese fifty-year-old woman with two ingrown toenails who had refused to be treated on an outpatient basis. The woman was deep in medicated sleep.

Stepping over to Judith, the nurse smoothed out some nonexistent wrinkles in her bedcovers.

She wore a name tag. Elizabeth O'Malley, R.N.

Just beneath the silver tag, the woman's heart thudded audibly in her chest. The enticing sound rang like a dinner gong in Judith's ears. She repressed the urge to lunge.

To the nurse, everything seemed fine. As quietly as she had entered the room, she slipped back out into the hall.

Judith heard her step back up to the nurses' station. A moment later, the woman headed down another corridor.

The instant she was out of earshot, Judith's perfect legs slipped out from beneath the sheets. Her feet made no sound as she stalked across the room to the small closet.

Finding her clothes, Judith suppressed an unhappy cluck. Too much blood on the blouse and jacket. Skirt was dark. At night, the stains wouldn't be visible.

She stuffed the hospital johnny she was wearing inside her short skirt. It gathered in bunches around the waist.

There was a large coat in the closet. No doubt the property of the patient in the next bed.

Judith turned to the gently snoring woman. She watched the sheet rise and fall over her ample belly.

A hungry purr rose from the throat of the geneticist.

Familiar footsteps suddenly registered in the hall outside. Judith spun rapidly back to the closet, throwing on the fat woman's coat.

She looked quickly around the room.

The footsteps were too close.

The door was out of the question.

There was only the window.

Judith made an instant decision. She spun on her heel and headed to the window. With one quick stop along the way.

WHEN NURSE O'MALLEY PASSED by the open door to Judith White's hospital room a few moments later, she glanced inside. She was startled to see both beds empty.

The nurse went into the dark room, not certain what to expect. A cursory examination revealed that neither patient was in the small bathroom.

The nylon curtains of the second-story room blew gently in the soft September breeze.

She looked out the window. Briefly, she thought she saw a dark figure moving quickly and stealthily beyond the lights of the parking lot two stories below. Whatever it was, it seemed to be carrying something large.

A practical woman, she dismissed the sighting as nothing more than her imagination giving in to all of the hysteria swirling around the wild animals that some local company had set loose on the streets of Boston.

Efficiently, Nurse O'Malley clamped the window shut. Leaving the empty room, she went off to search the floor for her two missing patients.

19

Judith White's parents were young urban professionals before anyone had even heard the term *yuppie*.

Her father was a successful corporate lawyer, her mother an executive in the same company.

Back when daddies generally played ball with the kids after coming home from work and mommies usually stayed at home, mother and father White were so busy they had to pencil little Judith in for appointments.

At least, that was what Mr. and Ms. White liked to call them—appointments. In point of fact, the periods of time spent with their only offspring were less appointments than intense, brutal lessons in how not to rear a child.

The point behind these sessions was simple. *They* had succeeded. *Judith* would succeed. End of bedtime story.

Mr. White kept his daughter up late the first nine months of her life trying to teach her to talk.

Mrs. White "walked" infant Judith around the

house until she was bowlegged and had to wear corrective leg braces.

Expensive tutors were hired to cram knowledge into a mind that—at the age of two—only wanted to play. Nannies were employed to take the place of a mother who, when home, acted more like a tyrant than a nurturer.

Little Judith was put on teams in order to round out her personality. Never mind the fact that she was much younger than the rest of the children and that the older kids taunted her. When she cried to stay home, her parents coldly told her that everything— good or bad—was a learning experience.

Judith's parents wanted her to have a life that neither of them had enjoyed. Mrs. White's father had been a minor city officer in a small town near Springfield, Massachusetts. Mr. White's father had been—to his son's eternal shame—a truck driver. According to the Whites, both of their mothers had never realized themselves as complete individuals, having stayed at home to raise their respective broods.

Judith would have the best. Just as they had not.

For the first year or so of grammar school, young Judith had worked hard to fulfill their expectations. In her parents' eyes, of course, she never succeeded but she tried her best. And for almost two years it appeared, at least on the surface, as if things were going perfectly well.

That is, until the first incident.

As with most parents who pushed too hard, the Whites found that their daughter eventually pushed back even harder.

The first time was small. Someone had gathered up all the toilet paper in the girls' lavatory in their daughter's public school and set it ablaze. The bathroom had gone up in flames. The school had to be shut down for the day.

Judith denied she was the culprit. And in spite of the testimony of the two other girls who had been with her and a teacher who had witnessed her leaving the smoking bathroom, her parents had insisted that their daughter was innocent. No matter what the others *thought* they'd seen, their precious Judith would *never* do such a thing.

The school had suspended her for a week. Her father had threatened to sue. Eventually, the school had given in.

During the two short days she was forced to stay home—for the very first time in her life—her parents had doted on her. At least it seemed that way to Judith.

They had come running to her defense. They had stood up for her when no one else would. They had become, for one brief moment, real parents.

Forget the fact that their chief concern was how the whole affair reflected on them. Judith's by-now-twisted mind saw their behavior as an act of love. For the first time in her life, she almost felt good. And she wanted the feeling to continue. In her next plea for attention, Judith used a pencil to stab one of the girls who'd squealed on her.

Everyone in class saw it clearly, including her teacher.

Judith was thrown out of school.

This time, her parents reacted differently. In the face of overwhelming evidence, they'd screamed bloody murder. Within forty-eight hours, Judith was shipped off to the Excelsior Academy for Young Women, deep in the woods of New Hampshire. She was seven years old.

At the school, Judith's young intellect was nurtured by stern yet caring teachers. Without the negative influence of her self-absorbed parents, Judith excelled. She graduated at the top of her class, moving on to a prestigious prep school. Four years later, Judith was valedictorian.

Her parents were there for graduation. Aside from her annual Thanksgiving and Christmas breaks, it was the only time she'd seen them since they'd shipped her off to Excelsior. Unlike those holiday visits, however, at graduation Judith didn't even try to be polite.

When Judith's father tried to hug her, she shoved him away. When her mother tried to kiss her, she spit in her face. It was the happiest day of her miserable life.

Judith could finally sever the tenuous ties with her unloving parents. She had gotten several scholarships to fine colleges. She no longer needed Mr. and Mrs. White.

College was a breeze. Judith had an exceptional intellect. She moved swiftly, achieving her B.A. in two years. After graduate school, her brilliance got Judith noticed by a bioengineering firm on the famed high-tech Route 128 north of Boston. It was a short jump from there to the Applied Genetic Research Department of BostonBio. Shorter still was the time it took Judith to develop the BBQ project.

As the guiding force behind the creation of the world's first fully genetically engineered animal, Judith White was unstoppable. She was also arrogant, single-minded, bossy and virtually impossible to get along with.

When some of the earliest prototypes of the creatures were developed—the ones with the equine DNA that would help name their successors—Judith wasn't averse to taking the weakest of the lot and strangling them in front of her team.

She would wrap her strong hands around their necks and squeeze in the cruelest, most giddily delighted way until the animals' tongues lolled from their mouths and they dropped over onto the floor.

When she was finished strangling one of the hapless creatures, Judith would always say the same thing.

"That felt great. Any coffee left?"

The carcass was left for an underling.

In this and in other matters, she gave off every

sign of a woman who was mentally unbalanced. If she'd been a man, Judith probably wouldn't have lasted long at her job. But she had one remarkable asset. In a field of nerdy men and beefy women, Dr. Judith White was an absolute stunner. She merely had to flash her perfect teeth or bat her long eyelashes, and the board of BostonBio would drop an inquiry before it even started. Of course, if she didn't get results, this brand of manipulation would have lasted just so long. But the fact was, Judith *did* get results.

In another corporate entity, BostonBio had once been the Boston Graduate School of Biological Sciences. BGSBS had been at the vanguard of genetic manipulating in the late 1970s, but had fallen on hard times after a freak accident involving one of its top geneticists. Judith had spent much of her early time at BostonBio exhuming and digesting the records of the earlier BGSBS experiments.

Judith had to admit, the research was brilliant. Flawed, but brilliant. She would have enjoyed meeting the woman responsible for the earlier exploration into breaking down the genetic differences in mammals, but her predecessor had vanished years ago under a cloud of controversy. The woman was presumed dead.

Still, her research lived on. Powerfully so.

The technology in the seventies wasn't what it was by the time Judith took over at BostonBio. Though the work of an obvious genius, the original breakthroughs at BGSBS had been misdirected. Judith had taken what she could learn from the dusty files she found hidden away in a secure basement and augmented it. Refined the procedure.

One of the results of her tireless efforts was the BBQ. The awkward, pathetic-looking creature that was ostensibly the savior of the starving world. The other, more important result was Dr. Judith White herself.

She was like a woman possessed. First, she meticulously reconstructed the circumstances of the original experiment. The one that had—in the minds of many at the old BGSBS—gone completely wrong.

For many months, Judith had no luck. The substance had been taken orally the first time years ago. She had tried that the first day.

Nothing happened.

According to the eyewitness accounts of the original incident, the effect had been virtually instantaneous.

It *should* have worked, but didn't.

Judith had tried various alterations in the formula. Still with no success.

It was maddening. The work with the BBQs proved that what she was trying to do was possible on one level. But the laboratory animals—at the time still very young—presented a less complex problem. The manipulation of their DNA had taken place prior to their conception. Judith was attempting to alter the entire system of an adult *living* organism.

Judith was almost ready to give up when she found something she hadn't seen before while re-reading one of the *Boston Blade* accounts of the time. The newspaper was from BostonBio's own archives. It had been preserved in thin plastic, yet had yellowed with age.

The reporter who had been on the scene described the thick brown substance that clung to the exterior of the test tubes. He told how it had slid like burned gelatinous fat down the woman's hand and into her mouth.

Into her mouth.

That was it!

Although the formula for the chemical compound used to retard temperature changes in scientific containers had been altered and improved over the years, Judith White was able to have some specially manufactured from the old formula. It was the same stuff that had clung to the test tube in the old newspaper account.

She had determined by her earlier experiments that human saliva was likely a catalyst to the change. Alone in her lab, Judith had carefully mixed specific DNA-altered genes, saliva and some of the gelatinous packing compound. Rather than swallow the vile mixture, she injected it into her arm.

The results were obvious and immediate.

Icy cold. Intense disorientation. And the change.

After her recovery from that first injection, she had prescribed a strict regimen of shots.

The formula as it now existed would destabilize after a few weeks. The original scientist would have eventually changed back. Judith didn't want that. She altered the formula to ensure that the change would be permanent.

And Dr. Judith White *had* changed. As a result, the world around her had changed, too. It was a change for the better.

Her perspective, while always warped, had altered dramatically. The evidence was everywhere.

It was in her attitude. In the way she moved. In the contempt she felt for humans. But at the moment, it seemed mostly to be in her appetite.

JUDITH WHITE AWOKE above a cluttered alley amid the overflowing rubbish barrels behind a Chinese restaurant.

She yawned expansively, tasting the paste of food still on her tongue.

The body of the woman who had been her roommate during her brief stay at St. Eligius lay beside a large open trash bin. Only her bare feet jutted into the alley. They were pale and unmoving.

Judith was perched on a fire escape above the body. One hand hung languidly down over the rusted metal side of the escape. The other scratched contentedly behind her ear as she considered the body.

It had been too fatty. She preferred leaner meat. Next time.

For now, she knew what she must do. A thinking animal, Judith found it difficult to focus when the cravings began. She knew that she shouldn't allow irrational desire to supersede rational thought. But with each subsequent injection, it had grown increasingly difficult to quell the urge to feed.

Judith yawned again, arching her back. She pushed her hands out before her, fingers splaying as she stretched.

She had almost been caught the night before. That nosy Department of Agriculture agent had shown up just as she was finishing her meal at the lab. She had barely enough time to get back to her office and clean up her face and hands before he came in.

Remo had fallen for her ruse. In his limited mind, he thought the blood on her clothes had been an accident. Humans were so eager to accept what they perceived as the obvious conclusion.

But that might not always be true.

She finished stretching.

They would probably come for her. It was only a matter of time before they connected her to all the deaths. She hated to admit it, but she had been careless.

She never should have taken her roommate.

Judith got up on all fours on the fire-escape landing. With a graceful leap, she hopped down to the alley floor. Landing, she barely made a sound.

Quickly, she padded over to the body.

The woman looked like the rest. Thick blood remnants coagulated in the hollow of her ripped-open abdomen.

Judith worked swiftly. Taking each of the woman's hands in turn, she chewed off all ten fingertips. The flesh was tough and cold.

"Blech," Judith complained. "I hate leftovers."

She swallowed the pudgy balls of skin.

With her fingernails, she shredded the woman's fleshy face until it was unrecognizable.

It would probably do no good. The missing organs would be a dead giveaway. Still, it might buy her some time.

Dawn had nearly begun to break over Boston.

Judith's underlings would be showing up to work within the next three hours. Before they did, she had to get back into BostonBio and destroy all evidence of what she had done. Perhaps there was a way to yet salvage the situation.

Judith spun away from the body. With catlike grace, she glided out of the desolate alley and onto the dark, silent street.

20

"Why are we here?" the Master of Sinanju complained.

They were driving along the desolate road where Mona and Huey Janner owned their farm. It was still several hours before dawn.

The wizened Asian's attitude had soured back at BostonBio. Whatever Chiun had discussed with Smith, it had turned the old Korean sullen and silent. Until this moment, he had remained thus for the entire ride to Medford.

"Smith thinks the rest of the missing BBQs might be here," Remo said, careful that by inflection he didn't appear to agree with the CURE director. His diplomatic tone didn't work.

"If your precious Smith directed you to leap from Yongjong Bridge with stones in the pockets of your kimono, would you?" Chiun challenged.

"How deep's the water?" Remo asked.

The old man's scowl could have cracked bedrock.

"Okay, okay," Remo relented. "Sheesh, Chiun, I don't know what he did to kick-start bile production, but I wasn't in on it, so could you cut me some slack?''

"And why should I?" Chiun demanded. "You are his lackey, are you not? He dispatches you hither and thither on his mad errands and you obey. You are the Divine Wind of America's pinchpenny emperor, Remo Williams. Do not pretend that you have a will of your own."

"Divine Wind?" Remo frowned. "Isn't that what *kamikaze* means?"

"If the Mitsubishi fits," Chiun sniffed.

"Should I even bother to argue?"

"No."

"Fine," Remo said. "If it'll keep peace, you're right. I don't have a will of my own."

The appalled expression that blossomed on the old Korean's face told Remo that he had answered wrong.

"I cannot believe what I am hearing," Chiun gasped. "Has a Master of Sinanju just admitted that he is little more than a puppet on a string?"

"I thought that's what you *wanted* me to say," Remo griped.

"What I wanted was for you to speak your mind, thus demonstrating your independence from Smith the Domineering. But I find that I must speak your mind for you. Repeat after me—I have a mind of my own."

"Fine, dammit," Remo snapped. "I've got a

mind of my own. There. Is that okay? Or did I get that wrong, too?''

"No," Chiun said.

"Good," Remo replied, fingers tightening on the wheel.

"Prove it," Chiun challenged.

Remo pulled his eyes from the road. "Huh? How?"

Chiun's hands slithered up opposing kimono sleeves. In the green wash of the dashboard's lights, the old man's self-satisfied mien was one of the most fear-inducing sights Remo had seen in all of his professional life.

"I will let you know."

Remo absolutely did not like the sound of that.

"Wait a minute…" he began, stomach sinking.

"Too late," Chiun interrupted, raising a silencing finger. His gaze was fixed on the dark woods beside the moving car. "We are being watched."

Remo had sensed the eyes upon them, as well. He found the Janner mailbox and turned onto the long dirt driveway that wound through the clump of dark trees.

They hadn't driven more than a few yards when the first figures appeared before them.

The two men were clad in body-hugging black leotards, faces obscured by black ski masks. In the pervasive gloom of the deep New England night, they stood like somber sentries before the gates of

Hell. Automatic weapons were aimed at Remo's car. They were a terrifying sight.

"How do you think they pee in those getups?" Remo asked.

"Who cares? Drive over them," Chiun replied.

"You want to hose blood off the grille?"

"I am an assassin, not a washer of cars," Chiun sniffed.

"Didn't think so," Remo said. He slowed to a stop.

As soon as the car stopped moving, a guard raced to either door. One grabbed Remo's door handle, wrenching it open.

"Get out," a muffled voice commanded.

Remo obliged. Even as he was stepping from the car, a similar command was being issued to the Master of Sinanju.

There was a grunt as the other commando pulled on the opposite door handle. It wouldn't budge. Inside the car, Chiun's pinkie pressed lightly on the inner handle. The commando cursed and yanked on the unmoving door.

"What do you want?" the man near Remo menaced.

"I want not to be manipulated all the time. I want to not be lonely when he's not around and then irritated when he is. But mostly, I want to know where you keep your car keys in that shrink-wrapped Union suit."

By now, the other man had dropped his gun. Both

hands and one foot were heavily involved in his game of tug-of-war with Chiun's door.

"Don't get smart with me," Remo's commando threatened. His gun jabbed at Remo's ribs.

"How about if I get fatal?" Remo suggested.

There came a blur of movement impossible for the HETA commando to follow.

He was stunned to find that his target had vanished. So, too, he realized with growing concern, had his gun. Frightened fingers gripped empty air.

A sudden coolness to his head and face. His mask gone, too. Whirling, the commando tried to shout a warning, but something blocked his throat. Something itchy.

And in a moment of horrifying realization, the HETA man didn't know which was worse: the fact that he was being force-fed his own hat, or the fact that the stranger was using the barrel of his own gun to tamp it down his throat.

"Junior eat up all him din-din," Remo enthused, stuffing the metal barrel deep into the man's esophagus.

"Blrff," the HETA commando gasped.

"Yum-yum. Eat 'em up," Remo agreed.

The man's eyes bugged. He couldn't breathe. The hat was wedged in a tight ball inside his throat. Remo pulled the barrel free, tossing the gun into the bushes.

The man immediately shoved his fingers into his mouth, probing for fabric. It was too far in. Clawing at his throat, the red-faced commando toppled over onto the road.

"Bon appétit," Remo declared, turning his attention back to the Master of Sinanju.

The other HETA man was still yanking on the door, his face red as that of his suffocating colleague.

"Perhaps it is rusted shut," Chiun was suggesting through his open car window.

"Chiun, quit clowning around," Remo complained.

The old Korean exhaled, bored. "Very well. But only because I grow weary of this buffoon."

As the commando gave the door one last mighty wrench, the Master of Sinanju lifted his pinkie, at the same time slapping a flat palm against the interior door panel. The crunch of bone on door was wince-inspiring.

The last Remo saw of the second HETA man, he was five feet off the ground and flying backward into a thick stand of midnight-shaded maples. Remo never heard him land.

Chiun joined his pupil outside the car.

"More up ahead," Remo informed him. The dark shapes of barn and farmhouse loomed up the road.

Chiun nodded. "Together or separate?" he asked.

"Together," Remo replied. "You haven't given us much of a chance to bond lately."

"I long for the day you finally get the hint," Chiun whispered, swirling from his pupil.

Side by side, the only two true living Masters of Sinanju began moving swiftly up the pitch-black road.

HUEY JANNER WAS DEEP in tofu-fueled REM sleep when he felt a firm hand clamp over his mouth.

"They're here," a voice whispered from the murky shadows.

Mona.

Huey pulled himself out of bed. In the dark, he fumbled off his pair of sweat pants. His unitard was underneath.

"How far?" he asked, sleep clogging his throat.

"Driveway," she replied tersely.

He could hardly see her. She was dressed in her black, formfitting leotard.

"Did you get them ready yet?"

"*No,*" Mona insisted. "I came for you first. Why, I'll never know. Move it!"

She hurried from the bedroom, slinking stealthily along the silent upstairs hallway. He heard one of the top steps creak as she crept to the ground floor.

Stumbling in the darkness, Huey chased after his wife.

THE SECOND WAVE of HETA commandos hid in a cluster of sickly elms that slouched up from the middle of the Janners' sprawling front lawn.

Not one of the three men saw even a flicker of

movement from the long driveway. Night skulked, dark and menacing.

"Are you *sure* somebody's here?" one commando whispered nervously as he studied the shadows.

"Sam yelled there was a car coming," the second replied.

"*I* heard a car," offered the third tense voice.

"Me, too," agreed the first man.

"Me, three," announced Remo Williams.

Panic. Gun barrels clattered loudly together as the men tripped and swirled around, looking for the owner of the strange voice in their midst. They found *two* men.

"Are you now the town crier, announcing our arrival to every lurking simpleton?" Chiun asked, brow creased in annoyance. He stood at Remo's elbow.

"I barely opened my mouth," Remo replied, equally annoyed.

"Silence is golden," Chiun retorted. "*Especially* coming from you."

Three sets of frightened eyes bounced from one intruder to the next. Finally, the jaw of one HETA man dropped open.

"Fire!" he screamed.

Two HETA commandos were accidentally slaughtered in the ensuing panicked shooting match. The roar of automatic-weapons fire was rattling off into the night as the third man checked the bodies at his ankles. Neither Remo nor Chiun was among the dead.

A finger tapped his shoulder. The remaining HETA man looked up dumbly. He found that he was staring into the deadest black eyes he had ever seen.

"Missed me," Remo said thinly.

A thick-wristed hand fluttered before the commando's face. The colors that danced across his field of vision in the next instant were more brilliant than anything the man had ever seen. First red, then blinding white, then black. Afterward, he saw nothing at all.

Remo let the body slip from his fingers.

"House or barn?" he asked the Master of Sinanju.

"Where does this kind belong?" Chiun asked dryly.

"Barn it is." Remo nodded.

Turning from the trio of bodies, the two men made their stealthy way toward the menacing dark structure.

HUEY JANNER NEARLY JUMPED out of his skin when he heard the gunfire.

"They're *close*," he whispered anxiously.

"Get a grip," Mona insisted. She kept her breathing level as they crept through the dark interior of the barn.

Huey had a difficult time following her. Though

he tripped frequently, Mona didn't slow her stride. She had exceptional night vision.

With Mona at point, they approached the old dairy stalls where the BBQs slept. Mona pulled two dark bundles from a wooden shelf. She tossed one to Huey.

"They're in for one hell of a surprise," Mona Janner whispered with certainty. Huey smiled weak agreement.

Wishing he shared his wife's confidence, Huey ducked inside a stall. Nearly purring in pleasure, Mona disappeared inside another.

"DINGBAT, twelve o'clock high," Remo commented as they slid up to the big barn door. His eyes were on the hayloft.

Chiun's narrowed eyes were fixed on the crouching figure. "I will deal with this one," the old man said.

Wordlessly, he melted into the shadows beside the barn. Remo continued on alone.

The barn door was open a hair. Remo slipped inside.

The big interior was drafty and dank. The thick smell of wet, molding hay clung to the air.

Remo's finely honed senses detected faint life signs coming from the long west wing of the barn. He slid across the packed earthen floor to the rear of the main building.

As he came upon the closed door that led to the old dairy stalls, he heard a new sound. A shout.

"Giddap!"

A woman's voice.

"Move, move, move!" a man yelled almost simultaneously.

Pushing open the door, Remo turned the old-fashioned crank light switch. Bulbs clicked on along the angled wood ceiling, flooding the old cow stalls with washed-out light.

"Giddap! Giddap, dammit!" the woman's voice shrieked.

Remo followed the shouting down to the third stall.

He found one of the missing BBQs. And, straddling its sagging back, perched on an animal-friendly faux-leather saddle, was a screaming Mona Janner.

"Hurry up and move, you stupid lummox!" the animal-rights activist yelled at the hapless BBQ. "They're *coming!*"

She tried to kick it in the sides to make it move. Her legs were too long, and the BBQ's were too short. She succeeded only in scuffing dirt.

"I'm trying to *save* your worthless hide," she snapped.

"Maybe it doesn't want to save yours," Remo suggested.

Mona's head snapped around. Her face hit one of

her own knees. The creature was so low to the ground they were up by her ears.

When she saw Remo, her eyes bugged in her ski mask. Wheeling, she shook the reins violently. "Hyah!" she urged.

The BBQ had had enough. Moaning, it settled to its ample belly. When its legs tucked up beneath its oblong body, Mona had no choice but to roll off. She shook a stirrup from one foot as she clambered to her feet.

"Please tell me this was a spontaneous getaway," Remo said from the door. "I'd hate to think it was planned."

Mona spun on him, hands held before her in a menacing posture. "Stay back!" she warned. "I know karate."

She demonstrated by attacking the air before her with her hands. Neither air nor Remo appeared very impressed.

As Mona attempted to bisect oxygen molecules, Remo heard a startled yelp from the adjacent stall. He'd become aware of the man and the second BBQ at the same time he'd found Mona. When the yelp was followed by a furious hiss, Remo suppressed a smile.

A few yards before him, Mona was still slashing away.

"I'm warning you, meat eater," she snarled.

"I always wondered something," Remo said, one eye trained on the wall of the stall. "If animals aren't supposed to be eaten, why are they made out of meat?''

His question had the precise desired effect. Eyes widening in horror, Mona froze in her tracks.

The HETA woman's mouth was in the earliest twitching stages of forming a furious, self-righteous O when there came a thunderous crash from her left. Mona twisted just in time to see the thin, unfinished pine that separated her stall from the next explode into a thousand shards of thorny kindling. And sweeping through the air amid the hail of wood fragments came a familiar shape.

Rocketing through the air, Huey Janner swept his wife off her feet in a way she hadn't allowed him to during their courtship. He slammed roughly into Mona, scooping her up and flinging her against the far wall. They hit with a crash, arms and legs tangling together as they collapsed, inert, to the hay-strewn floor.

As the dust was settling on the HETA activists across the stall, a familiar bald head jutted through the jagged hole made by Huey Janner's thrown body.

"Remo!" the Master of Sinanju wailed. "That savage was abusing one of these poor beasts!"

When he spied the saddle on Mona's BBQ, Chiun's eyes pinched to slits of fury. Flying through the hole, he bounded to the animal's side. Hands slashed with blinding fury, long nails severing the straps of the saddle. Chiun pulled the piece of molded plastic loose, flinging it across the stall. It landed on Huey's moaning, upturned face.

Squatting, the old Korean began stroking the long snout of the BBQ. "There, there," he said soothingly.

The BBQ seemed oblivious to Chiun's presence.

The Janners had landed near Remo. With one loafer, he toed the saddle off Huey's head. He frowned as he peered down at the unconscious HETA man.

"I know him." Remo nodded. "He was on TV a couple hours ago." He tugged off Mona's mask. "Her, too."

"Doubtless they were featured on *America's Most Hunted,*" Chiun said. "Do you think they will double the ten-thousand-dollar prize for apprehending *two* notorious animal abusers?"

"I think you're mixing up shows, Little Father," Remo said. "And these two were on the dais at a HETA press conference. It was on the news."

At his feet, Mona was groaning herself awake. Cradling her head in one hand, she pulled herself up on unsteady legs.

"What happened?" Mona muttered. When she dragged her lids open and saw Remo standing before her, her eyes sparked with sudden memory.

Mona lashed out at Remo. He plucked her hand from the air and patiently placed it back at her side.

She tried to kick him. He caught her leg and returned it to the floor. As he did so, she again tried to punch him. Remo snatched her hand once more, pushing it calmly away.

Mona tried to bite him. Remo finally lost his patience and knocked most of her front teeth to the back of her mouth.

This got Mona's attention.

"Chritht! Do you know what thith dental work cotht me?" Mona whistled angrily, sounding like the front man for an Ozarks jug band.

"Not caring," Remo said. "Annoyed. When it becomes 'angry,' I start collecting tongues. Where are the rest of the BBQs?"

It was more than a threat. It was a promise. Mona Janner suddenly became interested in the preservation of only one very specific animal.

"Right here," she enunciated carefully. Her tongue stuck uncomfortably through the hole in her bridgework. She was quick to close her lips over it.

"Stay put," Remo commanded, spinning on his heel.

He found the remaining BBQs in the last stall. All four were curled on a blanket of hay. They snored contentedly.

When he returned to the stall, Huey Janner was dragging himself to his knees. Mona glared at her husband.

"We've got 'em all, Little Father," Remo announced as he stepped back into the stall.

"Thanks to the demons of BostonBio," Mona snarled. She spit a mouthful of bloody saliva at the floor. "When we tried to release them, they wouldn't go. We left the barn wide open for two nights. Those Frankensteins at BostonBio robbed them of their natural urge to flee personkind."

"Did you consider that they might never have had it to begin with?" Remo said, irked.

"BostonBio again," Mona insisted. "They probably fed them, cared for them. Made them feel they had nothing to fear. Then bam! Hold the pickle, hold the lettuce."

Remo only shook his head. "Where's your truck?"

"What truck?" Mona sneered.

"The one you *brought* them here in," Remo said.

"We don't have a truck," Mona spit, a superior grin splitting her jack-o'-lantern mouth. "We only rent them when it's absolutely necessary."

"Mona doesn't believe in internal-combustion vehicles," Huey explained. "*We* don't believe in them," he amended, shrinking from his wife's dirty look.

"You're Mona?" Remo asked. "Now I know why Curt Tulle was more worried about you than getting mauled by a BBQ."

"Tulle?" she snapped. "You mean that little jerk gave us away? I gave him one of these monsters to take the heat *off* us. Why didn't I hire a skywriter to point a big, fat, greenhouse-gas-filled arrow straight to the barn?"

"Actually, we traced your husband's credit card." Remo smiled. "Start your engines."

As Mona twisted, face a mask of pure rage, to her cowering husband, Remo turned his attention to the Master of Sinanju and the resting *Bos camelus-whitus*.

"Any ideas how to get these things back, Little Father?"

Chiun was stroking the long nose of the BBQ.

"A vexing problem." The old Asian nodded thoughtfully. "I recommend we give them safe harbor at Castle Sinanju until we work out a solution. There is room in the fish cellar."

"No, there isn't," Remo said. "And if we can get them that far, we can get them to the lab."

"I will remove a tank or two," Chiun continued, as if he hadn't heard. "I have not had pickerel in ages. That one can go."

"I just had pickerel two days ago."

"As I said, *I* have not had pickerel in ages. We can eliminate that and your silly shark tank, thus opening up space near the furnace. They will enjoy the warmth."

"Okay, let's get on the same page here, shall we? We're not taking out any tanks, we're not bringing home any stray mutants, and we *still* don't have anything to carry them in even if we wanted to." He frowned as he looked down at the animal. It was well over a hundred pounds. "I can't squeeze six of them *and* us in that rental car," he complained.

"*Please,* Mona!"

The pleading voice behind Remo distracted him from his dilemma. He glanced back.

Huey Janner was lying in a fetal position on the earthen floor. Mona loomed above him, bruised face enraged.

"I...told...you...to...use...cash." Each word was punctuated by a fresh kick to the ribs.

"Okay, that's it, Punch and Judy," Remo announced. Stepping over, he coaxed Mona out of the way with one hand, lifting a grateful Huey to his feet with the other. "I need to think without distractions."

Over the objections of both animal-rights activists, he shooed the Janners out of the stall. He propelled them into the main barn.

A sturdy toolshed was set into one wall. He tossed Huey inside, where he landed on a pile of pitchforks and hoes.

"Serves you right," Mona snapped at her husband. But when Remo reached for her as well, she balked. Desperate to avoid confinement, she struck up a seductive pose. "Hey, baby," Mona said, using her best sexy voice. "I'm in HETA." Her tooth gap whistled.

"Take a cold shower," Remo suggested. He tossed her in atop her husband.

Slamming the door shut, Remo piled a few hundred-pound sacks of organic gardening compost in front of it. The sounds of Mona Janner pounding on her husband anew were issuing from the shed as he returned to the stalls.

In his absence, Chiun had led the BBQ from its stall. The creature looked exhausted. It wasn't the effort of walking that made the animal seem bone tired. It was the wearying burden of life itself. Its fat tongue lolled.

"Damn, these things are hideous," Remo commented. He pulled his eyes away from the sullen BBQ. "I'm gonna call Smith. He can figure out how to get these eyesores back."

But as he turned, the Master of Sinanju rose from his post next to the sad animal. "Hold," he commanded.

Remo turned. "What?"

"It is time," Chiun intoned. His expression was somber.

Remo's face scrunched. "Time for what?"

"Time to prove that you are not Smith's lapdog. You may demonstrate your independence *and* give the gift you failed to give me on my return." He cast a knowing eye down on the dismal form of the BBQ.

Remo followed Chiun's gaze. The BBQ stared at him with guileless brown eyes. When he looked back up to Chiun, the old man's hazel orbs were filled with sly hopefulness.

"Oh, no," Remo said with quiet dread.

"Prove to me, Remo, that you are better than a Japanese zealot," Chiun encouraged.

"Chiun, you already talked to Smith about this back at the lab, didn't you?" Remo said slowly.

"Smith," Chiun spit. "Do not invoke the name of the American Hirohito. Especially not at this time of your great liberation." He held aloft a fist of bone. "Remember Pearl Harbor!"

"You *can't* take one, Little Father," Remo stressed.

Chiun's face hardened to stone. "And why not?" His tone was ice.

"For one thing, what would we do with it?"

"We would bring it back to Sinanju, of course. My triumph of discovery would forever eclipse that of Na-Kup the Fraud and his diseased camel." There was passion in his singsong voice.

Remo raised an eyebrow. There was something more to this than just the BBQs.

"What's with you and Na-Kup?" he asked.

The old man's jaw tightened. His thread of beard quivered. "You never met him?" he asked tightly.

"Since he died about three thousand years before I was born, no," Remo replied.

"Consider yourself blessed. He is an arrogant braggart, even in death. He and that anthrax-laden beast of his."

"But you couldn't have met—" Remo stopped dead, the light finally dawning. "The Sinanju Rite of Attainment," he said. "The last rite of passage before full masterhood. You went through that mess when you were visited by the spirits of past Masters, just like me. I'm gonna go out on a limb here and say you met Na-Kup."

The dark storm cloud that passed over Chiun's silent face spoke volumes.

"History remembers the camel, but it doesn't remember the *Master*." Remo nodded, understanding at last. "Someone had something up someone's kimono sleeve that someone else didn't expect, huh?"

"Someone is an idiot," Chiun snapped. "And wipe that smug expression off your stupid, fat face. My reasons are my own. Besides, I only want one of these animals. Perhaps two. Five at most."

"I'm sorry, Chiun," Remo said, shaking his head.

"You would not do this simple thing for me?" Chiun demanded hotly.

"You *know* I'd do anything for you. But there's only a limited number of these. They'd miss one."

"It could have escaped," Chiun suggested.

"Chiun," Remo said, reasonable of tone, "Smith has been to Sinanju before, remember? We don't know that he'll never come back. What's he going to say when he sees that moaning lump of DNA schlepping down Main Street?" He nodded to the BBQ. It burped.

"He would say 'What joy and pride you must have felt, O great Master of Sinanju, that your son did honor you by granting you the single boon you desired during the five hundred years in which he abused you.'"

"First off, Smith doesn't say 'boon.' Second, I

doubt he'd take the theft of a phenomenally expensive animal that we're supposed to be returning to its rightful owners so lightly. Third, I don't know where you've been, but you've asked for a lot since I've known you. Fourth, it has *not* been five hundred years.''

''You have a facility for compressing much abuse into a short amount of time,'' Chiun said coldly. ''You will not help me?''

''I *can't*, Chiun,'' Remo said helplessly. ''I wish you could see that.''

''I see nothing but ingratitude,'' Chiun retorted, delivering his final word on the subject. Spinning, he offered his back to Remo. He squatted down beside his BBQ.

Remo stared for a long moment at the back of Chiun's ornate silk kimono. The old man's mood had soured so rapidly in the past four hours it would be a miracle if he didn't lock himself back in his bedroom for the next fifty years.

It made Remo feel terrible to deny his father in spirit one of the pathetic animals. But he had a job to do. If Chiun didn't understand that, it was his problem.

But as he looked down on the tiny Korean, Remo felt as if the problem were his own. Chiun had that knack. And it made Remo feel miserable.

Turning away from the wizened form of the man who had given him so much in life, Remo quietly left the Janner barn.

21

"Smith." The CURE director's voice was anxious.

"We got them all, Smitty," Remo announced.

"At the Janner farm, presumably," Smith said, relieved.

"They are—I'm not," Remo explained. "Those dopes don't believe in phones or lights or motorcars. They're like the Amish without the crack. I'm on a pay phone at a gas station down the street."

He glanced around the grimy black yard of the all-night station. Half-built cars—some with their hoods open—littered the area around the pay phone.

Smith's tone became concerned once more. "Where is Chiun?" he asked.

"Back at the farm," Remo answered, quickly adding, "and don't worry, I know he wants one of them and I told him no dice."

"Good," Smith said, exhaling.

"For you, maybe," Remo griped. "He made me feel like mountain-beast droppings."

"Neither your feelings nor Chiun's desires are important now."

"What else is new?" Remo replied caustically.

"I meant no offense," Smith said quickly. "But there has been another death in Boston."

Remo's back straightened. "Like the others?"

"Yes," Smith said. "An unidentified woman. The stomach cavity was consumed as in the previous attacks."

"Unless they were cross-pollinated with Houdini, it wasn't any of the BBQs," Remo said. "The two at the lab aren't going anywhere, and the six here were too far away."

"That's just the point," Smith said excitedly. "This last body is different than the rest. The woman's fingerprints and features were mutilated to complicate identification."

"So?"

"Remo, the mere act of the killer trying to cover his tracks proves *conscious* thought. Animals kill to survive. Only human beings worry about fingerprinting and police investigations."

Remo's brow furrowed. "I see your point," he admitted.

"That is not all," Smith said. "The latest body was found almost in the same location as the first."

"That was near BostonBio, wasn't it?" Remo queried.

"Within walking distance," Smith answered, his lemony tone betraying intrigue.

"So we're right back to square one," Remo said.

"We have narrowed our focus," Smith disagreed. "When I learned of the latest body, I checked with

St. Eligius. Judith White has not checked herself out of the hospital. Therefore, we can eliminate her as a suspect. That leaves someone else at the company. Possibly someone on her team.''

"Or someone with HETA.''

"That remains a possibility, as well,'' Smith admitted.

"Okay,'' Remo sighed. "I'll go back to BostonBio and see what's shaking there.''

"Stay there until something turns up,'' Smith instructed.

"Great,'' Remo said, with not a hint of enthusiasm. "I can pass the time between corpses hearing about how big an ingrate creep I am.''

He hung up the phone and trotted back to his parked car.

Chiun was sitting stoically in the passenger's seat.

"What are you doing here?'' Remo asked.

"Why?'' Chiun sniffed. "Was your intention to abandon me, as well? Forgive me, Remo, I did not know. If you but give me one moment, I will lie beneath the wheels of this carriage so that in your departure you might crumple my worthless shell.'' He stretched a bony hand to the door handle.

"Okay, okay,'' Remo muttered. "Sorry I asked.''

He started the car. Angling the vehicle out of the driveway, Remo headed into the brightening dawn.

After they'd left, a tiny moan rose from the back of the ill-lit office of the service station.

22

Terror Toll Mounting! screamed the headline in the *Boston Messenger*'s early edition. Beside the banner print, a picture of the latest victim stared out from every newspaper box in town. The worst of the mutilated body had been covered by strategically placed black bars. Small type below the headline read, "Killer creatures still stalk Hub."

For years, the *Messenger* sat alone on the sensationalistic limb. Of late, however, the local television stations had been clambering up the trunk. On the morning following the latest death, every syndicated or network program ordinarily broadcast on Boston's network affiliates was preempted for continuous coverage of the "Killer creatures."

Most of this coverage involved reporters marching around street corners and storming straight up to cameras in order to create a sense of frenetic excitement.

Boston's highly paid evening anchors had been awakened early, rapidly moussed, blushed and rolled out in front of the cameras. Eyes puffy with sleep and wardrobe consisting of flannel shirts with rolled-up sleeves to show that they were "down and dirty," the empty-skulled anchors spent most of the morning interviewing one another. On occasion, the zany weathermen would be hauled out to fill up dead time. During these painful-to-watch moments, everyone's brains would shift into overdrive as they tried desperately to remember that wacky quips and joking bon mots were probably not appropriate to coverage of a multiple-murder story.

Although there were now eleven confirmed deaths, the constant hyperbolic media coverage had dulled public concern. Many Boston residents had taken to the streets once more.

They found they were not alone.

Drawn in by the crisis, hunters from all over New England had converged on Boston. So far, local authorities were looking the other way. The police quietly defended this position of noninterference. After all, the killer here was an animal. And as yet, there was no law against shooting a *Bos camelus-whitus*.

On TV, HETA's newest spokesman claimed that the animals were being hunted out of season. When an NRA spokesman pointed out that there was no such thing as a *Bos camelus-whitus* season, the HETA man had responded by throwing red paint on the NRA man and tearing up a picture of the pope before storming off the set.

While the debate raged on Boston's airwaves and in its civic buildings, trucks filled with hunters patrolled the streets. As the pinkish predawn sky warmed to deeper shades of red, the light of the new day washed over many an ATV. Remo saw hundreds of them on his drive into the city.

The drivers wore garish orange hats adorned with laminated hunting licenses. Orange vests wrapped khaki or flannel shirts.

Remo found the outfits redundant. If the double-barreled shotguns jutting from open windows and over tailgates weren't enough to warn people that there were hunters in the area, the powerful aroma of beer-soaked fatigues should have been a dead giveaway.

"Has a brewery exploded?" the Master of Sinanju complained. His wizened face puckered in displeasure as they drove along Tremont Street.

"Beer." Remo nodded. A truck of rowdy men nearly sideswiped them as it flew past in the opposite direction. "The lifeblood of hunters. They must have declared open season on the BBQs. Good thing the animals are all locked up."

"Yes," Chiun said. His voice was vague as he stared out the window. "Why are these drunken fools adorned thusly?" he asked, nodding to a pair of men who were crouching down behind a mailbox. They sipped from a shared hip flask.

"You mean in orange?" Remo asked. Chiun nodded. "I think it makes it easier to shoot each other when they're drunk in the woods."

He was relieved the Master of Sinanju was talking

to him. The old man had remained silent since they'd left Medford.

On the street, one hunter was piddling on a lamp post. He staggered where he stood, getting as much on his trousers as on the ground.

"This is unpardonable," Chiun gasped. "A gamesman needs his wits about him at all times. These boomstick-carrying inebriates do not even know when they are soiling themselves. How do they expect to dispatch their prey?"

"And therein lies a riddle greater than that of the Sphinx," Remo intoned. "Does a hunter get drunk because he never catches anything, or does a hunter never catch anything because he's always drunk?"

The old Asian's lids pinched to razor slits. "If this is your feeble attempt to distract me from your ungratefulness..." he warned.

"You brought it up," Remo countered.

Chiun turned his attention back to the street.

The latest hunter they were passing was sprawled unconscious on the sidewalk. A stray dog was lapping at the puddle of beer that had spilled from the can still clasped in his hand.

"I will study the enigma further before rendering judgment," Chiun announced. And settling back into silence, the Master of Sinanju set his studious gaze on the men they passed.

It was still early morning by the time they reached the BostonBio parking lot. A few cars were already there, but at 6:30 a.m., most of the lot was empty.

Remo parked near a car that looked vaguely familiar. Early-morning sunlight gleamed off its windshield as he stepped into the adjacent empty space.

Chiun didn't follow.

"You coming?" Remo asked the Master of Sinanju, leaning down to the open door.

Chiun shook his head. "Observe," he whispered. He nodded toward the chain-link fence that marked the edge of BostonBio's property.

Remo saw a strange wooden kiosk on the street corner across from the lot. It took him a moment to realize that it had once been a newspaper stand. Branches broken from BostonBio's meticulously landscaped trees had been lashed to the exterior of the booth. Weeds and straw were thrown up on the roof. A pair of orange hats and attendant shotgun barrels bobbed up from behind the counter of the booth. Every once in a while, a pair of liquor-bleary eyes rose into view.

"Oh, brother," Remo said. "It's a duck blind."

The Master of Sinanju kept his voice low. "I will use this as an opportunity to solve your riddle," he said.

Remo heard the distant sound of two beer cans popping open. The gun barrels behind the counter began to weave with greater purpose.

"The only riddle you're apt to solve watching those booze-bags is the 'tastes great, less filling' mystery," he said.

"Whatever I learn will be of greater interest to

me than any of the interminable, pitiful excuses for your ingratitude you are likely to babble.''

Remo closed his eyes. ''Suit yourself,'' he sighed.

He left Chiun in the car and headed for the side door of the main research building.

The same guard was on duty as had been the first day Remo arrived at BostonBio. He didn't even look at Remo's bogus Department of Agriculture ID, passing Remo through with a bored wave.

Remo took the elevator to the third floor, crossing the hall to the closed and unmarked door to the genetics labs.

The sound of rapid typing issued from inside the otherwise silent lab. With all that had gone on, Remo wasn't eager to give some poor lab assistant a heart attack by breaking down the door. He rapped sharply.

No answer. At least not directly.

The speed of the typing increased, as keyboard keys rattled furiously.

Frowning, Remo pressed two fingers on the door's surface. The lock popped and the door sprang open into the room.

Startled eyes jumped in his direction. A mane of raven-black hair whipped wildly around.

Remo was as surprised to see Judith White sitting behind her office desk as she was to see him.

''Judith?'' Remo called, stepping across the lab to her open office door.

She pointedly ignored him. Her fingers continued flying furiously across her keyboard.

At her door, Remo noted the faint smell of stale blood in the air. He glanced back to the corridor where the BBQs were caged. A yellow band of police tape hung across the closed door.

The blood smell didn't seem to be coming from that direction. He stepped around Judith's desk.

"Shouldn't you be terrorizing the hospital staff right now?" Remo pressed.

The hand came out of nowhere. It thumped against his chest with shocking ferocity. Remo was thrown back against the office wall, crashing into an overflowing bookcase. Books and papers rained down on him.

It took his reeling mind a moment to register what had happened. Judith White had assaulted him. More incredible than anything, her blow had *landed.*

In Sinanju, breathing was everything. It was the thing from which all else flowed. And that single, awkward punch had forced the breath from him.

Lying on the floor, stunned, Remo pulled air deep into the pit of his stomach. It coursed through his body. Feeling some strength return, he rose to his feet, shaking off the bookshelf debris.

"You don't know when to stay down, brown eyes," Judith growled as he came toward her.

She was still typing madly away, confident that Remo posed no real threat. When he was within striking range, her hand lashed out again. It was the same move as before.

But this time, Remo was ready for it. He blocked the swinging hand with his wrist, deflecting it harmlessly. Pivoting on the ball of one foot, he launched a chopping hand at her temple. He intended only to knock her out. With Judith unconscious, he could take a step back. Figure out just what the hell was going on here.

All hope of a calm appraisal was shattered in the next instant.

A sharp-as-light pain in his shoulder. His hand still inches from her temple.

His own fault. He'd chalked up her first attack to blind luck. His overconfidence had allowed her to land another, more lethal blow. She had feinted with the right hand and attacked with the left.

Flesh ripped down to bone as fingernails tore from shoulder to chest. It was powerful, but not fatal. Almost too *much* force behind the blow. While her nails did lacerate the skin, the curled fist that followed the downward stroke pounded solidly into Remo's chest.

The force flung him back once more. Fortunately, Remo had centered himself this time. He didn't land as awkwardly as before, but his lungs still struggled for air as he struck the wall near the upended bookcase. Uncertain feet toppled a pile of medical texts.

Judith leaped into the breach left by Remo's moment of awkward hesitation. She flew to her feet, twisting in place. Grabbing at the base of her heavy leather office chair, she hauled the seat high above her head. With a deep, primordial scream that resounded off the pressboard office walls, Judith hurled the chair through the air.

It struck the blinds of her office window, rattling and bending them into knots of twisted tin. The blinds buckled out, and the chair crashed through the big window behind. Huge triangular shards of glass exploded out into the cool morning air. Judith followed immediately in the chair's wake. Bounding up into a squatting position on the office radiator, she flung herself through the rattling metal blinds. From his vantage point on the opposite side of the small office, Remo saw her dive out into open space. The twisted blinds clattered loudly back into place, obscuring his last view of the free-falling geneticist.

They were three stories up. Judith White had just committed certain suicide.

He forced her from his mind. At the moment, he had his own problems. He collapsed against the wall.

The raking blow had opened gouges several inches long across his shoulder and chest. His T-shirt was torn in four perfect parallel lines.

Although his body was already working to repair the damage, blood still oozed from the open gashes. Remo glanced around for something to staunch the flow.

He found a lump of cloth bunched up in the small

office wastebasket. When Remo pulled it out, he found that it was already soaked in blood. Although the sticky liquid was mostly dry, some blood had pooled and clotted. It remained largely wet in the creases.

The source of the distinct blood odor he'd noticed when he first stuck his head in the office.

He recognized the articles of clothing as some of the blood-soaked outfit Judith had worn to the hospital last night. There was even a blue-speckled gray johnny thrown in the trash. The hospital gown—like the rest of the clothing—was smeared with blood.

She had been wearing a new outfit just now. Judith must have kept a change of clothes in her office.

Remo dropped the clothes back in the barrel. Everything was becoming clearer to him. He was angry at himself for dismissing her as a drug-besotted academic. It was obvious now who was behind the slayings.

One hand held tightly over his wounds, Remo went out into the lab. He found a few sheets of sterilized cotton in a cabinet. Remo pushed one of these up underneath his shirt, pressing it into the injured area. Something jabbed painfully into his shoulder at two distinct points.

Reaching inside the first of the bloody gashes, Remo was surprised to find something embedded there. He pulled the object loose.

Between his fingers was the thin sliver of an artificial fingernail, identical to the one he'd pulled out of Billy Pierce's body. He found one more in one of the other wounds.

And like a flash, Remo suddenly remembered the violence and speed of the murders of Pierce and the other HETA members back in the Concord field. If Judith had strength *and* speed, it was possible...

Alarm. Hand holding gauze, Remo raced back to the office window, shoving the blinds roughly aside.

The sight below turned his stomach to water.

The office chair had survived the fall. It lay on its side on the damp green lawn. Around it, hundreds of shards of shattered glass were spread wide across the grass. That was it. There was no sign of Judith White.

"Damn!" Remo growled.

He couldn't risk scaling the wall. Not with a half-shredded shoulder. Cursing at himself for assuming the three-story drop would have killed her, Remo flew back through the lab, racing downstairs.

He exploded out into the parking lot.

The car he'd parked next to was gone. In a wave of self-recrimination, he realized why it had looked familiar to him. It was the same vehicle he had seen parked near his own on the lonely road near the cornfield.

The same car he had seen driving slowly away after the attack against the HETA people.

The same one in which Judith White had carted the first BBQ back to BostonBio.

As he ran over to his own vehicle, Remo realized

why the second set of tracks he'd discovered had ended so abruptly in the alley behind HETA headquarters. After killing Curt Tulle and Sadie Mayer, Judith had hauled the BBQ out to her waiting car, loaded it in and then climbed behind the wheel.

End of tracks.

The only mystery now was why her footprints weren't those of an ordinary human. He was thinking of this when he ran—still struggling for breath—to the Master of Sinanju.

"Did you see her?" Remo demanded, panting near Chiun's open car window. As he spoke, he glanced anxiously around the lot.

"See who?" Chiun asked blandly.

The old Korean was still peering at the pair of hunters crouching in their makeshift duck blind. After two more breakfast beers, one of the shotguns had sunk below counter level. Wobbling, the second seemed destined to follow.

When the Master of Sinanju turned a distracted eye on Remo, all thoughts of inebriated hunters evaporated. His eyes grew wide.

"You are injured!" Chiun cried out. The old man burst from the car, flouncing to Remo's side.

"It's nothing," Remo insisted, pushing away Chiun's ministering hands. "Did you see Judith White?"

"A *woman* did this to you?" Chiun asked, voice flirting with heretofore unknown octaves of shame. His eyes filled with sick horror. "Quickly, Remo, we must get you inside lest someone learn of your great disgrace.''

''Chiun!'' Remo snapped, his face severe.

''Yes, yes!'' Chiun retorted harshly. A leather hand waved angrily. ''I saw the woman. She bounced through the parking area like a crazed grasshopper.''

As the realization that he had failed began to sink in, helpless fatigue took hold of Remo. Before him, Chiun widened the T-shirt tears. The old man's mouth thinned when he saw the raking wounds beneath the cotton gauze.

''She took the car?'' Remo asked, voice growing weaker.

''She is well gone.'' Chiun nodded. His tone grew somber. Affected shame gave way to concern. ''Remo, we must tend to your wounds. Come.''

Remo's shoulders sagged in defeat. The movement caused him fresh pain. He tore his eyes from the street. Jaw flexing hard, he nodded assent.

Injured shoulder sensitive to every step, Remo allowed the Master of Sinanju to guide him back toward the BostonBio building.

23

Back in the lab, Remo sat up awkwardly on one of the desks. The Master of Sinanju instructed his pupil to strip off his shredded T-shirt.

The pain in his shoulder should have been far greater than it was, but Remo had long ago learned to control pain. He willed his body to numb the sharp stabs down to a dull ache. Still, the pain was such that he winced as Chiun probed the area with his fingers.

"You are fortunate," Chiun informed him. Tapered fingertips pressed the flesh between gouges.

"Yeah. I think I'll run out and buy a lottery ticket," Remo groused.

Chiun's gaze was level. "Another two inches and she would have severed the artery. Then you would have stumbled and blundered around, decorating these walls with your spurting blood. And when the woman-who-is-not-a-woman grew tired of the sport, she would have slaughtered you and consumed you. Tell me again, Remo, how you are not the beneficiary of dumb white luck."

Remo gave him a lopsided frown. "Since you put

it that way," he grumbled. "So I guess we kind of both decided she's behind the killings."

Chiun nodded tightly. "Had I not been distracted by the handsome creatures which her wicked animal mind did create, I would have realized it last night."

"Animal mind?" Remo asked.

Chiun's reply was matter-of-fact. "Could anything but a beast in human form lay a finger on a full Master of Sinanju?" the old man said simply.

Remo considered. "I guess it would explain the weird tracks," he admitted slowly.

Before him, the tiny Asian clucked unhappily. He was using Remo's sheet of cotton gauze to clean the wound.

"You know better than to bind an injury," Chiun remonstrated, face pinched.

"I know," Remo sighed, "but I was bleeding like a stuck pig." He winced as the blood-soaked cotton traced the deepest furrow. "How is it?" he asked.

Chiun dropped the soiled bandage to the floor. "You will live," he pronounced. "In spite of your best efforts to the contrary. Where did you find these dressings?"

Remo blinked, surprised. He pointed to the cabinet where he'd found the gauze. Going over to it, Chiun collected a fresh sheet of sterilized cotton. He placed it over the worst of Remo's wounds, holding it in place with a few strips of expertly positioned tape.

That Chiun would wrap the injured area told

Remo all he needed to know about the seriousness of the damage. Neither man said a word as the Master of Sinanju applied the last pieces of tape.

"These wounds run deep in several places," Chiun said softly once he was done. "We must return home at once so that I might apply the proper balms."

Remo nodded, climbing obediently down from the desk. "Just let me check one thing," he said.

"Let others check." The aged Korean waved. He took Remo by the arm.

"Chiun, I want to see what was so important to her. It'll only take a minute." There was urgency to his tone.

The Master of Sinanju's grip was firm. With a troubled scowl, he released Remo's arm.

"And I will get a mop to clean up behind you. Be quick about it," he pressed unhappily.

They went back to Judith White's office.

The computer was still on. Remo saw several floppy disks on the floor near her chair mat. They'd been dropped haphazardly to the rug.

Remo glanced at the text on the monitor. There wasn't much there he recognized. There were some chemical formulations, only two of which he remembered from high-school chemistry. The rest was gibberish.

Endless lines of letters on a pop-up window were separated by endless lines of dashes. He couldn't make head nor tail of that part of the screen.

Remo was about to turn away when something at the top of one of the files caught his eye.

It was a name. It had been used to label the last file that Judith White had pulled up from her hard drive.

Remo was already light-headed from loss of blood. For a moment, he wasn't sure whether he was in worse shape than he thought. He might have become delusional without even realizing it.

"Chiun," he called, voice hollow. "Take a look at this." He was staring at the screen.

Face tight, the Master of Sinanju joined him behind Judith's desk. "What is it?" he asked impatiently.

Remo's good arm reached out to the screen. His index finger extended to the glass.

"What does that say?" he asked.

Chiun's eyes narrowed as he scanned the line. No sooner had the words registered along his optic nerve than his eyes grew wide once more. And in their hazel depths was something almost bordering on fear.

"How can this be?" he hissed. His face looked as if the lab computer were home to some manner of electronic ghost.

Remo was lost for an explanation. He shook his head woodenly as he looked down at the screen. He read the words again, hoping they had changed. They had not.

The name on the top of the computer file read simply, "Sheila Feinberg, BGSBS78."

And a terror that he had thought long buried resurfaced in the cold, barren center of Remo Williams's soul.

THEY WOULD BE FOLLOWING HER. If not Remo, others of his species.

She'd been careless. In spite of her best efforts to quell her base urges, she had given herself away.

Judith White tried not to make the same mistake as she zipped quickly along Beacon Street. She forced herself to drive the speed limit. Although every animal instinct within her screamed "Run," she resisted the impulse to pound the gas pedal to the floor. She didn't want to attract the attention of the local police.

There were hunters everywhere.

It was funny. She had seen them many times over the years—in real life, on TV—yet they'd never caused her such visceral dread before. Trucks drove rapidly past her, offering fleeting flashes of bright orange.

At the moment, the men in khaki thought they were searching for her BBQs. She would be safe. Safe until word got out that it had been her all along.

They would come after her then. She'd have no problem dealing with a few. She had done that before. But she couldn't possibly handle so many. Humanity would not take kindly to a new, superior species rising up in its midst.

Drive slowly. Not too fast.

She'd been like this for months. Her first meals had been indigents and whores. People decent society wouldn't miss. Their bodies were buried in the soft dirt floor basement of a warehouse off Eastern Avenue in Chelsea.

So many bodies. So many she didn't really know *how many* there were. Nor did she care. They were only humans after all. Inferior to her in nearly every way. The only concern she'd ever felt as far as that other species was concerned was the fear of being discovered.

Had it been this way for the first in her species?

Judith White had mulled that question many times over the past few months. For though she was the first in many years, she was not the first ever.

Dr. Sheila Feinberg, late of the Boston Graduate School of Biological Sciences, had actually been the first. It was the Feinberg Method that Judith had employed to achieve the state of perfection she now enjoyed.

Dr. Feinberg's case had been accidental. She had been a mousy little scientist, a Goody Two-shoes who had never been involved in anything vile or depraved. When she had ingested tiger DNA as proof that it was not harmful to a doubting audience, she'd never anticipated that the chemical reaction between her saliva, the DNA itself and the packing gel around the test tube would cause a change.

Judith knew. She had gone into her experiments with both eyes wide open. She *wanted* the result she had gotten. *Craved* it.

But although she wanted the result of the experiments, she had not necessarily counted on this particular outcome.

A car came straight toward her. Judith snapped from her reverie, cutting her wheel sharply, swerving back into her own lane.

The driver of the other car leaned on his horn as he sped past her, flinging out his middle finger as the vehicles nearly collided.

Concentrate, *concentrate*.

She drove out of the city. Out toward I-90.

Although technically the first of mankind to change, Sheila Feinberg shouldn't have really counted as *the* first. She couldn't anticipate nor could she control what she had become. And she would have changed back eventually.

An accident. All just a stupid accident.

Accident!

On the highway now, Judith swerved again. She pulled away from the rear bumper of the car ahead of her at the last possible moment.

Think! Think! She fought to stay in the right lane.

The effects were temporary in the first experiment. An instability on the microcellular level. Unlike her hapless predecessor, Judith had found a way to stabilize the receptor strands of DNA to eliminate rejection. Using a simple form of bacteria—which was perhaps the first form of life ever to evolve on Earth—Judith had piggybacked the new genetic programming onto the old. In this way, the new DNA-bacteria hybrid was able to rewrite the original codes. And unlike Sheila Feinberg, Judith White hadn't settled for mere tiger genes. Although she did largely use them in the earliest stages of her experimentation, she was more than that now.

Much more.

Lights flashing behind her. A state police cruiser. For a moment, she wrestled with the notion of trying to outrun it.

Rational thought fought back irrational desire. To flee would invite more cruisers. They would empty the nearest state police barracks for the high-speed chase. They would catch her eventually. Too many of them then. Better to stop now. Only one officer to deal with. Two at most.

Judith steered the car into the breakdown lane. The cruiser tucked in neatly behind her.

Traffic whizzed by, seemingly at lightning speed. Taillights glowed as the speeding Massachusetts drivers continued the three-mile-long slowdown that began whenever a state police cruiser was spotted.

For a moment, Judith wrestled with the idea of trying to charm her way through, accept the ticket and go on.

The cop stayed in his car. It seemed to take forever.

Did he know? Had Remo alerted them already?

Judith licked her lips in nervous anticipation. The officer was talking on his car radio. She could see him clearly in her rearview mirror.

Was he receiving instructions? Waiting for backup?

Judith glanced to her right. A brush-covered hill rose beyond the passenger's-side window. At the top was a thick growth of trees.

Safety. The trees were a haven. The cruiser, the trooper, his fellow officers—if they came—they were a danger. They would do her harm.

A steady hand reached for the keys dangling from the steering column. Judith switched off the idling engine.

The officer seemed to take this as a signal. He got slowly out of his own car. Lights flashed around him as he made his way up to Judith's car. As he walked, he hitched up his belt with practiced arrogance.

His beefy red face was unreadable as he stepped up beside her window.

"Good morning, ma'am," the state policeman said.

They were his last words.

A hand lashed out through the open window, clamping roughly around the lower part of the man's thick neck. Eyes bulged at the sudden, intense pressure.

The officer scrabbled for his gun. Too late.

The other hand was out, grabbing at his jaw, forcing it upward. The wide area from Adam's apple to chin was exposed. Into this opening lunged Judith White, fangs bared.

Growling low, she latched on to a huge portion of flesh. With a jerk of her head, she wrenched it loose. Most of his throat was pulled free of his neck. Part of his tongue was dragged down from his mouth.

Judith forced her hands into both sides of the opening, ripping outward as if tearing at a gift-wrapped package. The trooper's neck burst apart. Blood dripped inside the opening like a trickling waterfall at the back of a damp cave.

The officer staggered back, gun long forgotten. He fumbled at his throat, feeling only an enormous wet hollow where it had once been.

As he dropped, Judith sprang from the car. Strong hands wrapped around the remains of the man's neck. Judith twisted savagely. Through the opening, she could see the white spine crack. The man grew limp.

Finishing him off was not a bow to compassion. If the man was alive when backup came, he could in his dying moments point out the direction she'd gone.

She only realized how far her rational mind had gone when she glanced up. The faces of passing motorists were utterly horrified.

They saw her. Clearly.

Think, *think!* It was as if she had to force her mind to do what had always come naturally to her. She was now making the same demands of herself her parents had made so many years before.

Judith quickly pulled the keys from the ignition. There was no fumbling. Just rapid, concise movements.

Racing to the rear of the vehicle, she popped the trunk. She gathered several large black cases into her arms.

They might not be enough. But they were all she had.

Leaving the dead state trooper and sickened passersby behind her, Judith loped up the grassy roadside hill.

A moment later, she vanished into the dense woods.

"SHEILA FEINBERG?" Smith asked, his lemony voice bordering on squeezed incredulity. "Are you certain?"

"Smitty, I *can* read," Remo replied aridly.

"Tell me what it says precisely on the computer screen," Smith instructed. "But please do not touch anything."

They both knew that Remo was not particularly skilled when it came to dealing with machines. Although Smith knew it was logically impossible to destroy all information on a computer by pressing a single button, he would never put it past Remo to find such a doomsday switch.

"The top one of those little separate box things—you know, the ones with the little box in the upper left corner?"

"The window," Smith explained.

"Yeah, that," Remo said. "It's just full of letters and dashes. *G* dash *C. G* dash *C. T* dash *A. C* dash *G.* It looks like it goes on like that forever."

"It has," Smith said somberly. "At least since life began on Earth. That sounds like a base pairing sequence in a double helix."

"That's DNA, right?" Remo asked.

"Yes," Smith said, concerned. "Two polynucleotide chains are twisted into a coil to form the helix. A common representation would be a spiral staircase, with each rung holding the genetic information for a single base pair."

"The letters and the dashes," Remo offered.

"Precisely," Smith said. "Remo, this is not unusual in and of itself. Any genetics laboratory would have this sort of information on hand."

"Top flap of the file," Remo said, reading off the screen. "Sheila Feinberg, BGSBS78. I'll bet you a duck dinner not everyone has *that* on hand."

"Seventy-eight," Smith repeated slowly. "Obviously that indicates the year of the accident concerning Dr. Feinberg."

"Accident?" Remo mocked. "Smitty, in case you forgot, Sheila Feinberg turned herself and a dozen other people into half-human–half-tiger mutants, she and her pride ran through Boston chewing up half the town *and* she capped off kitty's night out by kidnapping me and trying to turn me into her personal stud in order to create some new generation of *ueber*-mutant. *Accident* is to Sheila Feinberg what *sobriety* was to Dean Martin.''

Remo's voice rose in intensity as he ran through the litany of offenses Sheila Feinberg had committed against both the natural order and against him personally. For Smith, noticeably absent from Remo's list was the fact that Dr. Feinberg had nearly killed him in her initial attack.

Remo hadn't suspected a thing when she cornered him in a car in Boston. His stomach had been ripped open and its contents nearly removed. Only Chiun's expert ministrations had saved his life. But even with the Master of Sinanju's aid, Remo's body had gone into shock after the incident. He had completely lost his Sinanju skills. They had resurfaced barely in time to save his life.

Afterward, it had taken Remo many long months to fully recover from his physical wounds. Smith hoped that the psychological ones were healed, as well.

''Remo,'' the CURE director said evenly. ''It was not my intention to diminish the significance of those events. We *all* went through a lot back then.''

''Yeah, I know,'' Remo sighed, his voice softening. ''This whole thing's put me on edge.''

"That is not surprising," Smith said. "Given the fact that Dr. Feinberg's name has turned up after all this time." Smith allowed a thoughtful hum. "Let me check something," he announced all at once.

There followed several minutes of rapid typing. Remo stood behind Judith White's desk the entire time. At the office door, the Master of Sinanju stood at attention, a watchful sentry.

Chiun was guarding Remo against attack. The thought that this tiny figure—charged with frail determination—would place himself in the path of a perceived danger swelled Remo's heart.

In spite of the dull ache in his shoulder, Remo felt a little better by the time Smith returned to the phone.

"There is a link," Smith exhaled. It was obvious from his tone that he hoped he wouldn't find one. "After the incident with Sheila Feinberg, the Boston Graduate School of Biological Sciences was sold at auction. Thanks to Feinberg, for much less than it was worth. It became a teaching institution for a time until it was bought up by a fledgling genetics firm in the mid-1980s. It has followed a circuitous path since then, but suffice it to say that the current company of BostonBio is the owner of all that once was BGSBS."

"That would include the Feinberg info?" Remo said.

"Assuming it was not destroyed, yes," Smith replied.

"I *guarantee* you it wasn't destroyed."

Smith was never one to shrink from cold facts. Although he had wished it weren't so, it appeared as if the experiments of years before had resurfaced once again.

"It all begins to make sense now," Smith admitted.

"You're casting a pretty broad definitional net to say that *any* of this makes sense, Smitty," Remo replied.

"Remo, where did you last see Dr. White?" Smith pressed.

"Jumping out a three-story window," he answered dryly. "But Chiun saw her driving out of the lot here about twenty minutes ago. I assume it was her own car."

"I will put out an APB to the local and state police," Smith said.

"Tell them to arm themselves with bear traps and elephant guns," Remo warned him. "She's strong as an ox and quick as a cobra."

"I will alert them to use extreme caution," Smith said. "In the meantime, I will dispatch an FBI team to BostonBio to see if anything can be learned from the remaining files. There is nothing more you can do there. If she turns up anywhere, I will call you at home."

"Yeah, we'd better get going. Chiun's itching to whip up some ancient Korean poultice for me. Probably bat dung mixed with mouse spit."

"Why?" Smith said. The light dawned even as he asked the question. "You weren't injured?"

"It's nothing, Smitty," Remo assured him wearily. "Flesh wound. She took me by surprise. I just need a little time to mend, that's all. Call me if you hear anything."

Before Smith could press further, Remo hung up the phone. As he did so, Chiun turned around, face impassive.

"You are not as well as you have led Smith to believe," he said seriously.

"I feel fine," Remo dismissed. "And I don't need *two* Henny Pennys getting all worked up over nothing."

Chiun didn't argue. At the moment, he was more concerned with getting Remo back home.

As if leading a lost child, he took Remo by the wrist. Walking carefully, he escorted his pupil to the lab door.

The proof to both men that Remo was not as well as he boasted was that he allowed Chiun to guide him.

24

Two more bodies turned up over the next two days. One in Waltham, west of Boston, the other in Lexington.

By this point, it was no longer a mystery who was really to blame for the previous victims. The BBQs were exonerated. The police were now searching for Dr. Judith White.

BostonBio's history was exhumed and dissected by a slavering press. BGSBS might have been a different corporate entity, but the genetics firm was up to the same horrid business as its predecessor.

State, federal and local agencies, along with families of Judith White's victims, filed lawsuits against BostonBio. The company's stock plummeted. Because of the dreadful events swirling around the now discredited BBQ project, BostonBio had taken a giant leap toward bankruptcy.

And through all of the tumult and acrimonious public debate, Judith White continued to elude authorities.

Day had bled into night once more, and in his office at Folcroft Sanitarium, a weary Harold Smith fruitlessly scanned the latest news digests as they came in.

The CURE director was bone tired. The only sleep he'd gotten in the past forty-eight hours came during unplanned catnaps. The only real relief from the tedium had been a single trip home earlier that day for a shower and a change of clothes.

His suit jacket was draped over the back of his chair. Bleary eyes studied his submerged monitor.

Smith was helpless to act. All of the sophisticated technology at his fingertips could not be employed to track something that operated on instinct. If Judith White continued on her current course of behavior, he had as much of a chance of finding her as he had of tracking a wild bird in flight.

That Dr. White had carried through on Sheila Feinberg's original experiments was no longer in question. After he had hung up from Remo, Smith had surreptitiously ordered agents from Boston's FBI office into BostonBio. Computer experts for the federal agency had collected all available evidence from Judith White's office.

There hadn't been much left.

She had magnetized the floppy disks Remo had found on the floor. It would take weeks to piece together the small scraps of information that had not been destroyed utterly. But it turned out the disks offered a painstaking piece of electronic detective work that, in the end, was unnecessary. Unbeknownst to Dr. White, they had gotten most of what they needed without the floppies.

Although the files in her computer itself had been largely erased, she had failed to destroy her hard drive. The genius of BostonBio's top scientist apparently didn't extend to computers. All she would have had to do to wreck the internal system of the device would have been to engage the drive and then—while it was running—drop the whole machine on the floor. Her failure to do so had given Smith the information he needed. And did not want to hear. Many of the files she had tried to erase had already been undeleted. The story as it unfolded was horrific.

Judith White had made a deliberate effort to discover the old BGSBS files that dealt with the Feinberg Method. She had taken the original formula and had improved greatly on it. According to one of the nation's leading geneticists, who had been called in as a consultant by the FBI, Judith White had piled layers of genetic material from more than a dozen species onto her own DNA.

If her notes were any indication, she had started primarily with tiger genes, so they held the most powerful influence on this new creature. But she hadn't been satisfied to stop there. Other genetic material was thrown into the DNA cocktail at later dates. And this abomination was skulking with impunity around the streets and backyards of Massachusetts.

The thought chilled Smith.

There had been nothing new since the last body, which had been discovered more than fourteen hours ago.

According to the earlier body count, the creature that Judith White had become fed frequently. But that number had dwindled. The seemingly low death toll of the past two days likely meant that she was somehow disposing of the newest bodies in order to avoid capture.

Waltham and Lexington. One body in each town. There was nothing to go on from there. Smith couldn't hope to establish any kind of pattern with only two corpses.

Smith felt ghoulish thinking that more bodies would help the search. But it was a gruesome fact. More would steer a course directly to her. An arrow painted in blood across a map of eastern Massachusetts would point the way.

It was a horrible thought. Even so, it wasn't one the CURE director could easily dismiss.

Judith White represented a threat to mankind. Perhaps one more dangerous than the species *Homo sapiens* had ever before encountered.

A thinking animal. A threat in and of itself. But if Dr. White had only the physical characteristics of an ordinary animal, she could still be avoided or captured.

She did not. Unlike the rest of the lesser creatures in the animal kingdom, she possessed the perfect camouflage. A vicious remorseless killer wrapped in a human face.

Judith White could blend in with humanity. Disappear.

Until it was time to feed.

And if the Feinberg incident was anything by which to judge this new case, Judith White would want more than mere survival. Like all animals, she would want her species to thrive. She would want to create more of her own kind.

Weary from lack of sleep, Smith pulled up a file on his computer. It was a file that he had read and reread many times over the past twenty-four hours.

He had used the available time since Judith White's disappearance to order an autopsy on one of the two BBQs that had been returned to BostonBio. Smith had found the preliminary results disturbing, to say the least.

It was a matter of fact; Judith White would want more than mere survival. Much more. She wouldn't rest until her species dominated the world. And one of the two men who represented the last, best hope for humanity had already fallen victim to her.

In a phone conversation earlier in the evening, Chiun had assured the CURE director that Remo's physical wounds were healing. But there were deeper cuts than these. The topic of Remo's potential psychological wounds was left undiscussed by both Smith and the Master of Sinanju.

Smith turned abruptly away from his desk—away

from the technology that had failed him. He spun to the picture window. As he stared out across the endless black waters of Long Island Sound, he saw no lights above the waves. Only the blackness of eternity.

Mankind was alone.

And in the claustrophobic darkness of his lonely, Spartan office, Harold W. Smith prayed that Remo was up to the challenge that lay ahead. For humanity's sake.

25

"I feel fine," Remo groused, for what seemed like the millionth time in the past forty-eight hours.

"You look pale," Chiun told him.

"I'm not sick," Remo insisted.

"I was commenting on the ghostly pigmentation natural to white skin, and not on your state of health," the Master of Sinanju droned. "Honestly, Remo, I did not notice until the last two days how amazingly white you are. Is it possible you are the whitest white man on Earth?"

"Last I checked, it was still Pat Boone," Remo grumbled.

The insults had started dribbling out slowly that morning. By noon, they were a flood.

At first, he had welcomed the normalcy. For Chiun to stop doting and start insulting proved that Remo was well on the road to full recovery. But that was hours ago. Right around now, the Master of Sinanju's abuse was beginning to grate on him.

As they drove slowly through the streets of Lexington, Remo tried to ignore the tenderness in his shoulder. His Sinanju-trained body healed much faster than that of a normal man, but the wounds Judith White inflicted had been deep.

When they returned home after leaving BostonBio two days before, Chiun had stripped the cotton gauze away from Remo's lacerations. For the first time, Remo noticed the white bone of his clavicle peeking out through the deepest center gouges. The bone was coated with a watery pink film.

The dressing Chiun had applied to the brutal gashes smelled worse than a used diaper, but had obviously done the trick.

Flexing the muscle, Remo felt a tightness to his skin around the area where Judith's claws had raked. The tightness became more noticeable every time he turned the steering wheel on their aimless ride through the dark streets of Lexington.

Beside Remo, the Master of Sinanju gazed into the dull yellow glow cast by a streetlamp. Insects that did not yet know summer was over fluttered lazily around the light.

"What are we doing?" Chiun queried abruptly.

Remo was staring at the shadows beyond the windshield. "Twenty, twenty-five," he replied absently.

Chiun turned from the window, allowing the streetlight to slip into their wake. "I was not asking our speed," he said with bland irritation.

His tone shook Remo from his thoughts. He glanced at Chiun. "You *know* what we're doing," he said tightly.

"Pretend I do not."

Remo allowed a perturbed exhale to escape his thin lips. "We're looking for her."

"Ah." Chiun nodded. The ensuing silence lasted but a moment. "Her who?"

"Judith White," Remo snapped. "We're looking for Judith White, okay? Jeez." The tension made his shoulder ache.

"I see," Chiun said, as if finally realizing the point of their quest. "Forgive me for pressing, Remo, but I thought briefly that you might be on yet another futile search for your dream female. You can understand why I would not want to be in this vehicle while you violate local harlotry ordinances." Alert eyes locked on empty shadows. "What makes you believe this creature is nearby?"

"Smith said the last body turned up here. Some college kid going to work this morning."

"But did not Smith also say the previous victim of this iniquitous thing was found miles from here?"

"Waltham." Remo nodded. "It's the next town over."

"Then why are we looking here and not there? Or for that matter, in another hamlet altogether?"

"I don't know," Remo replied, gripping the wheel in frustration. "But it beats sitting around doing nothing."

"You are sitting now," Chiun pointed out.

When he turned to the Master of Sinanju, the shadows cast on Remo's cruel face were ominous.

"If you want to go home, I can flag down the next cab," he warned.

In his kimono sleeves, Chiun's hands sought opposing wrists. His tone softened. "You know as well as I, my son, that this creature will not spring from the night to chase after your automobile like an angry dog. It is clever. It will bide its time until it thinks that it is safe."

"And in the meantime, more people die. No way," Remo said firmly. "I'm not going to have that on my conscience."

Chiun examined Remo's dimly lit profile. The younger Master of Sinanju's face was resolute.

"If there is ever a prize for self-flagellation, you will surely win it, Remo Williams," the old man muttered.

"What the hell is that supposed to mean?"

"You feel that because of your encounter with the other tiger creature years ago that you alone should have seen what others did not."

"Shouldn't I have?" Remo demanded, frown lines deepening around his tense jaw. "I got more up close and personal with Sheila Feinberg than anyone. Of all people in the world, *I* should have seen what Judith White was."

They drove down Bedford Street, taking a left onto Burlington.

Chiun's parchment face was serious. "Do not let the memory of another dark time cloud your present judgment, Remo," he said quietly. "You are not what you were back then. Then you were but a child in Sinanju. Now you are Apprentice Reigning Master, destined to succeed Chiun the Great Teacher.'' Hazel eyes sparked with a father's pride.

Remo smiled wanly. "She ripped me up pretty good, Little Father," he said softly. "Just like the last time."

Chiun shook his head. Wisps of cotton-candy hair became angry thunderclouds. "For this thing we seek, there was no last time," he spit. "It is a new mongrel creation."

Remo couldn't let it go. He flexed his shoulder. "Sure feels like old times," he mumbled.

Chiun's folded arms dug deeper into his sleeves.

"I do not know why I waste my breath," the old man hissed. "If you cannot snap out of this for your own sake, do it for me. I am far too old to train another pupil. Our village will suffer if you waltz off to an encounter with this thing and get yourself killed."

"You're all heart."

"And stomach and liver and kidneys. And I intend to keep them all where they are. Take care that you do the same." He settled into perturbed silence.

Across the front seat from the Master of Sinanju, Remo bit the inside of his cheek in concentration.

Logically, he knew Chiun was right. But logic had no place in what he was now feeling. A small, tweaking pang of unaccustomed fear tugged at his belly. And in that fear, Remo knew, there nestled the possibility of failure. Even for an Apprentice Reigning Master of Sinanju.

They spent the rest of that night wordlessly prowling the empty streets.

26

Ted Holstein was a hunter who had never once fired his shotgun at a living thing.

"Unless you count trees," he'd once complained to his next-door neighbor. "Or shrubs. Wind takes hold of a—what's that one called?"

"A rhododendron," his neighbor replied tightly.

"Yeah, rotordentine. Anyway, wind grabs one of those suckers and you look at it the wrong way? *Man,* you'd swear those branch things were antlers. Know what I mean?"

"You shot my shrub," his irate neighbor pressed. He held two large branches in his hands, severed by a blast from Ted's bedroom window. The rest of the plant was scattered across his neighbor's front yard.

"Yeah. Gee. I *did,* didn't I?" Ted was standing in his pajamas near the fence that separated their properties. Weaving, he glanced down at the smoking shotgun in his hand. He glanced back up, suddenly inspired. "Hey, you want a beer?"

If hunting was Ted's avocation, drinking was his vocation. He was one of the lucky few people for whom work and hobby melded seamlessly.

Ted had been drinking since he was sixteen and hunting since his seventeenth birthday. Since the drinking had come first, he had worked it so that he couldn't clearly remember a single hunting trip.

As a result of his excessive tippling, aside from some unfortunate flora, Ted had never shot anything living.

Birds could have landed on his shotgun barrel without fear. Bunnies and squirrels pranced through his backyard and dreams with impunity.

He *had* bagged a deer once. Driving home drunk from an annual family Fourth of July party, he'd inadvertently taken the scenic route. Weaving through the woods, Ted managed to plow smack into an eight-point buck.

Unfortunately, since it was the off season, Ted couldn't mount his prize to the crumpled hood and drive back and forth through town. Instead, he rolled the huge animal down a nearby ravine, covered it with pine needles and took off in his smoking Chevy pickup before some nosy game warden slapped him with a fine.

That was ten years ago and it was beginning to look like the last chance he'd ever have of bagging something big. At least, until two nights ago.

Alone in his dingy living room, Ted flipped on the TV. He'd hoped to see the sports segment on the late news. Instead, he was dropped smack into the midst of the hysterical, wall-to-wall local coverage of the rampaging BostonBio killer BBQs.

From what he could glean from the news, there was some kind of vicious monster loose in Boston. Police were looking the other way as thousands of hunters descended on the city, hoping to bag the trophy of a lifetime.

In his boozy haze, Ted Holstein had decided right then and there that this prize and all its attendant glory would be his.

Pawing through his mountain of empty beer cans, he'd found his phone. He and his two closest drinking buddies soon settled on a simple plan. The three of them loaded up on beer and shotgun shells. As fast as Ted's battered truck would take them, they set off for Boston.

It was only a day into their expedition and the rules of the game had already changed. Their target was no longer the BBQs, but a female scientist named Dr. Judith White. The grainy black-and-white *Boston Blade* BBQ photograph that Ted had fastened to the dashboard with masking tape had been replaced by an equally grainy picture of Dr. White. The stunning good looks of the BostonBio geneticist stared out at him as he drove up Route 117 in Concord.

"What are we doing here?" asked Evan Cleaver, one of the other two men crammed in the cab of Ted's truck.

"We're looking for her, stupid," Ted said, tapping a finger against Judith White's reproduced face.

The man between them belched. His bleary eyes

were at half-mast as he looked out at the cornfields that lined the road. "This Boston?" he grumbled.

Ted had known Bob for fifteen years and only had a vague memory of his surname. The ability to remember such trivialities as the last names of good friends had been lost a decade's worth of Coors ago.

"Bob's up," Evan commented.

"Not for long," Bob slurred. He rummaged around in the cooler wedged at their feet. The ice had long since melted. The can he extracted was dripping wet. Bob popped the top on his warm beer and began sucking greedily at the can.

"Get me one of those," Ted ordered.

"Get it yourself," Bob replied.

"I'm *driving*," Ted complained.

Mumbling, Bob reached for another drenched can. He handed it over to Ted.

Ted tried to pop the top but couldn't. He was already at least a sheet and a half to the wind and had a difficult time manipulating both steering wheel and can. After a moment of awkward fumbling, he turned to the others.

"Open it for me, will you?" he asked.

"Screw you," Bob said, slurping at his beer.

"Give it here," Evan offered.

Ted passed the can over.

Apparently, while attempting to open it, Ted had shaken the can more than he thought. When Evan pulled the tab, beer began spraying up through the opening.

"Shit!" Evan yelled, holding the can away from his khaki hide-in-the-woods shirt.

"Shit!" Bob echoed, spitting out his own beer. "You're dumping it all over me!" Beer dribbled down his chin. He mopped at it with his sleeve.

"Gimme that," Ted insisted urgently. He hadn't had a beer in twenty minutes and, as a result, his driving skills were suffering.

Evan dutifully handed the can over, still overflowing.

"Get that frigging thing *away* from me!" Bob screamed as more beer fizzed out onto his lap.

"Calm down," Ted told Bob as he took the offered can.

"*You* calm down," Bob griped. He sniffed the tail of his untucked shirt. "Great. Now I stink like beer."

"No more than always," Evan commented.

Ted spit beer out his nose. Choking on his drink, he began laughing hysterically. He laughed so hard Evan joined in. They howled and guffawed in delight as they turned off 117 onto a long side road.

"That wasn't funny," Bob said morosely.

Evan wiped tears from his eyes. Behind the wheel, Ted sniffled happily.

"Guess you had to be there," Ted said.

"It *wasn't funny*," Bob insisted, angrier. A furious hand wiped the damp spot on his lap.

While Bob continued to groom himself, Ted stopped the truck. He took a few rapid gulps on his beer, emptying the can. Belching loudly, he tossed it through the sliding window at the rear of the cab. It joined the growing pile of empties.

The three men climbed out. As they were collecting their shotguns from behind the seat, Evan glanced around. Cornfields rose high on either side of the road. There was evidence that some of the fields had been trampled by trucks. Evan looked at the ruined sections of field through boozy eyes, wondering why someone would drive over perfectly good corn.

"Why *are* we here, Ted?" Evan asked as his shotgun was passed to him.

"This is where she killed a bunch of guys," Ted informed them. He handed a sullen Bob his shotgun.

"That tiger broad?" Bob asked. He balanced his beer on the roof of the cab as he fumbled with the safety switch. It took three tries to flip it off.

"Duh," Evan commented.

"Why are we looking here?" Bob pressed, squinting at the cornfield. "Everyone else is in Boston."

"Exactly," Ted said proudly. "If you were a tiger lady everyone was looking for, would you go where everyone was, or where everyone wasn't?"

"Wasn't," answered Bob with only a moment's hesitation.

"And where's the last place you'd think people would be looking for you?"

"Bob's bed," Evan offered, giggling.

"Shut up," Bob barked.

Ted was looking at the wide expanse of field crushed by police and rescue vehicles that had gone in after the HETA bodies.

"You think she'd come back here?" Bob asked.

"Let's find out," Ted replied. He had a tingling sensation below his belly that for once had nothing to do with his bladder.

They took the path of least resistance into the field, following the tracks made by authorities.

The toppled corn stalks were still fresh enough that they didn't crackle underfoot. Deep tire treads had torn into rich earth, creating muddy pools.

Several hundred feet in, the men took a left into the more dense field. Several even rows lined this vast section. A lot of ground for only three of them to cover.

They split up. Bob went alone down a long path. Evan took another. Ted struck off in the same direction as the others but several rows down.

As he walked along, he idly felt the safety latch on his shotgun with his thumb. Forward. The safety was off.

Ted pulled the switch back, just to make certain. It slid with a tiny click.

The metallic noise was answered by a rustle of movement somewhere up ahead.

He glanced to his right. The others were far away. Neither Evan nor Bob could have made the noise.

Carefully, Ted slid the safety off once more. With cautious steps, he closed slowly in on the spot from which the sound had originated.

The green stalks were dense and high. While bright sunlight streamed down from above, not much reached the ground. But beyond the stalks of corn to his left, the light seemed brighter.

It was the same impression Ted got standing at the last line of trees before a wooded lake. A sense of emptiness not present in the rest of the field. From this area, there issued a persistent humming.

Peering carefully, Ted noted an expanse of brightness beyond the nearest stalks. Like the area trampled by vehicles farther back in the field, someone had knocked over the corn here, as well.

Cautiously, slowly—adrenaline pounding in his ears—Ted eased apart the two nearest corn stalks.

The source of the humming noise became instantly apparent. A mass of black flies swarmed around the open area. Their collective buzzing was akin to the drone of a persistent, tiny motor.

The corn had been trampled flat in a circular area about the size of Ted's truck. As he stepped into the bowl-shaped zone, flies swarmed up around him.

Ted recoiled, stumbling backward. As he did so, his foot snagged in something.

For a moment, he thought he'd stepped in a hole. He soon realized that it couldn't be. Few holes in the ground could be lifted into the air along with one's foot.

He looked down, squinting through the fluttering haze of a thousand swirling insects. What he found made his alcohol-soaked stomach clench in a terrified knot.

His boot had caught in an open chest cavity. His toe was snagged up just under the sternum.

Ted saw the rest of the body then. The head had been concealed behind a mask of flies. It looked up at him now, eye sockets teeming with maggots.

Another body lay near the first. As stripped of life as an ear of shucked corn.

Ted was too horrified to scream. He exhaled puff after puff of frantic breath, never pulling in fresh air.

Shaking, he collapsed back into the corn. Crackling stalks snapped loudly beneath his deadweight.

Frantically, he shook his foot. Trying to knock loose the body that still clung furiously to him in some morbid final act of desperation.

His crazed, terrified blundering appeared to stir the very earth. As Ted watched in growing horror, the ground began to rise up before him.

No, not the *ground*. Something *beneath* the trampled corn. Something that had been lying in wait.

The thing that had been hiding in the corn stalks before him turned rapidly, fangs bared.

Even in his panic, Ted recognized the face from

his dashboard. The woman he was after. Judith White.

Sleep clung to her eyes as she dropped to her hands. Blood dripped from her open mouth as she shoved off on tightly coiled legs.

As she sprang toward him, she screamed loudly.

Ted screamed, as well. As he did so, there came a terrible explosion nearby. The sound rang in his ears.

Another explosion. This one close, too. Like the first, it came from somewhere near the end of his arm. A gunshot.

In his panic, he'd fired his shotgun.

Judith's expression changed from savage fury to cautious rage in midleap.

Ted was still lying on his back on the ground. She dropped beside him. Pummeled stalks were further crushed beneath her weight. A heavy paw clamped on his chest. She snarled menacingly, flashing blood-smeared teeth.

Footsteps. Running. Shouted voices.

Judith raised her nose in the air, wiggling her ears alertly. Her paw stayed pressed to Ted's unmoving chest. He held his breath.

A decision. Instinctive.

She turned. Bounding on all fours, Judith dived into the field in the direction opposite that of the voices. In a second, she was gone. The most brilliant geneticist of her generation had been forced to abandon her makeshift nest to hunters.

And flat on his back in her corpse-strewn lair, Ted Holstein could take no pride in successfully fending off the creature that had terrified so many.

He had passed out cold.

27

After a futile night of searching, Remo had finally given up hope of finding Judith White on his own. Defeated, he had returned home. Morning found Remo sitting morosely in his living room watching the back of Chiun's head.

The Master of Sinanju had brought a quill, an ink bottle and a few sheets of parchment down from his bedchambers. Sitting cross-legged on the floor, the old Korean was writing furiously. Every time Remo tried to steal a peek at what he was writing, Chiun hunched forward, blocking the papers with his frail body.

Remo finally gave up trying to see and instead turned his attention to the wide-screen TV, hoping for some fresh news concerning Judith White. If the latest reports were to be believed, there was nothing.

"I should have stapled one of those radio tags to her ear like they do on *Wild Kingdom*," Remo grumbled.

"Shush," the Master of Sinanju admonished. The great plume of his quill swooped gracefully.

Remo couldn't take it anymore.

He was sitting on the floor a few feet behind Chiun. He leaned forward as he had before in order to get a glimpse of the parchment. Mirroring his pupil's movements, the old man tipped farther over. As soon as he'd lowered himself enough, Remo slapped both palms to the floor and unscissored his legs. He executed a flawless somersault, twisting in midair. Briefly, both men were back-to-back as Remo slipped over his teacher. He dropped back, cross-legged to the floor.

"Ow." Remo cringed, now face-to-horrified-face with the wizened Korean. He clapped a hand to his injured shoulder even as he read some of the upside-down words on Chiun's parchment. "How are you eclipsing Na-Kup?" he asked.

The Master of Sinanju's shocked expression flashed to anger. "None of your business," he retorted. He snatched the parchments to him. Flipping them over, he hugged the papers to his narrow chest. "Instead of irritating me with acts of childish acrobatics, why not do something useful? The rain gutters need cleaning."

"Gonna hire someone," Remo informed him.

"Why? It is a job for a street arab or other common vulgarian. I will buy you a ladder."

"I think I liked you better when you were writing screenplays," Remo said as he pushed himself to his feet. A fresh ache ran from shoulder to chest along his healed scars. He headed for the living-room door.

As he passed the phone, it rang. When Remo scooped it up, Chiun was already spreading his parchments out once more.

"Judith White has been seen," Smith announced without preamble.

"Where?" Remo demanded.

"In Concord," Smith explained rapidly. "She had made a nest for herself in the same field where the HETA *Bos camelus-whitus* exchange was supposed to take place."

"I'm on my way."

"Wait," Smith called quickly. "She escaped on foot."

"Dammit," Remo complained, jamming the phone back to his ear.

"It is not as dire as it sounds," Smith explained. "She apparently feeds at night. I suspected as much before. That is why most of the murders took place after dark. She is no longer accustomed to daylight hours, as is a normal human."

"She's not a freaking vampire, Smitty."

"She might just as well be," Smith replied. "For in daylight, she is exposed. People will see her. More so now that she has been identified as the killer."

"But we still don't know where she is," Remo argued.

"We cannot pinpoint a precise location," Smith agreed, "but there have been three sightings since the incident this morning. One in Minute Man National Historic Park, one in Winchester and the third in the woods near Middlesex Fells Reservoir. She appears to be heading back to Boston.''

''I thought she was the thinking man's animal.'' Remo frowned. ''Doesn't she know there are hunters everywhere around here? What's she doing coming back?''

''I could not begin to speculate,'' Smith said. ''But that appears to be the pattern. Do you still have your Department of Agriculture identification?''

''Yeah, why?''

''I am sending an unmarked state police car for you and Chiun. It would be simpler if the officers believe you to be agriculture agents.''

''I've *got* a car, Smitty,'' Remo stressed.

''Yes, but no radio. I want you on the ground in case she makes an appearance.'' He hesitated for a moment. ''Remo, if you are not up to the challenge, I can send Chiun in alone,'' Smith suggested.

''If I'm healed enough to clean rain gutters, I'm healed enough to pull one measly cat out of a tree,'' Remo muttered.

But as he replaced the phone, he felt the unaccustomed tightness of the still healing scars on his shoulder.

Remo hoped his words to Smith were not simply idle boasting.

MASSACHUSETTS STATE TROOPER Dan MacGuire didn't know why he was being pulled away from his stakeout post outside the BostonBio complex. His was one of a number of unmarked vehicles that had been assigned to the area.

The FBI and Boston police had been having a pissing contest over who was in charge of the whole Judith White mess. No one seemed to be able to get the jurisdiction straight. While the agency infighting raged over the past two days, MacGuire had been waiting patiently in an empty lot across the street from the genetics firm.

He had heard several hours before that White had been spotted, seemingly en route to Boston. There were only two places she seemed likely to go. Her apartment—which was under around-the-clock surveillance—and BostonBio itself.

Dan was betting on BostonBio.

Laurels awaited the man who finally managed to bag the psycho doctor. Dan was already counting on the promotion that would come from being the one to take down the Beast of BostonBio.

He was understandably upset therefore when, after two days of sitting alone drinking stale coffee, the nasal voice of his shift supervisor informed him over his car radio that he was to go and pick up some Department of Agriculture agent. The man would be bringing along an assistant. Both had high security clearance.

Dan had objected strenuously, to no avail. He had his orders. Muttering something about being a ''goddamn taxi service,'' he abandoned his BostonBio post to collect his charges.

The Department of Agriculture agent wound up being some faggy-looking guy in a maroon T-shirt and tan chinos. Dan was a good half foot taller than him and had at least a hundred pounds of beefy muscle on the wimp.

The Agriculture guy's assistant was worse. The hundred-year-old man looked as frail as a wicker chair at an Overeaters Anonymous meeting. On top of that, he was dressed like Fu Manchu's grandmother.

Both men were waiting on the sidewalk in front of the address MacGuire had been given. As he pulled up to the curb, he noted that it was a hardware store.

''You Agent Post?'' Trooper MacGuire asked across the front seat, clearly hoping that he had the wrong man.

''Gimme a sec,'' Remo said seriously. He examined the last name on his own ID. It was hard to keep track of all his aliases. ''Guess that's me today.'' He nodded as he climbed in the front seat beside MacGuire.

''Great. A comedian,'' MacGuire muttered.

''What is this?''

The squeaky voice was so loud and so close MacGuire almost jumped out of his skin. He spun around.

The trooper was startled to see the old Asian sitting in the back seat. MacGuire hadn't heard the door open or close. The old man was aiming a slender finger at the bullet-proof shield that separated the rear seat from the front. It was a standard safety precaution. MacGuire told him this.

"Remove it," Chiun commanded.

"I can't," MacGuire replied, irked, as he turned back to the wheel. "It's permanently affixed."

"Why not just leave it, Chiun?" the skinny guy said over his shoulder, as if the old geezer could actually do something about the thick sheet of Plexiglas. By the looks of it, he was lucky just to haul himself out of bed in the morning.

"It annoys me," Chiun sniffed.

"So what?" Remo said.

"So, I already have to put up with you. One annoyance is quite enough."

As the two of them prattled on, Trooper MacGuire checked the traffic situation. He was about to pull out into the street when he was shocked by a horrible tearing sound over his right shoulder.

Spinning around, MacGuire was stunned to see that the protective shield—which could stop a .357 round fired point-blank—had been wrenched free from its casing.

The old man's hands were stretched out as wide as they could go. A set of bony fingers curled around each end of the shield.

As the state trooper watched in shock, the Asian brought his hands together. The sheet of thick plastic bent into a bowed U, straining until it could no longer take the pressure. All at once, it snapped with the report of a gunshot. MacGuire ducked behind the seat, hoping to avoid the inevitable spray of plastic shards he was sure would be launched forward.

There were none. Just another louder, quicker snap.

When he picked his head up over the seat, Trooper MacGuire found that the old man had placed the panes together, forming an inch-thick sheet of glass. These he had snapped, too. The four smaller sections he'd stacked atop one another. As MacGuire watched in amazement, he broke these, as well.

"Can we hurry up and go already?" the Department of Agriculture man complained from the seat next to MacGuire. "There aren't any doughnuts back there." He seemed oblivious to the action in the back seat.

Nodding dully, the trooper turned back around. He swallowed hard, forcing his Adam's apple back down his neck. It seemed suddenly to want to escape his throat.

As he pulled out into traffic, MacGuire heard the snap-snap-snap of increasingly-smaller sheets of Plexiglas coming from the rear seat.

TED HOLSTEIN HAD BEEN flown by helicopter to College Hospital in Boston. As the first known survivor of an attack by Dr. Judith White, it was feared by some authorities that the young hunter might begin to manifest some of the same man-eating characteristics as his assailant.

"She's not a freaking werewolf," Ted complained as blood was drawn from his arm for the umpteenth time.

"Yes, sir," replied the nurse. She appeared to not even be listening to him.

They held him for hours, testing and retesting, finally proclaiming that—in spite of having the liver of an eighty-year-old—he was perfectly normal. Ted was clearly not a threat to society at large.

The hospital released him. Directly into the grasping claws of the Boston press corps.

He granted dozens of impromptu interviews in the College Hospital emergency room.

"What was it like to be attacked by Judith White?"

"Did she say anything to you during the attack?"

"Are you afraid she might come back for you?"

Fortunately for Ted, five o'clock was approaching and most of the reporters had to get back to their respective stations to edit their miles of tape into the three seconds of material that would actually make it on the air.

Some of the stations tried to get him to come on the air live for their 5:00 and 6:00 p.m. news, but he'd firmly refused. Even so, a few cameras still lingered on him as he sat alone in the blue molded-plastic chair near the automatic doors of the emergency room.

Ted tried to ignore the glaring lights. His eyes and head hurt from not drinking. He hadn't had a beer since morning. All he wanted to do was to get away from here. Out of the public eye.

As he checked his watch for the hundredth time in the past half hour, the doors next to him slid open.

"Hey, hey, hey! There he is!" yelled a happy voice.

Bob came bounding through the doors, grinning broadly. The powerful stench of stale beer clung to his clothes and breath. Evan Cleaver trailed Bob into the hospital.

"It's about time," Ted said, annoyed. He got to his feet, stretching uncomfortably.

"Hey, the Feds were asking us all kinds of questions," Bob said defensively. "You ain't the only celebrity here."

"At least they weren't jabbing you with needles," Ted replied. He rubbed his pin-cushioned arm.

"Needles schmeedles," Bob dismissed. "You ready to go, or what? Guns are in the truck." This he said loudly, jerking a too casual thumb over his shoulder. He smiled at the remaining cameras.

The few reporters in the emergency room began to circle around the trio.

"Are you going after Judith White again?" a reporter asked, shoving a microphone in Ted's face.

"Damn straight," announced Bob, belching

loudly as he spoke. "Hi, Mom." He waved at the camera.

"*No,*" Ted stated firmly.

"We've *got* to, man," Bob insisted.

"They've tracked her as far as Malden, last I heard," Evan said excitedly. "She's looping around this way."

"Maybe she wants you." Bob leered, elbowing Ted.

"Aren't you afraid of what might happen?" a reporter questioned Ted.

The answer was written on his face. Even the *question* seemed to terrify Ted.

Bob answered for him. "No way," Bob insisted.

"He's not afraid of *anything,*" Evan agreed.

"Well…" Ted began timidly.

But Bob and Evan were already bullying him to the emergency-room doors. The glass panes slid silently open.

"What makes you think you can survive another round with the Beast of BostonBio?" the reporter asked, employing his profession's tired and tested technique of turning something serious into a frivolous sports metaphor.

"Hey, we've got the most famous hunter in New England on our side," Bob boasted loudly. "How can we lose?"

"Actually…" Ted started.

"Shut up," Bob and Evan instructed.

And as the hospital doors slid efficiently shut, fear

rang like a desperate clanging gong in the ears of New England's most famous hunter.

"WHAT ARE WE DOING?" the Master of Sinanju asked.

He was perched in the back seat of Trooper MacGuire's unmarked car. A pile of inch-wide, two-foot-long strips of plastic sat on the seat beside him.

"Don't you start again," Remo cautioned.

"I was asking the constable, O Nosy One," Chiun sniffed.

"We're waiting for that lady scientist," the state trooper offered.

Chiun leaned over into the front seat until his head was between the two men. He looked out the windshield at the high-tech glass exterior of the BostonBio building.

The Master of Sinanju frowned. "Is she inside?"

"No," Trooper MacGuire admitted.

Chiun paused, allowing the trooper's answer to hang in the air. He turned to Remo.

"What are we doing?" he repeated.

"She might come back," the trooper replied. "When she does, we'll be waiting for her."

Chiun sank back into his seat. "She has gotten all that she requires from this place. The creature will not return."

A horn suddenly honked loudly down the block. For what seemed like the millionth time that day, a truck loaded with rowdy hunters drove past the parked cruiser. It disappeared around the next corner.

"Looks like you're alone in that opinion," Trooper MacGuire mumbled.

"I think so, too," Remo offered, uninterested.

MacGuire frowned. "What makes you think that?"

"Because *he* thinks that," Remo said, nodding back to the Master of Sinanju.

The trooper raised an eyebrow. "I suppose he's an expert on human behavior?"

Remo nodded. "He knows more about behavior than a library full of psychology textbooks. Human or otherwise."

In the back, Chiun had grown bored. He began snapping apart the thick strips of bulletproof shielding.

"You'll forgive me if I reserve judgment?" MacGuire asked doubtfully.

Remo only shrugged. The movement reminded him of the tenderness in his shoulder.

MacGuire watched obliquely as the agriculture man probed at his left shoulder once more. It appeared to be causing him some kind of discomfort. He'd been poking absently at the same spot all afternoon.

The trooper was about to ask him what was wrong when the car radio squawked to life.

It was MacGuire's supervisor. The trooper was surprised it wasn't a dispatcher calling him.

"Special orders," the state police supervisor announced after reading off the car's ID number in a bored monotone. "Proceed to Eastern Ave, Chelsea. Over."

"Chelsea?" Dan asked, glancing at Remo. He picked up his microphone. "What—?"

He was instantly cut off.

"I have been instructed to say no more. Over."

The radio went dead.

"Must be something too hot to broadcast," MacGuire mused. He glanced at Remo for agreement as he hooked the mike back in place.

Remo wasn't paying attention. He was still rubbing at his shoulder. As he did so, Chiun continued to work away in the back seat, snapping his plastic Plexiglas strips into credit-card-size fragments. The old man yawned.

"So much for that promotion," MacGuire grumbled, turning the key in the ignition.

He had to wait for another truckload of hunters to pass before he could pull out onto the street.

28

They would be impossible to avoid forever. She had tried for days, even succeeded for a time, but she knew it couldn't last. Their single-mindedness was unmatched in the animal kingdom.

Humans.

It disgusted Judith White to know that she had once been one of them.

They were weak. Any strength they had came from sheer numbers. As a species, it was a miracle they had survived. And they hadn't merely survived—they had *thrived*.

No more.

Judith bounded through a few square yards of woods that had reclaimed a section of abandoned parking lot. She ran on two legs, keeping her back nearly parallel to the ground. Her head was up—face forward—as she reached the edge of the tightly packed trees.

She sniffed the air. Not sensing any humans, she broke her cover, racing across the cracked asphalt toward another, thicker strip of woods.

Judith ducked between the low branches, feeling the instinctive safety of the forest swallow her up.

She moved on.

The scientist in her was still lucid enough to see what was going on. It was a classic internal struggle. She was rational when calm. But in anything remotely resembling a pressure situation, her instinctual self reared its head.

That was why she had fled the hunters in Concord. If her rational mind had been in control at that moment, she would have stayed and fought.

There were only three of them. None of them had ever met anything like her before. Even when the first one had started shooting in panic, the element of surprise would have remained on her side.

The problem was, even as the hunter had panicked, and begun blindly shooting, Judith had panicked, as well.

Stupid, stupid, stupid!

If she had killed them and buried them somewhere, they never would have gotten word out about her.

Judith had broken into the house of an elderly shut-in in Melrose earlier that afternoon. While she was munching on her lunch of stringy retiree, she had seen video of Ted Holstein on the local news.

She recognized him right away. He was the one who had stumbled into her nest.

If she had only killed him!

It was her own fault. When Holstein showed up

she had been groggy from her previous night's meal. In her lazy sleeping stage, she thought she had heard a noise. Her animal self had been alarmed, but her vestigial human side had convinced her that there was probably nothing to worry about. After all, she had been in the same nest for two days without incident. She went back to sleep, only to be awakened by the human's stumbling and screaming.

Afterward, she had run, propelled by pure instinct and adrenaline.

She had been seen. Several times. The last no more than ten minutes ago. All because she could not yet control the unreasoning animal within her.

Now she was on the run. On *their* terms.

That wouldn't last. Judith White would not allow it. She was still more clever by far than almost any human alive. She would win. Her species would thrive. But she had work to do first. And now they knew roughly where she was. It made her work all the more imperative.

Running still, Judith came to the edge of this latest strip of woods. She poked her face through the brush.

There was a street beyond. Tired brick warehouses slouched along the sides of the road. Some were used for storage, but most were in various states of disrepair.

The wind brought the scent of water. Mildly polluted.

As she watched the road, few cars drove past. It

was as she remembered it. The lack of traffic was the reason she'd chosen this area originally.

She waited for a lone car to pass and was about to make a break across the street when she heard a loud noise coming from around the corner.

Constantly suspicious now, Judith sank back into the undergrowth. She trained a single wary eye through the tangle of bushes.

A truck drove into view. Judith felt the short hairs rise on the back of her neck as she saw who was in it.

Hunters. Five, six...eight of them in all. They screamed and hooted and waved their guns as they sped madly along. A cloud of asphalt-flecked dust rose in the truck's wake as the vehicle skidded to a stop at the side of the road near the old parking lot. The men piled out into the street.

No sooner had this truck arrived than another pulled around the corner. It stopped near the first.

Two more followed, one trying to pass the other. The men inside shouted curses at one another as they flew past the other vehicles.

Although they disappeared beyond the nearest warehouse, Judith heard these two vehicles stop, as well.

More were coming. She could sense the rumble of trucks through the sensitive pads of her bare feet. Raucous shouts rolled toward her, vibrations in the air.

The humans who had seen her ten minutes before

must have already contacted the authorities. And the human police—incompetent as usual—must have announced their findings to the world.

The hunters were here now. Reporters would follow in their wake. Eventually, the authorities would also arrive on the scene.

Judith had no desire to meet up with any of them.

Not yet, anyway. Not until she could work this to her advantage. And the thinking part of her was certain that she still could. After all, they didn't know that she had an ace up her sleeve.

Judith felt at the black case under her arm. It was one of the plastic boxes she'd brought with her from BostonBio. One of the ones she'd rescued from her trunk after her attack on the state trooper.

She *would* save herself. Her species *would* survive.

And multiply.

She pushed deep into her belly the alarm she felt at seeing so many hunters, all looking for her. Judith White melted back into the woods. Ducking east, she headed in through the crumbling pile of bricks that lay at the rear of the closest warehouse.

29

Remo knew word had gotten out the moment he saw so many Coors and Budweiser cans lining the road. The alcoholic's equivalent of Hansel and Gretel's bread crumbs.

"Uh-oh," he said in the front seat of the state police car.

"What?" Trooper MacGuire asked. They were cruising down Eastern Avenue in Chelsea.

"Party crashers," Remo informed him. "Take a left."

They hadn't gone much farther before the Master of Sinanju chimed in.

"Must these swill-pots pollute the air everywhere we go?" Chiun complained from the back seat. He was surrounded by tiny plastic fragments. Nose upturned, he sniffed through a tiny space in the window.

"BYOB, Little Father. The hunter's credo."

A turn onto a side street led them between two rows of crumbling warehouses. The roadway was lined on both sides with trucks.

Bright orange caps moved furtively all around the

area. A pointless effort since they were, after all, bright orange. The shade of orange was so vivid it would have been visible from space.

"How did they find out?" Trooper MacGuire griped.

"Everyone and his brother has a scanner," Remo commented. "That goes double for these Billy Beer types."

They parked behind the last truck in line. Remo climbed out onto the curb. Road sand that hadn't yet been swept up from the past ten winters filled the gutter.

"I'll let you out in a minute, sir," Trooper MacGuire called back to Chiun as he unlatched his seat belt.

"You are polite," a squeaky voice said from outside the car. "The Magyars of Kocs were such reinsmen. Remo, give this young man a generous tip."

When he looked, MacGuire saw that the Asian had somehow let himself out of the rear of the car. Impossible, since the door locked from the outside and there was no latch inside.

Chiun was standing on the curb next to Remo.

"Not too generous," Chiun said to Remo, sotto voce. "He is only a taxi driver, after all."

"We don't have to tip him," Remo said. Hands on hips, he was surveying the area.

"We *must* give him something," Chiun cautioned. "Without retainer, these mercenary hacks would strand their own mothers."

"It's all right, sir," the trooper called from inside the car. "You don't have to give me anything."

Since his bulletproof shield now lay in fragments on the back seat, he'd decided against asking Chiun how he'd gotten out of the car without ripping the door off. The trooper's main worry was backup. He appeared to be the only police officer in the area. MacGuire gathered up his radio microphone.

"Did you hear that, Remo?" Chiun enthused. "Our driver is better than the greedy Magyars. They always had one hand on the reins and the other in a traveler's purse. Hail to you, stout coachman!" In Korean, he said to Remo, "Give the fool a nickel. I do not feel like walking home."

"He's all set, Chiun," Remo insisted. He was still looking around the area, concern creasing his face. The hunters everywhere weren't going to make things easy. Brow furrowed, he turned to Chiun. "Where do you want to start?" he asked.

The Master of Sinanju sensed Remo's inner disharmony. Though he tried to mask the feeling, it was there. Lurking just beneath the surface. Although it would be easier to dismiss his pupil's concern as unwarranted, the fact of the matter was, Chiun felt it, too. The old man masked his own unease.

"One direction is the same as the next," Chiun said, an indifferent shrug raising his bony shoulders.

"Okay." Remo considered. "Uh…that way?" He pointed over toward a pair of warehouses.

Chiun nodded his agreement.

Inner thoughts of worry left unspoken, the two men struck off together toward the dilapidated buildings. And in spite of their training, neither felt the pair of narrowed eyes focused on their retreating backs.

JUDITH WHITE PERCHED easily atop the creosote-soaked rafter in the old warehouse nearest the parked police car.

She watched Remo and Chiun cross the street. They were four stories below and heading off in the opposite direction.

Good. That meant that they hadn't sensed her.

Frankly, Judith was surprised Remo was here. She had given him what she thought was a disabling, possibly *fatal* injury back at the lab. A normal man would have been in the hospital for days following such an attack. But Remo wasn't normal.

Judith had known it the moment she first met him. She sensed things on a different level than normal humans. She could tell that he was something special. And dangerous.

The old one accompanying Remo gave her the same impression. There was a complete stillness, an all-pervasive confidence about the ancient Asian that defied explanation.

These two were the best mankind had to offer. Her reasoning mind told her that if she could defeat them, she could ultimately defeat Man.

The two men stepped through a break in a rusted, half-torn chain-link fence and into an old parking lot. They disappeared around the side of a building.

After they'd gone, Judith crept back along the beam.

The attic floor was more than eight feet below her. Neither the narrowness of the beam nor the distance she would fall if she took a single misstep was a factor in her thinking. The skill to perch atop a high rafter and to keep perfect balance while doing so was innate.

Judith moved easily to the spot where she knew the rotting attic floor was strongest. Leaning to one side, she let her body fall from the beam.

One hand continued to grip the softened wood as she swung around like the pendulum on a clock. When her toes were dangling a foot above the floor, she simply let go, dropping lightly to the soles of her bare feet.

Remo and Chiun weren't her only concerns, she knew. There were many men around her now. Closing in for the kill.

There was a strong impulse within her to panic. The same instinct that would grip any trapped animal. She would have to use *reason* to get out of this situation alive.

She heard a noise. Scuffling feet in the parking lot far below. Afterward, the sound of humans arguing.

Hunters.

Remo was still across the street. He was far enough away. Her plan had a good chance of succeeding.

Judith gathered up the box she'd carried with her all the way from its hiding place near her Concord nest. She tucked it tightly under her arm.

Moving through the late-afternoon shadows that stretched across her large attic room, she slipped stealthily toward the rotted wooden door.

TED HOLSTEIN FELT like he was going to throw up. All he wanted to do was go home. But Bob and Evan refused to hear it.

"Are you *kidding?*" Evan said in disbelief. "After the great day we've had so far?"

"He's kidding." Bob nodded with certainty.

"Maybe if I laid down for a little while," Ted said weakly. They'd just driven into the crumbling area of Chelsea, pulling in behind the line of parked trucks. Out of Ted's truck now, they were loading up on shells.

Ted was like a prisoner walking the last mile.

"You heard the guys on the radio," Evan said to Ted, his tone reasonable. "They tracked her here. You don't want someone else to snag her, do you?"

"They took a lot of blood at the hospital," Ted offered.

"Stop being a faggot," Bob barked, annoyed.

It was the "faggot" comment that did it. Ted was terrified at the prospect of meeting up with Judith

White again, but he was more fearful that his masculinity might be brought into question. Stuffing his hands into the ammo box, he filled his pockets with shells. Gun in hand, Ted followed the others toward the cluster of warehouses.

"You look a little green," Bob commented as they walked through the bombed-out parking lot. "Wanna beer?"

He reached a hand around to the emergency six-pack he'd slung from the back of his belt.

"Hell, no," Ted insisted.

"Don't tell me you got religion on us," Bob said. His tone was vaguely disgusted.

"No way," Ted declared. "It's just I don't feel like it. Not after this morning."

"I've been drinking *more* because of this morning," Evan boasted. In fact, he hadn't had a drop, either.

"That's 'cause you're not a faggot like Ted," Bob said with a smirk.

"Shut up," Ted complained.

"Yeah, Bob," Evan echoed. "Why don't you shut up?"

They'd nearly reached the first warehouse. The big brick building was four stories tall and looked as if it had been built somewhere in the earliest days of the twentieth century. The facade was crumbling. Chunks of mortar and redbrick fragments were spread all around the lot before it.

Bob stopped near the closed warehouse door.

"Are you two queer for each other?" Bob asked, turning on the others. "You sound like you're married or something."

"Just lighten up," Evan insisted.

"*You* lighten up," Bob snapped back.

"Maybe we should keep it down," Ted offered warily. The morning's events had begun playing anew in his frightened mind. He felt woozy. His stomach fluttered in fear as added adrenaline pumped frantically through his system.

"I'm sick of you two always ganging up on me," Bob groused. "You think you're so much better than me. Well, I got news for you. At least *I* got a real live deer once, Teddy boy. And it wasn't with the front of my car." He glanced over his shoulder. Woods crept out around the side of the building. "I'm going to see what's going on back there," he announced, a sneer stretching his lip. "If I find her this time, maybe *I* can keep from pissing my pants and actually shoot her."

Grumbling to himself, Bob stormed off. After he'd disappeared around the side of the building, Evan shrugged.

"He'll be okay," Evan assured Ted. "It's just the beer talking."

"Yeah," Ted nodded. Getting yelled at by Bob had only increased his apprehension level. He felt the powerful tingling of pure terror in his groin. He wanted to pee, but dared not suggest it. Not after what Bob had just said.

Evan crept to the front of the building. With the flat of his hand, he tested the door. It was unlocked.

He turned back around. "You want to flip for who goes in first?" he asked, lips twisted into a devilish smile.

"Hurry up," Ted urged.

And before his faked courage fled him completely, Ted used the broad side of his shotgun to bully his friend into the warehouse. He followed close behind.

The door creaked shut with eerie finality.

WHEN REMO AND CHIUN ROUNDED the corner, they found the rear parking lot of the old warehouse teeming with hunters. Men with shotguns scurried all around them, like ants fleeing a dropped shoe. The hunters paid the two Masters of Sinanju little heed, so busy were they stalking sand and stones.

"I will never understand this nation," the Master of Sinanju commented as they waded through the armed throng. His wrinkled face was puckered in disgust. "There has never been a land as rich in food as America. Your markets are even given the boasting prefix *super*." His voice dropped. "It is amazing to me, Remo, that the American ego extends even to something as trivial as your grocery stores."

Remo's eyes were trained ahead, his senses strained to their maximum. "And?" he asked, distracted.

"Why do these simpletons dress up like clowns

and clomp around in the woods with their boom-sticks when they need only stop at the nearest supermarket?''

Chiun indicated some hunters who were trying to hide in the thin brush at the edge of the parking lot. The woods might have been enough to conceal two or three. There were eighteen of them.

''Gives them something to do,'' Remo explained. ''You know, I went hunting a couple of times years ago.''

''That does not surprise me,'' Chiun said, nodding sadly. ''After all, you were a barbarian when I met you. However, I had hoped that you had not sunk so low into depravity that you would shoot Bambi's mother.''

''I never actually shot anything,'' Remo pointed out.

''Not only did you use firearms—you were untalented with them. The pride I feel at this moment is underwhelming.''

It was as if Remo didn't hear. The two of them traced a path around the perimeter of the parking lot. Remo had already described to Chiun the tracks he'd seen in the Concord field and in the alley behind the HETA office. So far, there was no sign of Judith White's distinctive paw prints in the film of dirt and sand.

''I see nothing here,'' Chiun announced once they'd completed their circuit around the parking lot's edge.

"Me, neither," Remo said, disappointed. "These boot marks all over the place don't help."

He waved a hand at the kicks and scuffs that dozens of hunters' heels had made in the soft sand.

The fence along the side of the lot nearest them had collapsed. It opened into another, larger parking area.

"Guess we move on," Remo said glumly.

Chiun nodded agreement.

The two men clambered across the toppled chain link and into the adjacent lot. Moving ever farther away from their quarry.

"DID YOU HEAR THAT?" Evan whispered urgently.

"Hear what?" Ted asked.

Evan's voice was a hoarse rasp. "Sounded like digging."

The air was thick with dust. Tiny particles danced in the few beams of light that penetrated the spaces in the boarded-up first-floor windows. The smell of decay hung heavy in the wooden interior of the big brick building.

As they stepped gingerly through the large rooms of the old warehouse, both men found it difficult to breathe. They pulled air into their lungs in shallow, nervous spurts, exhaling almost as soon as they had inhaled.

Ted was an anxious wreck. The cavernous warehouse was spooky, like something out of a Saturday-afternoon horror movie. His head swirled as much from blood loss as from fear. They'd drained too much at the hospital. What little was left thundered in his ears.

Evan had taken point. A few yards ahead, he stepped cautiously over a rotted beam that had fallen to the floor. Years of settling dust and cobwebs formed a thick coat on its decayed surface.

As Evan's toes brushed the floor on the far side of the beam, there came a gentle creak beneath him.

Evan froze. Behind him, Ted stopped, too.

"What?" Ted whispered anxiously.

"*Shh,*" Evan stressed. He started to pick his foot up. The floorboards creaked greater protest. Worried, Evan stood stock-still.

"*Go,*" Ted insisted, pressing the length of his gun barrel against Evan's tense shoulder blades.

Hesitantly, Evan brought his foot down flat on the old warehouse floor. The creak from the wood came sharp and quick, stopping abruptly. Hoping the noise hadn't been loud enough to scare off their prey, Evan dropped his other foot next to the first.

A muted sound came from beneath. Not a creak this time. More like a tired groan. It flashed to a roar.

The creaky old floor vanished from beneath them. Helpless as the world collapsed around them, Evan and Ted felt an instant of weightlessness followed by the remorseless tug of gravity.

The blackness of eternity swallowed them.

Boards bounced around and off them as they

plunged into the basement. Guns were dropped; frightened hands grabbed instinctively for faces and heads.

A jarring stop. Crashing all around.

They hit the dirt floor hard. Rotting wood rained down, bouncing off their heads and shoulders.

Ted did a belly flop onto the musty earthen floor.

Striking ground, Evan tried to scramble to his knees. Heavy timber smashed his back, knocking him face first into the dirt.

It was over as quickly as it had begun.

Dust settled around them as the two men lay groaning on the basement floor. A lone nail clattered loudly down the length of a long, angled board, smacking lightly into the soft dirt floor.

After a long moment, Evan pushed himself up through the pile of debris. Dust fell as thick as flour from his hair.

"Ted?" he panted, voice small. He felt around his back where the beam had struck. Wincing, he hoped he hadn't broken anything.

Evan stumbled to his feet. Floorboards clattered away, settling on other sections of rotting wood. He looked up at the hole through which they'd fallen. It seemed a mile away.

"Man, we're lucky...we're lucky we weren't *killed*," he breathed.

Evan glanced around for his gun. He didn't see it anywhere. Probably buried under the avalanche of junk.

"You lose your gun, too, Ted?" he asked.

No answer.

"Ted?" he called again, the first hint of concern creeping into his voice. He suddenly felt very alone. It was dark in the basement. There was no sign of a door anywhere nearby. The only light spilled down from the hole through which they'd fallen.

As he tripped anxiously through the awkward piles of wood, Evan spied Ted. He was kneeling a few feet from the pile of rubble.

Ted's back was to Evan. Unmoving, he appeared to be engrossed in a spot on the floor.

"You scared the shit out of me, Ted," Evan exhaled, relieved. "Hey, have you seen my gun anywhere?"

One floorboard was jammed into the soft dirt floor, angled up over another. When Evan tried to climb over it, he tripped, slamming down onto the angled wood. The far end rose out of the dirt, dragging something into the air behind it.

Sprawled over one end of the long board, Evan glanced up at the thing that had risen from the soil...

And felt his heart freeze.

The board had impaled the corpse in its hollowed stomach cavity. The body hung from the rotten board—a gruesome playmate on the far end of a macabre teeter-totter.

And as the first brush of shock and horror pummeled Evan's reeling mind, he realized he knew the man.

Bob. His friend's head hung slack over his dirt-smeared chest.

In panic, Evan scurried off the board. The bloodied body collapsed with a horrible, meaty sigh to the dusty floor.

"Ted!" Evan gasped, backing away on palms and feet. His hand sank into something slimy.

With sick eyes, he looked down. A face stared up at him through the earth. Rictus-tight lips curled away from yellowed teeth. Mottled hair dragged across gray flesh.

There were more. Hands here. Legs there. All exposed by the collapsed ceiling.

They had fallen into a graveyard.

Fear overpowering horror, Evan stumbled over to Ted. He found his friend still kneeling in the same spot. Ted's gun rested on the floor near his boots.

Beside him now, Evan finally saw the thing that had turned Ted into a terrified statue.

A tiny hand poked up from the floor. The face and torso of a young child had been exposed by a falling rafter. The stomach had been ripped open. Dirt filled the hollow cavity.

Ted was clearly in shock. Frightened, Evan was trying to figure out how to get him out of there when he heard a soft footfall behind them.

On his knees, Evan wheeled. And felt the world drop out from beneath him again.

Judith White had crept stealthily from the shadows at the periphery of the basement. She stood a breath away from both hunters, teeth bared. In the wan light, her green eyes glowed red.

"Nice of you boys to drop in," she growled softly.

Evan dove for Ted's shotgun.

Clawing hands were snatching for the stock when he felt a blinding pressure at the side of his head.

He was too slow. She'd clubbed him over his left ear. And as the blackness of eternity collapsed around him, Evan Cleaver prayed for swift death. He did not wish to awaken on Judith White's buffet table.

The hunter crumpled to the wood-strewn cellar floor without so much as a sigh.

Abandoning the unconscious Evan, Judith padded up to the kneeling shape of Ted Holstein.

"Remember me?" she taunted, stealing around from behind.

His glazed eyes gained focus. Something seemed to spark far back in their shocked depths. He blinked, as if awakening from a long sleep. It was as if he were seeing Judith White for the first time.

Ted's expression instantly switched from one of shock to one of horrid fear. His next reaction was instinctive.

Ted screamed. His voice was loud and piercing, carrying out beyond the confines of the basement mausoleum.

Judith leaped forward. Unfolding fingers revealed

something in her hand. A test tube. Thin light from upstairs reflected yellow off its glass surface.

While Ted continued screaming, Judith dumped the thick brown liquid from the test tube down the hunter's throat.

Quickly, she clapped her hands over his nose and mouth, forcing him to swallow the sick-tasting fluid.

"You've sobered up since this morning," she hissed approvingly in his ear. Her breath was hot and vile. "That'll make this that much easier."

Ted heard the words as if they were coming at him down a long tunnel. The liquid had hit his stomach. The reaction was instantaneous. His rapidly beating heart spread the brackish fluid throughout his body.

He shivered uncontrollably. His head felt as if it were being whipped around the confines of the cellar—a lead weight swung on a long rope. It spun away, coiled, then whipped back in. In all, it took no more than ten seconds.

When it was over, a menacing calmness overtook Ted. A low rumble rose from the primitive depths of his empty belly. A growl.

Judith released her grip. She smiled a gleaming row of white teeth. Human flesh filled the spaces between.

"Doesn't that feel a whole lot better?" she purred.

Ted nodded, arching his back. He began sniffing

the air experimentally. A tantalizing smell filled the musty basement. It was human blood.

As Ted padded over to the corpse of Bob, Judith hopped on all fours over to the unconscious form of Evan Cleaver. While Ted began gnawing at the belly of his dead friend, she pulled another test tube from the pocket of her tight slacks.

"Don't get too settled over there," she warned Ted. He looked up, a sheet of dirt-smeared flesh hanging from his mouth. "You have work to do," Judith directed.

Picking Evan's head off the floor, Judith dumped some of the brown liquid into his mouth. She massaged his throat as he slept, forcing the syrupy fluid down into his stomach.

As she worked, Judith raised her nose, sniffing carefully. The hunters were getting far too close. Including Remo and Chiun.

"High time I evened these odds," she purred.

With an open paw, she slapped awake the creature that had been Evan Cleaver.

THE GROUND around the muddy pothole yielded nothing but hunters' boot marks. Near Remo and Chiun, water seeped up into a fresh Survivor sole imprint. A crushed Budweiser can lay next to it.

"Dammit, why don't these rummies take their clog-dancing chorus line to the nearest bar?" Remo complained.

He had grown more irritated as their search wore on.

"These lummoxes do not drop their clumsy hooves everywhere," Chiun said. "I see no evidence of the tracks you describe."

"Me, either," Remo relented. "But it'd sure as hell be easier to look if Bob and Doug McKenzie weren't here."

As they turned from the puddle, Remo rubbed his shoulder absently. It was a habit he'd developed after the attack and one that caused him irritation whenever he caught himself doing it. When he suddenly realized he was rubbing his shoulder yet again, he pulled his hand away, dropping it abruptly to his side.

A few yards away, four hunters sloshed through a puddle. They ducked inside an old boiler room that was attached to one of the bigger buildings.

Remo stopped dead. "This is ridiculous," he announced angrily. "Where are the cops? They should be rounding these rum hounds into paddy wagons."

Beside him, the Master of Sinanju cocked a sudden ear.

"Silence!" the old man hissed. A raised hand halted all objections.

The Master of Sinanju's head was tipped to one side. He seemed to be listening intently.

Remo trained an ear in the same direction. It took him a moment to filter out all the extraneous sounds, but once he'd cleared everything else away, he heard it, too.

A scream.

The glance they exchanged was swift and knowing.

Their feet did not disturb a single particle of dirt, so swiftly did they move. Without a word, the two men flew off in the direction of the terrified sound.

30

Trooper Dan MacGuire couldn't believe what he'd just been told. There was no backup coming.

Eyewitnesses had confirmed the initial reports. Killer scientist Dr. Judith White—who had murdered a fellow Massachusetts state trooper no less—was suspected to be at large in this very area. And there were no other police units being sent in.

The place should have been swarming with cops by now. But the only people here were civilians. Even news people were being kept out of the area. Although some police had been deployed to Chelsea, it had been to cordon off the area. They were sitting this one out.

This lunacy was all because of some crazy, mysterious order out of Washington. No one even seemed to know where the command had originated.

And while the brass tried to figure out what the hell was going on up the chain of command, Dan MacGuire was left hanging. A lone sitting duck for the deranged, gene-sucking tiger woman of BostonBio.

Well, not entirely alone. There was always the

skinny guy from the Department of Agriculture and his two-thousand-year-old assistant. If push came to shove, *they'd* be a big help, Dan thought sarcastically.

His negative opinion of the two agriculture men wasn't altered by their sudden appearance around the side of the warehouse across the street from MacGuire's unmarked car.

The trooper had been sitting in his sedan, door open, black-booted feet planted on the road. He rose from the vehicle when he saw the two men appear.

They came at him much faster than men should have been able to travel on foot. They were both flying along as if Dr. White were hot on their heels.

MacGuire quickly pulled his side arm as they approached, half-expecting to see a loping Judith White racing in for the kill behind them.

Remo and Chiun flew out of the parking lot and across the street, racing up to the parked state police car.

MacGuire had his gun leveled at a point behind them. But there was nothing there.

"Where is she?" the trooper shouted, crouched and alert as they soared across the street. His gun swept left, then right. Still nothing visible.

"Where'd that scream come from?" Remo demanded, skidding to an abrupt stop next to the trooper. Alert eyes raked the immediate area.

"Scream?" the trooper asked, confused. "What scream?"

Remo ignored MacGuire. "It was over here somewhere," he said to Chiun.

"*What* scream?" MacGuire repeated. He lowered his gun as he glanced from Remo to Chiun.

"There," Chiun decided, pointing to a large warehouse.

"Could be that one," Remo replied, indicating the next building over.

"Yes," Chiun agreed, "but this one is closer."

Dan MacGuire's head bounced back and forth between each man as they spoke. "Somebody screamed?" the trooper asked.

"Okay." Remo nodded. "Big one first. You take the front—I'll take the back."

Chiun hesitated a fraction of a second. Given what had happened during his pupil's first encounter with Judith White, he didn't want to abandon Remo now.

Remo sensed his teacher's unease. "Look, I'll be fine, Chiun. *Really.*"

The hesitation passed. Nodding, the Master of Sinanju set his frail shoulders firmly. "Remember, my son," he intoned. "Man holds dominion over all beasts. And you are far greater than any mere man. You are Sinanju."

Remo smiled tightly. "I'll do you proud, Little Father," he assured his teacher.

"Aim for an attainable goal," Chiun retorted. "I will be satisfied if you do not get yourself killed."

With a sharp nod they separated, each tearing off to an opposite end of the warehouse.

Trooper MacGuire could only stand by his car and watch as the two men flew away from him at impossible speed. Not a single puff of dust rose in their wake.

"Who screamed?" MacGuire yelled helplessly after them.

SHE HAD TO WORK QUICKLY.

Judith White gathered up a few more test tubes from the one case she'd carried to the warehouse. She slipped them into the front pockets of her slacks, careful to keep the old-fashioned corks in place.

There wasn't a lot of the formula to go around. And what she had was inferior to the solution she'd used on herself. This was only the original mixture. A poor substitute for her refined blend. But while it didn't have the same long-lasting effects as the formula she'd taken, it would be good enough.

She had almost dumped the older stuff out after her breakthrough with the newer formula. Lucky for her, she hadn't. Right now, she was glad to have it.

Bent low at the waist, she ran through the empty rooms at the back of the warehouse. Light streamed in through the dust-smeared windows, filtering down through the thick canopy of green-turning-to-orange autumn leaves.

The woods that grew up around the small tributary that fed into the larger Chelsea Creek had been her refuge for much of the time during her change. It was through them that she'd carried the many bodies buried in the basement.

As with all animals, the jungle had a powerful draw on Judith White. It was a haven. The thick cover meant safety.

But there were things to do first.

She needed to create more like her. Needed to give herself more of an edge.

Though her heart pounded madly, it was no longer from fear. It was the thrill of action that impelled her.

Judith leaped over a few old crates, landing softly in the interior of an old office. She paused, sniffing the air.

She was about to move on when she heard a noise. A footfall sounded through the thin wall to her left. A branch cracked beneath the tread. Someone was coming through the woods.

Another victim.

The window in the office was partially open. Judith White hopped lightly to the sill. Careful to not break the glass tubes in her pockets, she eased herself to the moist ground outside.

The figure she saw creeping through the woods surprised her. He was familiar. She'd watched him arrive from her rafter in the attic.

He was oblivious to her presence. Too easy.

Slipping one of the vials from her pocket, she palmed it. On confident, gliding paws, she stole quickly up on the newest unsuspecting member of her superior species.

THE MASTER OF SINANJU HAD waited long enough for Remo to reach the rear of the building. He was stretching one hand to the door of the warehouse when he saw a flash of movement in the woods at the back of the neighboring building.

It was a fleeting glimpse. But it was enough.

Whoever it was moved much faster than a normal human being. So quickly, in fact, Chiun's well-trained eyes almost didn't detect the motion.

The figure had darted out of sight in an instant.

He paused, considering for a moment if he should not go back and collect Remo.

This whole affair had been a strain on his pupil. The attack by Judith White would not ordinarily have been enough in isolation to cause Remo concern. But Chiun knew that he had dredged up long buried memories of his last encounter with one of these tiger creatures. Remo's old fears could blind him to the current problem. A single distraction at the wrong moment could prove fatal.

And something else had apparently not occurred to Remo during this time of crisis. For years, Chiun had tried to convince Remo that he was the fulfillment of a prophesy that asserted that a Master of Sinanju would one day train the avatar of Shiva, the Hindu god of destruction. This dead night tiger would be brought to fullness in Sinanju.

To Chiun, Remo was fulfillment of the legend. However, for most of their association, Remo—in his typical white, Western, lunkheaded way—had deemed the legend "a big, fat, smelly load of doo-hickey." Nonetheless, Chiun persisted. Certain factors in recent years had caused Remo to argue less strenuously against the prophesy. In a very small way, he had allowed the glimmer of a possibility that the legend might actually be true. It was a step in the right direction, as well as a step to fulfilling the legend.

But there was another aspect to the ancient story.

As the dead night tiger trained in Sinanju, it was said that Shiva could only be sent to death again by his own kind.

"Shiva must walk with care when he passes the jungle where lurk the other night tigers," were the words Chiun had intoned to Remo years before when first they had encountered the tiger creatures. Hand in hand with the Shiva prophesy, it was one of the most ancient legends of the House of Sinanju.

Perhaps Remo had thought of this and hadn't mentioned it for fear of worrying Chiun. However, given Remo's monkeylike attention span, it was more likely he hadn't been paying attention when the Master of Sinanju was relating the tale. To someone who knew the truth of the legends, Chiun alone appreciated the danger his pupil now faced.

Poised to enter the dusty old warehouse, Chiun

thought of all these things in a fraction of a millisecond.

The decision was made in an instant. Remo's life was too important to risk. The legend did not affect Chiun. And the Master of Sinanju didn't carry the same emotional baggage as his pupil. Chiun would deal with Judith White on his own.

Spinning abruptly, the old Asian left the front of the first warehouse. Kimono skirts billowing, he raced across the barren space to the next building.

REMO CREPT STEALTHILY through the thick underbrush at the rear of the first warehouse.

As he stepped carefully over the moss-slick stones that lined the trickling brook behind the building, he scanned the high wall, looking for the best route of entry.

There were high windows all along the back. A lot had been broken, but not as many as at the front. Vandals didn't have as easy a time getting back here and so left the rear largely untouched.

Graffiti artists had decorated the brick foundation, as well as the clapboards that encased what appeared to be the old office wing.

Remo wasn't surprised to find that the sprayed words were illegible. In a state where most teachers spent half the year filing phony grievances and the other half complaining about the latest basic-competency test they'd all just failed, simple things like teaching spelling and penmanship had a tendency to get lost in the classroom shuffle.

A few yards along the rear wall, Remo found an open door set into the foundation. It was coated with moss and propped against a jagged rock. As he approached the doorway, Remo's heart skipped a beat.

Tracks in the mud. *Hundreds* of them.

They were identical to those he'd seen in the cornfield back in Concord. Judith White had apparently been using the rear warehouse door to come and go unseen. For *months,* if the dried prints at the edge of the muddy path were any indication.

The path she regularly took carried her out into the center of the stream. Judith was evidently trying to mask her scent in the water. A distinctly human act.

Remo glanced into the dark interior of the warehouse.

The ground angled down along the rear of the structure. This was the basement. Chiun would be entering on the first-floor level.

For a moment, Remo contemplated going back for Chiun. The Master of Sinanju expected to meet up with Remo on the ground floor, not the basement. And Remo had no great desire to stumble on Judith on his own.

And in that instant of hesitation, Remo was ashamed of his own apprehension.

No. To go back for Chiun now would be a surrender to fear. Not only that, but he would also be abandoning Judith White's probable escape route.

Remo steeled himself.

"I am *not* cleaning out her litter box," he muttered under his breath.

Without a backward glance, he plunged into the darkness...

And the figure that had been trailing him stealthily along the rear of the building followed swiftly behind.

CHIUN DIDN'T SEE Judith White anywhere.

The woods near the small stream were overgrown, making visibility poor. In the distance, he heard the sound of lumbering hunters. Closer still was the sound of the roaring river into which the small tributary fed.

Surely his eyes had not deceived him. She was here. Somewhere.

The figure he had seen moved with the grace and speed of a big cat. It had slipped into the late-afternoon shadows somewhere nearby.

A filthy mattress lay on the ground in a small clearing near the brook. Around it, shattered beer bottles mixed with rotting leaves from years gone by. Chiun stepped past these, glancing first to woods then to building.

And in that sliver of time when his eyes were trained on the warehouse, a figure emerged from out of the thicket.

So soft were his footfalls, Chiun hadn't heard him moving in the woods. He wheeled on the sudden sound.

When he spied Trooper Dan MacGuire, the old man's alert features relaxed to annoyance.

"Why are you not at your carriage?" Chiun demanded.

"You said someone screamed," MacGuire replied, his voice a harsh whisper. He was slipping quietly and confidently away from the tree cover, gun clutched in his hand. "I can't let that psycho doctor escape, with or without backup."

"Put that noisemaker away," Chiun commanded, nodding to the trooper's gun.

"Sorry, Pops," MacGuire said, shaking his head. "You do what you want, but I'm not getting killed."

Chiun's brow creased. "The Magyars were grasping, but at least they had sense to guard their coaches from bands of roving drunkards."

"Hey, cruiser gets trashed, they give me another one." MacGuire smiled tightly.

Chiun had no time to deal with foolish taxi drivers. Frowning, the Master of Sinanju turned away from the trooper.

Judith White could *only* have come this way, Chiun reasoned. But a rapid scan revealed no doors on the rear of the building. The only windows were too high for her to reach. That left the woods. But as he listened, he heard no sounds coming from the nearby copse of trees.

As he contemplated this riddle, Chiun was distracted by the soft sound of the Massachusetts state trooper gliding in behind him.

MacGuire moved gracefully. Almost as effortlessly as Chiun himself. It was strange for a man as beefy as MacGuire to be so light on his feet. It was almost as if...

And in a flash, Chiun finally understood.

He wheeled in place. Just in time to see MacGuire make his final animal lunge. His gun had been dropped. The trooper's teeth were bared, head tipped as it thrust forward at Chiun's exposed throat.

And a single powerful hand—curled like a tiger's paw—swept down in a furious killing blow at the shocked upturned face of the Master of Sinanju.

THE REAR DOOR LED into a dank corridor. The wet concrete walls were covered with moss. The floor was earthen, packed firmly into a level path. Even so, the paw prints of Judith White were clear to Remo as he walked carefully into the bowels of the warehouse.

His eyes pulled in ambient light. Enough so that the dark corridor appeared as bright as midday.

The corridor broke into a vast interior chamber, so wide it seemed to encompass most of the area beneath the main warehouse. Wooden columns spaced evenly throughout the cellar kept the ceiling from collapsing.

Most of the ceiling. As he stepped inside, Remo saw that a good-sized chunk of the first floor had crashed into the basement. Recently, judging by the level of disturbed dust that was swirling through the fetid air.

He caught the stench of rotting human flesh the moment he walked into the large cellar room.

A body was impaled on a board near the debris. Even from this distance, sharp eyes saw evidence of more corpses.

A breeze pushed in from the long corridor behind him. It carried a hint of fresh air into the foul-smelling basement. The clean air made the smell in the cellar seem all the worse.

As Remo stepped farther into the room, his senses detected something more in the cool wind on his back.

A stronger pressure of air. Something pushing through the natural breeze. Something *fast.*

And in that moment of realization, the thing became airborne.

Remo flung himself to the dirt floor. Parallel to the earth, he tucked his shoulder sharply in, executing a tight roll. He ignored the fresh stabs of pain in his scars.

Flipping to a crouching position, he was just in time to see the startled face of Ted Holstein soar overhead.

Ted had thrown himself at Remo's back with such ferocity that he flew several yards into the dank cellar. He dropped to all fours, springing to his feet the instant he'd landed. He wheeled around, snarling angrily.

"You're fast," Ted commented.

The hunter's face was smeared with dirt. His eyes were wide, staring blind hatred at Remo.

Behind him, another creature dropped through the ceiling hole. Evan Cleaver skulked rapidly forward.

"You were supposed to lead him over to me," Evan growled, flashing fangs.

"He moved too fast," Ted replied, voice low.

Evan kept coming, moving out around Remo. He was trying to get their prey between them.

Remo noted the effortless movements of the two tiger creatures. But though they had grace, they were not artful. It was all pure instinct with them. And in that moment, Remo knew that this was not like before.

When Sheila Feinberg had created her army of tiger people years ago, Remo had been injured. His Sinanju abilities had already deserted him. He had stood helplessly by as Chiun fought the battle that he could not join. But these creatures were nothing special. He saw that now. With their snarling and snapping, they were little more than wild beasts. Certainly nothing to be feared.

And as the dawning knowledge that all his worries had been for naught began to set firmly in,

Remo Williams did something the beasts before him did not expect. He laughed. Long and loud.

"What's so funny?" Ted Holstein demanded, confused.

"You, snagglepuss," Remo sniffed, tears of mirth in his eyes. "You're already dead and you don't even know it."

"He's bluffing," Evan hissed. He was between Remo and the rear door. Blocking escape.

Remo took a deep breath, feeling the power that was his Sinanju training flood every corpuscle of his being.

The pain in his shoulder had fled. He was alert, infinitely aware. Every movement they took—every soft pad that dropped to the floor—he heard.

His senses were alive in Sinanju.

Remo kept his arms away from his body, hands open. He watched Ted, but kept his body attuned to Evan, still moving behind him. He smiled.

"Try me, puddytats," Remo challenged.

And as one, the two tiger creatures lunged.

CHIUN BOUNDED BACK from the swinging paw.

MacGuire's hand swept viciously past, throwing a wild gust of air into the Master of Sinanju's face. Thin beard fluttering in the wind, Chiun's eyes grew wide.

"You are in league with the fiend!" he cried.

"I am now," MacGuire snarled. "I just met Dr. White. Nice woman. Don't much like her taste in beverages.'' He made a show of tasting the vile potion, the aftertaste of which still coated his tongue. "But I think I found a chew toy to cleanse my palate.''

He sent another hand toward Chiun, fingers curved in a move as old as the jungle itself. Splayed claws were meant to rip open the flesh of prey. But unfortunately for Trooper MacGuire, Massachusetts did not yet allow its state troopers to grow claws.

Chiun snagged the hand as it swung toward him, arresting its motion. Bony fingers encircling the trooper's hand, he applied pressure with his own clenching fist.

Bones crunched audibly.

Yelping in pain, MacGuire flung out his free hand.

Chiun's countermovement was invisible to the beast before him. But its effect was obvious.

A sharp tug. Trailed by a horrid, wrenching pain. MacGuire was left staring dumbly at the bloody stump where his hand had been. The severed hand dropped to the bed of rotting leaves at his feet, fingers still curled in attack.

The trooper let out a shriek of agony that ended with the sharp point of a single long fingernail in the center of his broad forehead.

Animal scream dying in his lungs, MacGuire crumpled in a heap to the moss-coated ground.

The Master of Sinanju let the body drop.

MacGuire had been changed since their arrival.

Judith White was not only close by, but she also had a fast-working version of her formula. And Chiun had allowed himself to be lured away from Remo.

The old man left the state trooper to be reclaimed by the earth. Hands clenched in knots of furious ivory, the Master of Sinanju raced from the rear of the crumbling warehouse.

REMO DUCKED BELOW the two springing hunters, rolling to the right.

The two hunters had launched themselves head-long at him from opposite directions and were moving too quickly to arrest their forward momentum. Their great surprise at the sudden absence of their quarry turned to yelps of pain as they plowed into one another headfirst. Together, they tumbled to the dirt floor. They rolled back to their feet with surprising swiftness.

"Did puddy get a bang on him head?" Remo sympathized.

"Asshole," Evan snarled.

"Hey, I don't remember Sylvester ever calling Tweety an asshole." Remo frowned.

Beside him, Ted lunged forward, both hands clawing down at Remo's chest.

He was fast. Remo was faster.

"Do I look like a ball of yarn to you?" Remo asked.

One forearm swept Ted's hands harmlessly away. With his arms no longer stretched out before him,

Ted lost his balance. And in that split second, Remo launched a balled fist into his attacker's chest.

Bones crunched audibly. Splintered sternum and ribs exploded into heart and lungs. Ted was dead before he hit the ground.

Even as his partner fell, Evan sprang forward, teeth bared menacingly.

There was no need to play with this one. The movements of these creatures weren't as graceful as Remo had thought. As Evan thrust his fangs toward Remo's neck, Remo realized he was facing nothing more than a poor dumb animal whose behavior was programmed by twisted science. It wasn't Evan's fault he was what he was.

Remo showed Evan the compassion that Man alone of all the creatures on Earth could demonstrate to a lesser animal. As he flashed forward for the kill, Remo's flattened palm caught Evan just above his slathering fangs. Facial bones cracked, shattering to jelly. Evan had struck a solid wall. He joined Ted Holstein on the dirt floor.

Remo looked down upon the bodies. It was a victory without satisfaction. These men weren't to blame for what they'd become. The responsibility for all of this rested squarely on a single set of shoulders.

A fresh sound came from far above.

A few more gunshots followed the first.

Shouting voices. Panicked.

Remo spun from the hunters' remains. Racing to

the pile of collapsed debris, he scampered to the top. Flexing calf muscles propelled him up out of the basement and onto the ground-floor level. He ran to the source of the commotion.

In his wake, silence flooded the macabre grave-yard.

31

The first floor of the warehouse split off in two separate wings. The main section was the large part of the building that faced the street. The other was a long addition that extended over the waters of Chelsea Creek at the rear of the property.

The gunshots he'd heard came from the direction of the river and so when he jumped up through the basement hole Remo struck off into the narrower wing of the musty old building.

He found a group of hunters hustling away from an alleylike loading-dock tunnel. Beams had collapsed from the low roof. The men were forced to climb awkwardly as they hurried back toward Remo.

There were six of them in all. Three trained their shotguns back on the door through which they'd just come. The other two bore one of their fellow hunters.

The man they were carrying had a vicious chest wound. Blood seeped into the cloth of his gray shirt, staining it black.

"What happened?" Remo demanded, racing up to the men.

Darting eyes were terrified. Orange, late-afternoon sun shone through dirty windows, illuminating faces shiny with frightened perspiration.

"It was *her!*" one of the men panted fearfully.

"Where?" Remo pressed.

"The stairs. She jumped us before we could stop her. I think the shots might have scared her off."

They hurried past him, hauling their bleeding friend.

When they realized Remo wasn't with them, two of the men glanced back. They were just in time to see the old wooden stairway door sigh softly shut.

JUDITH WHITE MOUNTED the stairs five at a time.

Her heart thudded madly. It was the fear of a hunted animal.

She was the mouse, cornered by the cat. A fox chased by hounds. A gazelle stalked by a lion.

It was a horrible feeling. A complete loss of control. Utter, utter helplessness and abandonment.

She had seen Remo in the basement. Unbeknownst to him, she had watched through a crack in the baseboard on the far side of the cellar as he went up against her two sacrificial lambs.

It hadn't been much of a fight. Ted was dispatched so quickly she didn't even see Remo move. Judith fled before he finished off Evan. She didn't need to stay. She knew what the eventual outcome would be.

Hit the landing running.

Up the next flight.

Six steps at a time now. Faster, *faster*.

Next landing, next flight.

Barely slowing, barely *breathing*.

She had more of the original tiger solution but she now knew that it would do her no good. The old files of BGSBS stated very clearly that alcohol dulled or even killed the bacteria on which the new gene coding lived. Most of the men in the area had a blood-alcohol level high enough to blind a herd of bull elephants.

Judith had lucked out with the ones she did find. Ted Holstein had sobered up after her morning attack. Evan Cleaver appeared to have dried out a bit, as well. Trooper MacGuire had been unquestionably sober.

The rest?

Drunks. All drunks.

Last landing.

Judith pounced forward, slapping a palm against the creaky old door. A plume of displaced dust flew up into the air as the door swung wildly open. She moved inside, quickly shutting the door behind her.

Her attic room.

High above her, the tired wooden beams on which she had spent many a night sleeping off her ghoulish feedings stretched toward the distant wall.

Windows lined all but the wall directly behind her. To her left was the parking lot, to her right, woods.

Judith raced toward the last set of windows.

During more prosperous times, the long dead business that had once occupied the warehouse had built a new wing out over Chelsea Creek. The four-story wood addition rested on huge pylons that had been constructed atop concrete platforms in the river far below.

At the grimy windows, Judith looked down at the river. Overflow from a dam farther upstream made this area of the waterway treacherous. It was a long drop into swift-moving rapids.

Judith spun from the window, looking desperately across the big empty attic. There was nowhere else she could go. She was trapped.

"Some plan," she muttered to herself.

Footfalls on the stairs. Light as air. Inaudible to a common human. She might have missed them herself if she hadn't been specifically listening for them.

Two fingers poked into her pocket and removed one of the slender tubes of tiger-gene formula.

Her plan was bleak. No matter how she looked at it. But perhaps there was another way.

Wild-eyed, she waited for the door to open. And for her new species's final reckoning.

REMO SENSED THE MOVEMENTS coming from the attic room. From the way the animal carried itself, it was either Judith White or another of her tiger creatures.

At the moment, the animal that lurked before him wasn't his primary concern.

He had smelled the smoke before he'd even gotten to the staircase. The gunshots of the retreating hunters had drawn others. Huddled together in the parking lot far below, the men had apparently gotten the bright idea to smoke Judith White out. To this end, they'd set fire to the building.

The wood was catching quickly, too fast for Remo's liking. The stairwell was already filling with black smoke by the time he reached the closed attic door.

The first hints of flame at the bottom of the stairwell four stories below crackled into his peripheral vision as he pushed the old warped door open.

Inside, he found nothing but four empty walls. Judith White was nowhere to be seen. Ever cautious—sensitive to the flames licking up below him—Remo stepped into the vast, airy room. In his wake, smoke wafted into the chamber.

"Here, kitty-kitty-kitty," Remo called.

A creak from above his head.

She'd been hiding on the rafter directly above him. Judith dropped, deadweight.

Remo bent double, catching her falling bulk on the meaty part of his back.

As her claws brushed the cotton cloth of his T-shirt, Remo flexed his back muscles and jerked left. Judith White flipped off his shoulders. Twisting, she landed solidly on both feet, facing Remo, her teeth bared viciously.

"You heal quickly," Judith commented, nodding to the spot where her claws had raked his shoulder and chest.

"Good genes," Remo explained thinly.

Her smile was feral. "*Better* genes," she replied. She dived at him again.

Remo had prepared for her. He was ready to stop her forward momentum as he had with the hunters in the cellar. But as his hand flew out from his side, Judith White did something unexpected.

At the last minute, she dropped low, beneath his rocketing fist.

The command had been sent. Remo's hand was already locked into an unstoppable motion. It flew forward, but with nothing to contact it struck only air. It was all he could do to keep his arm from tearing out of its socket.

He lurched forward as the force of the missed blow knocked him off balance.

Before Remo could regain his equilibrium, Judith sprang up at the inside of his outstretched arm. Both hands balled tightly, she shoved Remo's chest with a strength far greater than her slight form would have indicated. As he toppled backward to the floor, she leaped forward, collapsing on his prone form.

In her hand, Judith held a test tube filled with brown, brackish genetic formula. With a savage grin of victory, she tipped the thick liquid into Remo's open mouth.

CHIUN SPIED THE CROWD of rowdy hunters the instant he broke from the wooded area behind the adjoining building. They surrounded the warehouse into which Remo had gone.

Much of the ground floor was already engulfed in flame. Acrid smoke hung heavy in the afternoon air.

Arms pumping furiously, he raced across the vast space that separated the two warehouses. By the time he reached the building, the second story had already ignited. Flames were racing up to the third.

Near the old loading dock, the hunters were enjoying a celebratory drink. Someone had retrieved a bottle of Jack Daniel's from one of the trucks. They were trying to figure out how to pour the liquor into their open beer cans without spilling a drop when Chiun raced up behind them.

"Where is my son?" the Master of Sinanju cried.

The voice startled them. Jumping, the hunter with the bottle splashed some whiskey on his hand.

"Watch it, Grampa," the man threatened. He slurped the spilled liquid off his thumb.

"Hey, tha' counts ash your helping," another slurred.

Chiun had neither time nor patience. Plucking a shotgun from the concrete dock, he wrapped a hand around each barrel. He pulled.

With a pained wrench of metal, the two barrels tore up the length of the weapon.

The men were only just becoming aware of what was happening when Chiun's hands became sweeping blurs. The hunter with the bottle felt a tightness at his throat. He only realized that his shotgun had been knotted around his neck when he looked down and saw the stock jutting out beneath his chin. A single skeletal finger brushed the trigger.

"My son, grog-belly," Chiun repeated savagely.

"There was a guy in there," the hunter panted. "Heading for the stairs. After White." Tense fingers groped the shotgun knot at the back of his neck. "*Please.* You can have the bottle. Just don't pull the trigger."

His plea fell on deaf ears. Chiun was already gone.

None of the hunters could say for certain where the old Asian went, but a few swore they saw a flash of silk kimono hurtling like a fired cannonball into the growing wall of orange flame.

REMO JERKED HIS HEAD to one side. The gene-altering liquid splattered thickly to the dirty floor.

Above him, Judith White growled in anger. Her breath was rancid.

The crazed geneticist's elbows were bent and jammed against his biceps, pinning him down. There was a surprising amount of weight to her.

Without his hands free, Remo used the next-best

thing. As Judith repositioned her test tube, he bent his knees sharply, stabbing them up into her pelvis.

The weight lifted. Judith flew off him, landing in a heap near the stairs.

Remo completed the motion with his legs, slapping soles to the floor. Upright, he spun to Judith as she was scampering to her feet.

Black smoke poured up around her. Flames licked at the wooden door casing. Framed in fire, Judith White was a hell-sent demon.

Judith sensed the fire at her back. It clearly frightened her. Keeping her back to the walls, she moved quickly and cautiously away from the open flames.

She stepped around Remo, leaving a wide space between them at all times.

"You should have taken a sip, brown eyes," she said, hurling the near empty test tube away. The frail glass shattered against the brick wall. "You could have been on the ground floor of the new era. You'd be one of the first successors to mankind."

Remo's gaze was level. "Been there, done that," he said coldly.

Her green eyes betrayed suspicion. "What do you mean?" she asked.

"I met your predecessor, Sheila Feinberg, years ago. She tried using me like a scratching post, too."

For the first time, uncertainty clouded Judith White's features. "What happened?" she asked.

Remo smiled thinly. "I don't see old Sheila on 'Stupid Pet Tricks,' do you?"

Judith had continued sidestepping in a wide arc around Remo. She was moving toward the river side of the attic room.

"She wasn't me," Judith sneered.

"Yeah," Remo replied. "What happened to her was an accident. You deliberately did this to yourself."

Remo's eyes strayed over her shoulder.

Apparently, the hunters hadn't been satisfied with simply setting fire to the front of the building. They had torched this rear section of the warehouse, as well. Orange flames had just begun to peek up over the sills of the attic windows behind Judith. She didn't seem aware of the flames at her back.

"Is this the point where you give me the big speech on the immorality of tampering with God's grand scheme?" Judith White said sarcastically.

"No," Remo said. "You've been a bad kitty. This is the point where I put you to sleep."

He'd had enough of Judith White's attacks. It was Remo's turn to act.

She was still several yards away from the rear wall. Remo tensed his legs and sprang.

He was off the floor in a shot. Whirring like an airborne top, he chewed up distance faster than the animal eye could perceive. Only when his feet struck her solidly in the chest did she realize he'd even moved. By then it was too late.

Judith was thrown back by the force of the blow. She landed roughly against the wall, one elbow crashing through a filthy windowpane. Flames instantly began licking up through the new hole.

Judith jumped back from the fire, shocked.

"Tigger doesn't like fire," Remo observed. He was standing before her in the smoke-filled room.

Flames erupted along the staircase wall. The wooden structure of the building was igniting like a struck match. Sections of brick wall began falling away, tumbling to the ground four stories below.

And through it all, Remo stood. Mocking her. Mocking that which she had become. And in the primal heart of the animal that had once been Dr. Judith White, a rage as ancient as the oldest living beasts exploded in violent fury.

Careless, unthinking, propelled by hatred, she flew at Remo, face twisted with vicious passion.

Hands flew up with blinding ferocity. She was no longer rational. She was a beast, lashing out in hate and fear and rage.

Remo stood his ground, allowing her to fly to him. When she was close enough, he simply reached out and grabbed hold of one of her mauling raised arms.

One foot shot into the air, bracing against her sternum. With a horrible twist and wrench, Remo ripped the arm from its socket. It tore free like an overcooked turkey leg.

Judith shrieked in pain. Shoulder bleeding, she swept the other hand toward him.

Although Remo could have stopped the blow easily, he never got the chance.

All at once, the floor buckled beneath them. The room suddenly listed like a boat caught in a gale. Remo kept his footing, but Judith was thrown from her feet. She fell to the angled floor, rolling down toward the far wall. When she struck the wall, dozens of bricks broke loose and tumbled out into wide-open space.

She pulled herself awkwardly to her feet. It was difficult to stand. Judith turned back to him.

Remo realized what had happened. The ground floor had collapsed around the wooden columns that supported this section of the building. This wing of the warehouse was preparing to fall into the river.

The heat from the fire grew in wicked intensity. Remo ignored it.

Mindless of all but the creature before him, he began to advance on Judith White.

The room around him creaked in pain. The entire building seemed on the verge of collapse. Flames erupted in wild bursts through holes along floor and walls.

"Remo!"

The voice came from above. Louder than the symphony of noise all around him. When he looked up, he saw the frantic face of the Master of Sinanju peering down through a wide hole in the ceiling. Flames curled around his tufts of smoke-tossed hair. Chiun waved them away.

"Hurry," Chiun called. He beckoned urgently.

The flames were everywhere now. Wafting clouds of smoke partially blocked his view of the old Korean.

"In a minute," Remo called back.

"This building is collapsing!" Chiun pleaded. "We must flee! Now!"

Remo hesitated. He knew Chiun was right. But he also wished to finish off Judith White once and for all. There would be no satisfaction in letting the fire do the work for him.

She was watching him with her big cat's eyes. A whimper of fear rose from her throat as she hugged her knees close to her chest with her one good arm. Blood poured from the vacant socket of her other shoulder.

In the end, good sense won out. Remo spun from the mad scientist. He left her cowering against the distant wall. With a leap, he made it up to the hole. Chiun grabbed hold of him. Firm hands dragged him onto the roof.

The coolness of the air outside shocked him. His body had compensated for the heat of the flames. The room had been like an inferno. Sweat beads evaporated from his skin.

Remo paused at the top of the brick wall. When he looked back through the hole, he saw the rear of the building give way. The entire row of windows, the bricks and Dr. Judith White tumbled out together. Moments later, they crashed into the rocks of the Chelsea Creek rapids.

"This is no time for sight-seeing," Chiun snapped. "If you get injured again, you may tend to your own wounds."

Whirling, the old Asian bounded along the length of the brick wall, unmindful of the sheer drop to the woods below. Fire erupted through holes in the broad flat roof.

Remo raced after him to the main warehouse.

As he sprang over to the largest part of the building, the rest of the office wing behind him collapsed onto the floating figure of Dr. Judith White. Her battered carcass vanished beneath a ton of bricks and burning wood.

32

Dr. Judith White's body turned up five days later.

"It washed up on Deer Island," Smith explained to Remo over the phone. "Her name tag from BostonBio was in her pocket, as well as a few credit cards."

"They're sure it's her?" Remo asked. He was sitting on the floor in his living room.

The Master of Sinanju sat on a simple reed mat across from him. Chiun's parchments were laid out carefully at his knees. A quill danced in his bony hand as he sketched Korean characters.

"The coroner says that her arm was wrenched off with what they are terming 'inhuman strength,'" Smith said dryly. "I doubt it is necessary to go much further than that."

"What about the other hand? Did you check fingerprints?" Remo asked suspiciously.

"Unfortunately, Dr. White never had prints taken," Smith said slowly.

"At a high-tech joint like BostonBio?" Remo asked.

"It is not part of their normal procedure," Smith

explained. "And anyway, they did not regard her as a security risk."

Remo snorted derisively at this. "What about dental records?" he asked.

Smith was growing concerned now, as well. "Her face was mangled in the fall. The teeth were shattered. What are you getting at, Remo?" he asked. "You do not believe she could have escaped?"

"I guess not, Smitty," he admitted reluctantly. "It's just she was awfully resilient."

"Not this resilient," Smith stated firmly. "The genetic formulas of BostonBio died with her. The BGSBS material confiscated from BostonBio that detailed the so-called Feinberg Method has been destroyed. No one will be able to duplicate the formula. Nor, I suspect, will anyone want to."

"Amen to that," Remo echoed. "What I can't figure out is why she was so fired up to help out humanity."

"What do you mean?" Smith asked.

"That was the point of the whole BBQ project," Remo reminded him.

"I didn't tell you?" Smith said, surprised.

"Tell me what?"

"An autopsy was performed on one of the animals Dr. White brought back to BostonBio. There was a deliberate destructive code buried in the DNA of the animals."

Remo blinked. "Are you saying the BBQs really *would* have killed people?"

Across the room, Chiun's head snapped up. Remo shot a glance at his teacher.

"Worse," Smith intoned gravely. "She heralded them as the cure for world hunger. However, that was not their only purpose. Dr. White's cure would have turned mankind into creatures like her. The genetic code contained in the animals was a variant of the old Feinberg bacteria formula. If consumed, the meat of the *Bos camelus-whitus* would have transformed people into things like her. If enough meat was eaten, the change over time would have been permanent."

"So we saved the human race one giant step back down the evolutionary ladder," Remo said. One eye was trained on the Master of Sinanju.

Finding nothing of interest in Smith's explanation, the old man had returned to his writing.

"I had the remaining creature at BostonBio destroyed," the CURE director said. "Since you eliminated the ones in the possession of HETA, every loose end should be tied up."

"Me?" Remo frowned. "I thought you did it."

Smith's voice was level. "Are you joking?" he asked.

"No," Remo insisted. "I told you where they were. I figured you'd take care of them. I said I wasn't going to kill them, Smitty."

"Yes, but surely under the circumstances…" Smith paused, thinking. "It has been several days since you left Medford," he said, his tone reasonable. "With no one to take care of them, perhaps the animals have died already."

"If you do send someone out there, you might want to check the toolshed in the barn," Remo suggested, thinking of Mona and Huey Janner. "And make sure they don't get within sniffing distance when they crack the door."

"Why?" Smith asked.

But Remo had already hung up the phone.

"What's your problem?" Remo asked the Master of Sinanju once he'd dropped the phone in its cradle.

"*Besides* you?" Chiun asked aridly. He didn't look up from his work.

"Ha-ha," Remo said. "You acted like you'd been gut-stabbed when I said the BBQs could kill people."

"A Master of Sinanju cannot be stabbed. Oh, the clumsiest of us has been known on occasion to be mauled by feral kittens, as has been noted in the annals of the House, but stabbed? Never."

"Judith White was no kitten, Little Father," Remo said.

"Perhaps," Chiun replied vaguely.

He wrote for a few long minutes, quill prancing merrily as his knotted hand traced perfect lines. Remo stared at the top of his bowed head the entire time.

As the time wore on, Chiun grew more annoyed. Though he tried to mask it, the quivering tufts of hair above his ears belied his increasing agitation.

At the point when the old Asian could take it no longer, Remo spoke.

"You boxed one of them up and shipped it back to Sinanju somehow, didn't you?"

The shock on Chiun's face faded the instant he glanced up at Remo. He saw that his pupil was only guessing.

"Pah, leave me," he spit, turning back to his scrolls. "You are interrupting my train of thought. I was just at the point in the history where the kitten trapped the foolish assassin in a burning building." He waved a dismissive hand.

Remo got to his feet. He began walking slowly to the hall. In the doorway, he paused.

"You know, Chiun, between the BBQs and this mysterious movie deal of yours, you're building up a lot of secrets lately," Remo warned. "You just better hope Smith doesn't find out."

"Smith knows only that which I tell him," Chiun said with indifferent confidence.

"If you say so," Remo replied. "Just don't say I didn't warn you."

Chiun looked up in time to see his pupil leave the room. His aged face puckered in displeasure.

Remo could be so irritating at times.

The old Korean returned to his work. On the paper, he wrote the Korean symbol for *ingrate*. Although it wasn't much, the mark did help to ease a bit of his great burden of suffering. But only a bit.

EPILOGUE

In a few short weeks, the gruesome murders in Boston passed into the realm of local folklore. Dr. Judith White joined the ranks of the Boston Strangler and Lizzie Borden as citizens of the Hub and surrounding Essex, Middlesex and Norfolk Counties vied to outdo one another over the backyard fence with tales of how they had almost encountered the "killer doctor." Around the rest of the nation, things returned to normal.

In a small room in a strip motel in rural North Dakota—away from all the idle gossip—a lone figure looked critically at herself in the long bathroom-door mirror. She had requested the room farthest away from the office. It offered the kind of privacy she liked.

She had ordered dinner not long before and didn't want to be disturbed while she was eating. The human predilection for rudeness was one of the things about them she most despised.

Judith White examined the sprouting mound of pink flesh at her shoulder. At the moment, it was as large as a baby's arm and hand, but that would change quickly enough.

She considered herself lucky to have had the foresight to include starfish DNA in her new genetic code. The sea creatures were able to regenerate parts that had been torn off. Now she could, as well.

Hers had been a daring plan. One that involved great personal risk. But it had worked. She hadn't been followed. The world thought that Dr. Judith White was dead. She would allow mankind that small luxury. For now.

She flexed and opened the small hand. It was important for its growth that she exercise the new limb. How long it would take to mature, she had no clear idea. But so far, eating seemed to help its growth spurts.

As she wiggled her tiny pink fingers, she heard a car slow down outside her motel room. Rapid feet ran across the gravel drive. All at once, there came a sharp knock at the door.

"Pepe's Pizza!" a harried young voice called from outside. A cold wind rattled the motel windows.

She draped a robe over her shoulder, covering her tiny baby arm. Judith stepped from the bathroom.

It was time for Judith White to feed. And she had no intention of having pizza for supper.

With the purpose of a hungry feline, she stalked over to the closed motel door, purring gently.

The ultimate weapon of terror...

JAMES AXLER

DEATH LANDS®

Dark Reckoning

A secret community of scientists gains control of an orbiting transformer that could become the ultimate weapon of terror—and it's up to Ryan Cawdor to halt the evil mastermind before he can incinerate Front Royal.

Book 3 in the Baronies Trilogy, three books that chronicle the strange attempts to unify the East Coast baronies. Who (or what) is behind this coercive process?

Follow Remo and Chiun on more of their extraordinary adventures....

#63220	SCORCHED EARTH	$5.50 U.S. ☐
		$6.50 CAN. ☐
#63221	WHITE WATER	$5.50 U.S. ☐
		$6.50 CAN. ☐
#63222	FEAST OR FAMINE	$5.50 U.S. ☐
		$6.50 CAN. ☐
#63223	BAMBOO DRAGON	$5.50 U.S. ☐
		$6.50 CAN. ☐
#63224	AMERICAN OBSESSION	$5.50 U.S. ☐
		$6.50 CAN. ☐

(limited quantities available on certain titles)

TOTAL AMOUNT	$
POSTAGE & HANDLING	$
($1.00 for one book, 50¢ for each additional)	
APPLICABLE TAXES*	$ _____
TOTAL PAYABLE	$ _____

(check or money order—please do not send cash)

To order, complete this form and send it, along with a check or money order for the total above, payable to Gold Eagle Books, to: **In the U.S.:** 3010 Walden Avenue, P.O. Box 9077, Buffalo, NY 14269-9077; **In Canada:** P.O. Box 636, Fort Erie, Ontario, L2A 5X3.

Name: _____

Address: _____ City: _____

State/Prov.: _____ Zip/Postal Code: _____

*New York residents remit applicable sales taxes.
 Canadian residents remit applicable GST and provincial taxes.

GDEBACK1